ASAR EPPEL

Born in 1935 in Moscow, Eppel graduated from
the Institute of Civil Engineering, majoring in
Architecture. Unpublished in Soviet times due to
his unorthodox views of Russian life he made
his living as a literary translator, mainly from
the Polish. His translations of Bruno Schultz
and Wislava Simborska won him the Polish Medal
"For the Service to Polish Culture". He also has
to his credit translations of poetry such as
Petrarch, Boccaccio, Scottish and Irish ballads,
Bertolt Brecht, Kipling, 18th century American
poets, to name a few. Today he is the
vice-president of the Literary Translators' Guild
and winner of the **Foreign Literature** magazine's
literary award.

Eppel wrote the libretto and the lyrics for the
musical based on Isaak Babel's **Odessa Stories**,
produced by 20 theatres in Russia, and also
by the Philadelphia Walnut Street Theatre under
the title **How It Was Done in Odessa**.

His original works include **The Grassy Street**
(also published in French by Robert Laffont,
in Italian by Einaudi, in German by Suhrkamp,
and in Polish by Czytelnik); **The Mushroom of
My Life**, a collection of long stories; and a
number of stories published in the leading
Russian journals.

D1528197

Glas New Russian Writing

a book series of contemporary Russian writing
in English translation
edited by Natasha Perova & Arch Tait

volume 18

Back issues of Glas:

Translated by Joanne Turnbull | **18**

ΛSΛR EPPEL

The Grassy Street

N E W   R U S S I A N   W R I T I N G

glas

GLAS Publishers (Russia)
Moscow 119517, P.O.Box 47, Russia
Tel./Fax: +7 (095) 441 9157
E-mail: perova@glas.msk.su

GLAS Publishers (UK)
Dept. of Russian Literature,
University of Birmingham, Birmingham, B15 2TT, UK
Tel/Fax: +44 (0) 121-414 6047
E-mail: a.l.tait@bham.ac.uk

world wide web:
http://www.bham.ac.uk/russian/glascover.html

USA and Canada:
Ivan R. Dee Inc
1332 North Halsted St., Chicago, Illinois 60622-2637, USA
Tel: 1-312-787 6262
Fax: 1-312-787 6269
Toll-free: 1-800-462-6420

Cover design: Andrei Bondarenko
Camera-ready copy: Tatiana Shaposhnikova

First publication in English

Published in Russian in: Asar Eppel, *Travyanaya Ulitsa*,
Moscow, Tretia Volna, 1994

Contents

To my parents

RED CAVIAR SANDWICHES

As you approached Ostankino Park, coming from Mariyna Roshcha along the wide Novo-Moskovskaya Street, on your right you would soon see the Pushkin student dorm, an accumulation of stuccoed barracks. A barracks is done fast and slapdash. And always for drastic action. Like a barricade, its direct predecessor. But a barricade may fall, and then be taken down, whereas a barracks will never fall, and never be taken down, witness that heir to the barricade, the Pushkin student dorm.

Having at some point performed its panicky mission, become a shelter for faceless working-class students, and cast the ones who finished out into the world of socialist achievements and rah-rah Soviet songs, it did not fall and was not taken down, but occupied: by the ones who never finished, by all manner of riffraff, and by good souls. Occupied permanently and in perpetuity.

I had various acquaintances there. Of the first, second, and third ilk. Take, say, of the third, the amazing Samson Yeseich. But about him later. Not here. Instead I'll tell you about Aunt Dusya who took care of him. And not just about her. First, however, let's celebrate the barracks. The Pushkin student dorm.

The barracks is an oblong two-story structure crouched low to the ground with two entrances along the front and two outside wooden staircases going to the second floor. It is a barely whitewashed construction under a black tar-paper hat inside which people walk, sit, lie down, and out of which they peer.

I couldn't tell you the length of the barracks today, but we can easily establish the width. Since the plaster walls were nothing but timber inside, the barracks' butt-end could not have been more than twenty-four or twenty-five feet wide; or rather, that's exactly what it was since that is the length of a timber. Said feet contained the lengths of two rooms plus the width of the corridor. Allow five feet for the latter, and that leaves eight feet for each room. That's right! Along the length you may fit a working-class student's bed (six-and-a-half feet) and, at the head or foot of the bed, a nightstand in which the working-class student may keep his Marx or his tattered little tome with the disturbing, but trivial title *Without the Bird Cherries*.

On each floor, you have a corridor five feet wide and, on either side of this corridor, opening onto it, you have rooms stretched the length of their beds and, crammed into these rooms, people, children, and belongings.

The corridor, which is also the kitchen, is absolutely endless, for beneath its ceiling burn only two yellow ten-watt bulbs, sooty as oil-stoves, and in the smoke and steam the nightmarish chiaroscuro from many different objects creates countless screens and cul-de-sacs, and all of this corroded by the rich, fetid, murky air.

Smoke and stench pervade. Along the walls loom washtubs, rags on nails, twig baskets, two-handled saws wrapped in dusty, brittle yellowed newspapers wound round with twine; the floor is a sea of trunks piled one on top of another, little padlocked cupboards painted white, and damp soapy stools supporting basins under small hanging washstands. There is no rule or rest from the dimly glinting buckets of water, the trash buckets, and the buckets of slops for the pig which someone's godmother is fattening in a nearby village, from the old-fashioned camp-beds (canvas on crosspieces), from the sleds, the vats, the barrels, the bowls, from the shovels caked with yellow clay, the pitchforks and the rakes, for the ground-floor tenants have vegetable patches under their windows, and some keep rabbits or chickens. There are children's skis, faded and flat as boards, one ski shorter than the other for lack of means. And there are plain boards, also of different sizes, with crooked brown nails bowed down to their rough surfaces.

There are even some things – marvelous but unsuited to the needs of barracks troglodytes – that once belonged to the ruling class: a broken chair lined with cord on velvet upholstery, a stand for walking-sticks, and a settee (facing the wall) whose rounded back in tandem with the wall makes a marvelous receptacle for storing potatoes.

A frightful corridor, a foul labyrinth, no end to it! But even its endlessness is not beyond reproach, for it is broken up by open doors, by the odd conversation, always more akin to an argument, or by the um-pa-ra um-pa-ra-ra of an accordion, and from one of the rooms comes the astonishing voice of a portable gramophone which goes on valiantly playing the same popular tune from the last war on the same dull needle (sad to say, the record cracked badly not long ago).

Aunt Dusya lives in the cornermost and most pitiful room. The eight linear feet abovementioned multiplied simply by five become forty square feet, and anyone who has occupied such a room knows that opposite the door is the window, that to the left you sleep and rummage in your trunk, while to the right you sit at the table and keep moths in the closet. A treadle sewing machine, if you have one, may stand by the window; if not, you may put, say, a stool there.

The bedding on Aunt Dusya's cot forms a hummock since nonseasonal things and big bunches of torn brownish stockings, the raw material for darning heels, are stowed under the mattress. The stockings tend to contain flakes of the epidermis of the once-young Aunt Dusya; the stockings are all knitted, though an occasional exhibit is of Lisle or even Persian thread.

The ceiling is low, 6 feet 10 inches, but that doesn't bother anyone because people were short and stumpy then, like the Orel peasants in Turgenev's novels. Turgenev's stately Kaluga peasants did not settle here and were found no closer than Grokholsky Lane, and that was miles and miles away.

So then, on the bed there was a hummock and this caused us – me, pressing against my girlfriend, so as to die, and my girlfriend, pressing against me, so as to restore me to life, my girlfriend who, unlike me, knew wide beds and how best to use them — various (we won't go into it!) inconveniences frustrating the ancient and inarticulate rite of embrace.

The barracks, its corridor, Aunt Dusya... My blindingly beautiful girlfriend who knew other — Oh God, I slid down again! — much wider beds, and I, who knew only trestle-beds, — Oh God, you slid down again! — but who also knew that my blindingly beautiful girlfriend, who knew other wider beds, had come to see me. Why all this together? Why did all this couple, combine, connect on the ground floor of a barracks, more specifically in its right-hand rear corner, if facing the barracks from the front? — oh God, we slid down again! — here's why.

Little, wheezing, old Aunt Dusya took care of my old friend, the never-married physics teacher Samson Yeseich, who lived in the barracks across the road. But about him, as I said, later and not here. So now, Aunt Dusya, who considered friendship with me good for the brilliant Samson Yeseich (about which also later and not here), and therefore respected me, had supplied me with the key to her tiny room through the kind offices of Samson Yeseich. She was in the habit — for a little something or simply for a word of thanks — of loaning her key to friends of the physicist, probably because the carnal life of others excited pleasant thoughts in her.

People with good memories will never forget how hopeless it was in those days to find a corner in which to consummate the unbearable half-meetings begun in bushes, in building entrances, on park benches, or in dormitories when the room-mates had fallen asleep — as if they ever did! So to land on Aunt Dusya's lumpy bunk, while Aunt Dusya herself went to her employer's to tidy up or just dashed out somewhere, was a rare and welcome piece of luck.

Now about the one for whose sake I had gotten hold of Aunt Dusya's key.

We trudged, lamenting long since, up the hill. The climb up the rough, rutted road, studded with round flat sea stones and pebbles, on which one's feet constantly twisted, was a very bad idea of mine, and it seemed that she, my new girl-friend, a Calypso-like beauty with fear in her eyes, was on the point of rebelling and wanting to turn back, for even the pretext for our ascent had been unclear and unconvincing: either to survey the sea from on high, or to see what the new fruit on a tangerine tree looked like.

But my companion did not rebel, though she could have turned right around, and I waited in dread for her indignation, for her acquiescence to cease: I was young then but I knew that acquiescence could easily turn to indignation. After all, she suspected, or rather understood our secret, or rather my intention — my clammy and intolerable hope. Of course she, too, was involved in our tacit compact. If not for that torrid climb! At first she agreed to look at the new fruit, then she changed her mind.

We sat down under a tangerine tree on the baked earth, on the dry hot clods, and my hand began to insinuate itself between her softish, slightly cool, but also slightly flushed thighs. My five-fingered touch was discovering the longed-for world tucked between these stunning buttresses; suddenly my wrist was creeping along the dry hot clods of cultivated earth under the tangerine tree, and my fingers were squeezing in between her thighs, now relaxed, now clenched, and burying themselves like pups in the damp, vast — after the closeness of her thighs — tangle of the thickets attained. My girl was quivering, twitching, and protesting, "Don't, or else I'll get a headache, a really bad one!" Yet she went on, with her slender, ringed fingers, squeezing whatever she liked. "Let's wait," she whispered, "this isn't the place. People will see us, and the sun... Let's wait!" And she went on twitching her legs irrevocably parted, but she was right, and the arid incline under the wayside tangerine tree was wilting and dying under the sun.

Wait till Moscow? Which one of us was going away that day, I don't remember. Let's wait till Moscow!

We walked to Aunt Dusya's at the end of a warm summer day past the barracks and the mangy little vegetable patches, fenced in, or rather off from one another with all sorts of junk. Standing in the windows of the low ground floors were people and insipid indoor plants, growing out of cans either rusty, or once gold, now peeling.

Note: Russian cans have always been the color of tin, and it was only the war, on top of all its meager miracles, that produced the gilt, black-lettered cans of saving stewed pork. And though the war was over, and though it was already so over that we had somehow decided to return the Dresden art collection to the Germans, once we had shown it to all comers, these cans still rotted in the windows of the Pushkin student dorm, though some were wrapped in pretty white paper cut-outs, now shrivelled from the sun, mildew, and water.

We walked to Aunt Dusya's past low buildings in the windows of which stood people who seemed not to know me, though my acquaintances might just as easily have been standing there. Our skillfully chosen route allowed us to avoid meeting anyone since, in the first place, I was with a woman and, in the second place, a woman utterly unheard of in these parts.

People's first and most correct thought would be that she was a spy since she was dressed and adorned as no woman to this day has ever been dressed and adorned, save the heroine of that universal film favorite *The Girl of My Dreams*. Even I, whose fingers retained the memory of her bathing suit, wondrous for those days, heavy to the touch, like a portiere, and phosphorescent beneath the stars of our nighttide swim, when everything was beginning and when she kissed me with a kiss unknown in my once and future life, well... even I, who knew her sartorial means, was stunned by what I saw.

As I said, the war had ended to such an extent that it was remembered as a time of hunger, but hunger with stewed pork, as opposed to the hunger after the war without stewed pork. The wartime styles (noted for battle-field chic) varied with American gifts (by those who had them) had ended, and the captured finery — fabulous for its elegance, its shimmering linings, its neat seams, its lacy underthings, and the many possible ways of wearing all this even inside out if you liked — had faded. The wartime styles had ended for everyone, and everyone was arrayed in their own, homemade clothes. But not my girl. She came to me in a fantastic guise, which one I no longer recall, though she had her own, very good reasons for her appearance.

Women came to Blok wafting perfume and mist. This I learned later. She came to me sparkling with rings, earrings, necklaces. All this would become known as costume jewellery and over the years people would get used to it, despite their shame and prejudices, they would get used to wearing this stuff that made broads look like ladies.

But where could it have come from when it wasn't supposed to exist yet? Where did she get it all: the strange dress, the shoes with golden clasps glittering with glass beads? Where? Here's where: she was with the occupation forces in the East bloc, had lived a long time in East Germany, and recently come from there, where she worked as a staff translator and lived with her husband, an officer in the secret service.

She was deathly afraid of her spook. With his secretive way of life and omniscience, he compelled her soul and flesh to suffer, generally relating to the latter with an unbearable brittleness. This flesh did not seethe by the warm sea, or under the tangerine tree for fear of being seen by some acquaintance, a junior officer, say, dispatched by the spook.

We couldn't arrange a meeting in Moscow either. Couldn't for a long time. But now Aunt Dusya had given me her key, had gone out somewhere, and I was walking with my girl, a little to one side and a step ahead or, you could say, behind, along the little paths and backways around the Pushkin student dorm to Aunt Dusya's barracks. It certainly tests a man's mettle: trying to sneak a glittering woman in the door of a teeming barracks right on the main street.

As it is, people are lolling dumbstruck in every window, old women perched on mounds of earth are combing out wisps of grey hair with fine-tooth combs, former classmates may appear, and then there's the man by the shed who has been fixing his bicycle for a year now.

The summer street is light and sunny, and behind another shed boys are mating rabbits. Girls huddle at a deliberate distance, but still see how the rabbit, raptly nibbling grass beside the doe one instant, rears up on her the next, one of the long-eared little beasts squeals, then both wiggle their noses, and resume eating. The boys insist that the rabbits are *fucking.* The girls, watching from afar, know what the rabbits are doing but don't use the word *fucking.* The brazen boys, wanting the girls' attention, make circles with thumb and forefinger, then insert the other forefinger, and slide it back and forth. The girls walk off.

Thus I lead my girl through my childhood, but she neither sees nor cares, she walks beside me in silence, thinking only of how her spook may have had her shadowed.

She walks with amazing calm. She is simply numb and blind with fear. *Her* fear. *My* fear has made me monstrously sharp-eyed and, when we pass from the daylight into the barracks' pitch-dark corridor, I manage to make out someone's slummy laundry, hanging at the far end and a man sorting maggots for bait in a tin can.

Some trouble with Aunt Dusya's key... and we're in the room. I've brought sandwiches. Red caviar. Five of them. Cheap eats in those days. And she produces wine! She produces... wine... Never in my wildest dreams would I have expected such a thing. She produces a wine I don't know, the only wines I know (and those by hearsay) are Cahors and "three-sevens" port, highly regarded by local experts in anything you like, but not that.

"Wait a moment!" she says when I, having drunk a little wine and eaten half a sandwich, begin aquiver to embrace her, freely fondling the heavy warm folds of her soft dress, in itself a voluptuous sensation. "Wait a moment!" she says.

"I have to run out first!"

"Run out?"

"I have to! Or else I can't..."

I am crushed. In the Pushkin student dorm they run out, here's where: for the entire barracks there are all of two outhouses, resembling, as it were, rural granaries. Each one is high and light on account of the chinks in the walls and a lone dormer window. The outhouses are bleached with lime which drools down the dingy old boards to create a unique atmosphere of slovenliness and untouchability. Each outhouse is divided by a wall that would have reached the ceiling, had there been one, but above the wall is empty, and higher still one can see the inside of the finial atop the gable roof.

On either side of the wall – in the male and female halves – there is a platform made out of thick boards in which a series of eight holes has been cut. The effect of another presence is total. First, because of the low partition; second, because if you stand slightly back from the platform, the product of the performer on the other side of the partition is visible in the pit.

As if this weren't enough, huge holes have been punched in the wall at different levels. Here and there the holes have been boarded up with whatever came to hand. But only here and there. Now I was not born in a palace, and I have visited my share of latrines, and that one is supposed to sit, not stand on a toilet seat, I figured out all by myself at the age of twenty-three, but I never ventured into those monstrous outhouses except in dire need, though on sultry days the stench in their simmering semi-darkness grew somehow languorous, and through the breaches in the partition one could observe the determined squatting and listen to intriguing bits of female conversation. But that was in summer.

As we know, our people are uncommonly careless and sloppy with regard to earth closets. It costs our people nothing, given their disdain for basic aiming skills, to foul the rim of the orifice, soak the floor, and leave fingerprints on the wall. The boards absorb everything, everything sticks to them, deliberate sloppiness begets forced sloppiness, and it becomes harder and harder to position oneself over the hole. Puddles further frustrate one's approach to the sloping grey gutter, especially if one is in soft soles or slippers.

And now, the cold is upon us. Everything that has been absorbed begins to freeze and form layers. By late December, crossing the ice crust to a hole is out of the question. There is less and less room for maneuver. The visiting public retreats closer and closer to the door, fouling the floor higgledy-piggledy. The walls (inside only, so far) are caked with tall ice crusts the color of whey, rising up out of the floor like stalagmites, interspersed with fossilized brown clumps. The hoarfrost on the boards, the yellow newspapers frozen in the ice, the yellow crystals forming under the roof: nothing deters our people – where else can they go? By mid-February, only by standing in the doorway may one celebrate the call of nature in the murk of the fossil world.

This circumstance decidedly alters the daily rhythms of the Pushkin student dorm. People put off going until dusk or after dark. By now the walls are caked even on the outside with turbid ice crusts, by now the expanse around the walls, if not covered with snow, is you can well imagine what.

But here spring arrives. Someone, cursing wildly, is cleaning out all this muck. Who, I don't know. For half an hour after it has been hosed down the granary looks human, then it begins all over again, and towards evening masturbator Mitrokhin walks in and takes a swift chisel to the rough-hewn wall's most promising hole. In no time at all, he is convulsing in a corner in response to the rustling behind the partition.

To this granary then my girl is calmly proceeding. In haste and confusion, I explain the long way round, unable to imagine how she will get there, and if she does, how she, wafting perfume and mist, will react to the shame, how she will ford the swollen floor in her velvet slippers?

I cannot take her there, for I simply cannot imagine how anyone could take a woman to that place, and so become unwittingly initiated into this utterly secret necessity, into this apotheosis of awkwardness and discouraged dignity.

She goes. I wait. I get it! Walking through the settlement, humiliated by the road to Aunt Dusya's, stunned by her forty-square-foot burrow – I'm used to it, but she's seeing it for the first time – by the musty humpbacked bed on which *we will*, by the table with the caviar sandwiches, red-and-white and sparkling beside the cloudy tumbler in whose putrid water a dirty swollen onion, now limp and splayed, has disgorged the repulsive greenish bud of an onion leaf... seeing all this made her change her mind. She's gone. She's just up and gone! She took her purse, didn't she! True, she left the wine... she brought wine... It never, ever occurred to me that anyone would bring wine on my account. She's gone! And if she's not gone, then she's lost, and if she's not lost then somebody's picked her up: as I said, the neighbors might easily think she was a spy. Only recently, loyal and concerned citizens not far from here caught a spy, apparently American. Or even two.

"Hey, Kalinych, you mother, why'd you block my wood-pile with your bicycle? Ain't you ever gonna be done with that thing?" the cheerful start of a friendly exchange by the shed can be heard outside the window. I startle, freeze, steal up to the window, and peek through the slit between the gauze curtain and the peeling wood.

A rivulet of tiny ants streams by my eye, skirting a stony tumor of oil paint on Aunt Dusya's window frame. They stream out of one chink and disappear an inch or so later into another. That's nothing! At this point, my eyes could make out an amoeba. My ears could pick up ultrasound.

"Kalinych, you fuck..." the usual sounds from the vicinity of the shed and then my pounding heart stops as the door, just behind me, opens with a jolt. I jerk round and am amazed to see my girl slip quietly into the room.

"Here I am," she says, and I fasten my sharp eyes on her velvet slippers, especially the delicate line of her pretty dyed-black sole.

"Where can I wash my hands?"

Oh God! It will never end! I don't know where Aunt Dusya's washstand is in the endless corridor or which shard of soap on which of the thirty-three shelves belongs to her or what sort of soap it is. Maybe it's the marble soap sold by weight and boiled by the Ruzhansky soap-boiler, but out of what, about that later and not here. What if the basin under the washstand is full and has to be emptied? And if it's full, then of what?

"*Unmoeglich!*" I say because my girl speaks German beautifully and at the time I too could get along in this language fairly well which, incidentally, is largely what drew me to her there, where the tangerine trees bear fruit.

"*Unmoeglich, weil ich weiss nicht wo ist der* Aunt Dusya's washstand *und Seife!*" I play the fool, and she, smiling, takes a sparkling perfume bottle from her bag, then some cotton wool and neatly wipes her fingers with the many magnificent rings, among them a thick band binding her to her spook – not the custom then and also a surprising thing.

She went to the window, glanced through the slit to one side of the curtain, then turned around, undid her dress, took it off, then took off some other mysterious underthings, then took off everything else, and for the first time I saw a woman who had undressed for me.

"Now you take everything off!" said this miracle when I went up to her, embraced her and dazedly pressed myself into this unbearably various nakedness so unlike my own uniformity.

"Wait a moment! Stop! Metal inhibits love!" And she began to remove the sparkling objects from her neck, from her wrists, from her fingers, from her ears, and put them on the oil-cloth-covered table where there soon accrued a small heap of watches, earrings, bracelets, rings – one rolled away under the bed. By her exquisite legs I, like the young Actaeon, found the gossamer ring in the desolation under the bed, and as I pulled my head out, I saw, still on my hands and my knees, that the exquisite legs had been tucked up out of my way – taken off the floor: she had sat down on the humpbacked bed, and then lain down. I quietly placed the ring on the oil-cloth. The ring clung trustingly to the others, and I just as trustingly entered the land where they kiss strangers sweetly, caress them, enchant them and yet sob, clinging to these strangers, – the land of ripening tangerines and dry hot earth, the land of two, along whose damp sandy shores the wanderer Odysseus bends his firm steps towards Calypso languishing in the tangled thickets of her hair.

This was *free* love. All my previous conquests, hurried, prehensile, greedy and pitiful, were under-love compared with what happened in the land of the tangerine sun. Outside it was getting dark, in the room it was twilight, and this dusk increasingly isolated the land I had entered over and again, always to the sound of muffled laughter, muffled sobs, muffled words, and where I suddenly sensed moist lips humbly kissing my regal hand.

This was a meeting of two people who, for different reasons, dearly needed each other. A woman, who needed me, and I, who needed this woman most in the world. A meeting without shame, or rather, outside shame, celebrating with muffled sobs our triumph over the foul surround and over the hero of these out-of-the-way places, the spook; a meeting joining experience of vast Pomeranian beds with the entertaining erotica of Russian suburbs, slaking Mitrokhin's unbearable reverie, and sanctifying the ancient gesture made by the brazen boys in front of the girls at the rabbits' wedding.

The weary tangerine sun was already sinking when we heard a polite little cough outside the door.

"Your landlady! She's been sitting there a long time, I think!"

We issued forth, leaving behind two whole sandwiches and one almost whole, plus half a bottle of wine in thanks, and found Aunt Dusya slumped on a sack of bran in the now empty corridor. Aunt Dusya was dozing, and softly grunting.

I touched her padded jacket, I had to return the key. She jumped up, grinned slyly, and surprised us with this phrase worthy of Sumarokov:

"Love is by nature inherent in people!"

On the eveninged street, my girl and I quickly went our separate ways because she might run into undesirable acquaintances at the tram stop, she said, scraping a fleck of red caviar off her teeth.

I walked away from the Pushkin student dorm and, by the last barracks, ran into Nasibullin, a shy and very modest Tatar boy who enrolled voluntarily in a secret service college after school.

"Good evening!" he said politely because he always strove to associate his cultivation, assiduously earned thanks to society's concern, with my own innate cultivation, and, by way of continuing this association, asked shyly:

"Been to the Dresden show yet?"

"Na-a-ah!"

"Go, don't miss it!" And so as to pique my interest, he glanced down the dusky alleys, looked terribly embarrassed and said: "Lots of bare bodies!"

SEMYON'S LONELY SOUL

*S*emyon set off for the umpteenth time since he had begun living in Moscow to get his hair cut at that barber's. The No. 39 tram rattled away from the three train stations at first along good streets, then began clanging beyond the Rzhevsky bridge and rolled into moldering wooden outskirts without end. Semyon got on at the Novo-Alekseyevskaya stop. On the way to the barber's the tram did pass three big buildings – two on the right, one on the left – and these, this time too, Semyon registered as harbingers of the new.

Nearer the barber's, to the left of the accelerating tram, empty expanses appeared in the midst of which grew – on a hillock or not? – a magnificent pine. The rumbling No. 39 passed the tree, as lonely as Semyon's soul, and stopped. When Semyon got down, the tram bowled off in the direction of some place called Ostankino, and again Semyon's heart, just like the last time, began to pound: again he had a vision of a hill with a church on its crown, and all over the hill brown hovels huddled. In his confusion, Semyon wanted to dash towards the last house by the church, where they had tired of waiting for him, but then he remembered. The church didn't seem like the one by which they had tired of waiting for him, and though everything else did seem almost the same, it wasn't *that*, for of *that*, it seems, there wasn't a trace.

That didn't exist – *that* wasn't there any more! – but Semyon, being young and inexperienced, hadn't yet been able to ascertain how something could just disappear, and although he was generally a sensible person, in this case he was laboring under a delusion, hoping for something, though he was right to do so, to hope for something. So long as *that* existed in him, so long as he was alive, *that* couldn't disappear, only he, in his innocence, didn't know what to do about it. Semyon didn't know, though somebody else did. But Semyon didn't know this somebody else and had never heard of him. And he never would.

Semyon asked for a crew cut but refused the eau-de-Cologne so as not to bring shame on himself and not to make people laugh. Then he went to get his cap in the cloakroom – black tufts of his own hair crunching underfoot – and met an intent stare created by the anxious, if all-knowing eyes of the stumpy cloakroom attendant who asked very intently:

"Still no wife, young man? What's keeping you? Enough already, stop with those chance meetings of yours!"

How the cloakroom attendant knew that he had had a chance meeting, Semyon hadn't the faintest!

Semyon is walking along the edge of a potato field; he is on his way to the ravine to dig up the clay he needs to rebuild the drying-shed stove which is stopped up with broken bricks from the flue and hasn't been fired in a year. Semyon has been walking a long time, he's even tired. The place is deserted: there's no one around. Then he sees two girls sitting on the boundary strip; they are convicts who have been left there to earth up potatoes until evening. When he comes up to them, one girl says:

"Hold it, boy! Sit right down here with us, boy!"

When he sits down, they begin scoffing, laughing and jostling him with their shoulders. He laughs, too, and jostles them back, but the hussies stop laughing and start snorting, pinching and pressing him to their jackets.

"What's with you? What's with you? Come on and diddle us quick!" snorting, they mutter incomprehensible words. "Come on and diddle us, you little sonuvabitch! Come on!"

Then, realizing something and laughing hoarsely, one girl pushes him over sideways, falls heavily on top of him and sucks his mouth into hers while the other girl fumbles with Semyon's pants.

"Hold on, boy, hold on, stop your squirming!" breathes the first, slobbering over Semyon with her wet lips, while the other, finding no buttons, rips the shrivelled elastic holding up his loose trousers, and straddles him.

"Hold'm now, Varya, hold'm!" she half snorts and begins gyrating wildly while Varya holds Semyon down, leaning on his chest like a weight, and snorts too:

"Me next! Me too, you little sonuvabitch... right after my girlfriend here!" And she shoves her fat tongue into Semyon's gaping mouth.

"It's time you got married, young man! What's keeping you?" says the cloakroom attendant confidentially and then confidentially tells Semyon that he personally doesn't have a stomach, that a medical professor cut it out, that he wouldn't wish his digestion on his worst enemy, but at least he's alive, and thank God for that.

At the request of the man without a stomach, Semyon tells him something about himself while the man, twirling Semyon's eight-gore cap disapprovingly, listens most intently, however the news that the master craftsman comrade Rossisky works at Semyon's factory, of which Semyon is rightfully proud, makes no impression for some reason; instead the man asks:

"What job did they give you?"

On hearing that Semyon is a turner-modeller, his new acquaintance says:

"You related to Faina Turner, the one who lives next to the post office? No? You surprise me, but so be it! And, may I get my stomach back, do I have a bride for you!"

He takes out a thick checked copy-book, the kind they only dreamed about where Semyon went to school, and, glancing into it, begins muttering:

"You see, I, thank God, can still see without glasses. But what's this here? Two degrees, father owns his own store... that's not for you... And this? They're offering a piano... also not for you; they want Misha Fikhtengolts... Nice eyes... lives with her sister, can't guarantee she'll take you in... Ha! And what's this... Honest girl, mother teaches into German... here

I know who to tell... She's a doctor, husband was killed... that I'll have to think about... Here they're not offering even a kopek... Loud-mouthed mother in Pervomaika, but you don't need a loud-mouthed mother, you're an orphan... Here! This I think is for you! You said you're a turner? They'll be happy to have a turner here!"

The man without a stomach knew what he was doing, and Semyon moved to Ostankino, a little to the left of those places where the No. 39 rolled after the barber's.

Semyon was married off to Eva, past her prime and uncouth. When Eva was still a little girl, her name, strange even for our grassy street, inspired the rhyme: "Eva is a spinsta", which with time seemed to come true.

Semyon's marriage had been brought about by various circumstances, including the seemingly secondary fact that the bride's family came from that same place gone up in smoke where Semyon had wanted to dash when he got off at the stop by the barber's.

This family was highly unattractive. Mama, Sozilvovna, with her nasal voice and bedbug-colored shawl, did not make a good impression. The younger sister, Polya, though not a hunchback, looked like one nevertheless: the lack of a neck, the stubbiness, the short trunk, long legs, and matronly chest jutting out in front were a far cry from the traditional proportions. The culprit, of course, was her father. He was the first to turn out stumpy, with his very short trunk and long legs in dark blue jodhpurs tucked into narrow boxcalf boots with galoshes.

He worked in a kerosene store. He ladled out kerosene and sold chandleries: wicks, candles, when they had them, and they almost never did, shoe polish, flake camphor, insect powder, string, when they had any, waxed thread, barn hinges, and nails.

The whole family had strange skin: slightly greasy, it seemed as if it had been filled with a fine layer of marsh water, translucent under a fine film, and this produced a transparent brownish slick that turned shiny when one of them sweated. And they tended to sweat.

The kerosene store also sold putty, but putty is a heavy commodity and you have to know how to weigh it. For the benefit of all and your own benefit, too. This is why Eva's father did not foresee any financial difficulty in giving his daughters away. He just needed takers. As soon as they were married, Semyon and Eva moved into a room bought for the young couple at considerable cost.

Eva's family lived on the mezzanine of Darivanna's house. Truth to tell, neither Eva, nor her family, nor, for that matter, the rest of the grassy street's residents had any idea that the upper quarters in Darivanna's spacious house were called the mezzanine, and they called it "upstairs"; but even if they had known they wouldn't have attached any meaning or importance to this and certainly would have forgotten this untenable word.

Although Eva's papa had money, it was impossible to squeeze much out of him: a three-leaved mirror, all right; a couple of lengths of fabric, all right; a wardrobe, all right! To buy the family another apartment made no sense: "upstairs" was warm even if downstairs at Darivanna's was cold. Her flue went through their wall. And after all, whether you live upstairs or down, you're not going to go out into the yard at night when it's freezing cold, for that there is a chamber pot. On the other hand, no one will rob you "upstairs": the whole street would see.

The girls grew and grew up. They both needed husbands. Eva had been on the shelf far too long. She had to be married off no matter what: there were as many other girls as you could want on the grassy street. True, the street had always known that no one would pick the sallow-skinned Eva, and besides, her papa's capital wasn't even the twentieth largest in the district.

But there is a God, and there is a man without a stomach. The first willed it, while the second made a commendable effort for which he was rewarded with sixty rubles in today's money.

In the house across the way, where the room for the young couple had been bought from the Smykovs, distinctly reduced after the revolution but well-to-do petty bourgeois before, the remaining lodgings had been sold off long since. Upstairs, for instance – there was an "upstairs" there, too – lived Tatyana Turkina with a small son, but no husband. She was a bird of passage. She had a particular style of dress, was not afraid to go out in her opera cloak, and even painted her lips though she was not a streetwalker; she worked in a People's Commissariat.

There was also a tender schoolgirl who lived with her mama and granny. She had only to walk out onto the grassy street and set off somewhere for the boy from the fine house opposite to appear with his blue accordion, sit down on a bench and, without paying her any attention, play something.

The left side of the house – at the back – was occupied by a taciturn mother and daughter, the Bogdanovs. The back yard with its small cherry orchard belonged to them.

Cavity-like cracks appear on the branches of the cherry-trees: the lips are twisted inside out like those of, say, a sea shell, to reveal the intimate yellowish strip of the under side. From out of these cracks appear excrescences, transparent and darkish, resembling resin: a peculiar sort of cherry gum. One of the great pleasures in finding such an excrescence is to peal it off the bluish-black cherry bark. One can and must chew it, especially as a child. Because only at a tender age can one detect and savor the strange, faint taste of this wood drop. Semyon remembered this taste and once brought Eva a turbid cherry jelly, but she said:

"I don't eat just anything!"

Semyon had not expected the severed connection to his past to be somehow restored on this street. True, he knew of no such connection, it is we tellers of the tale of Semyon's lonely soul who know of it, but Semyon felt at home on the grassy street. Or rather, *almost* at home.

Let me explain: Semyon's harmonious world was perfectly unsurprised by the goat tied to the peg at the end of the street. This was normal: there should be a goat on the grassy street, but as for the two cows and their mistresses or the little boys who sprayed each other with fire extinguishers salvaged from lend-lease Studebaker trucks, they struck Semyon's intuition as in some way disturbing. Little things like these, however hazy in his perception, willfully pressed Semyon to remain aloof.

How did Semyon become Semyon? That's hard to say. He was a rare sort of young man. Not only could he not distinguish good from evil, he didn't know they existed, for he wasn't the least inclined to analyze events or anyone's actions, including his own. He was lucky: people rarely hurt his feelings in earnest, and those small hurts he had the good fortune to endure taught him neither caution nor circumspection.

One could not say that Semyon made friends easily or that, being good-hearted, he became kind-hearted. He kept to himself. But not out of bitterness, not out of a desire to protect himself, not out of orneriness. He was a congenital loner and doomed to loneliness, what's more, by the circumstances that had conspired in a little abandoned monastery outside Penza where there was a trade school with only ten apprentices and four adults.

The monastery was a long way from Penza itself: neither the passions, nor the influences of that small town reached the boys, all of a similarly sluggish nature, while kind and quiet people taught them their trade.

This is why Semyon's childhood and youth, though meager, though isolated, were nevertheless tranquil. The poor food, the apprenticeship, the having to repair their ancient accommodations themselves, the vegetable garden for subsistence, and the laying in of wood for the long winters, all of this held the boys back from becoming men even; the devil had nothing to do in the trade school, within the walls of the little monastery that is, for there was nowhere and no one from whom to learn voluptuousness and lust. True, there was some talk: for instance, if a girl allowed herself to be kissed on her wrist watch, that meant that she would let you embrace her and so on. The adolescents had some dreams but all this was as normal as breathing.

And so Semyon, virtually untaught in any of the passions that propel society either forward or backward (it's still unclear which), was nevertheless disposed to certain things by God.

Semyon was drawn to the beautiful. This does not mean he recognized the beautiful despite the ugly. Never having been taught to prefer, he did not prefer the former to the latter, though all five of his senses perceived first what was most beautiful in the world around him.

This is why he didn't understand that he had been bought as a husband, this is why he wasn't at all dismayed by Eva's appearance, this is why he wasn't overjoyed by the upholstered chairs, the three-leaved mirror, and the couch with the built-in shelf which he gained in addition to Eva. This is why he didn't feel the amazement or the censure excited by such a mercenary (even from the grassy street's point of view) marriage, and didn't catch what Rebecca Markovna said once: "Sponger with a hat full of holes!" Eva, though, she caught it.

But, say what you like, he married and began living with a woman who said for a week out of every month: "You can't come near me now!" and Semyon didn't go near her. On the other hand, the first time he was alone with Eva after the wedding, he kissed her on her ZIF watch, and it worked: she let him come near her.

Semyon married and began living in one room with another person. This did not bother him in the least because he had lived his whole life, as is the way in hostels, in rooms with other people, so when he began living with Eva he didn't notice any particular difference, just as he didn't notice Eva's missing virginity, for he was simply unversed in this matter so vital to a man's self-respect, and if he had heard anything then he either hadn't taken it in or hadn't understood.

Neither did he notice Eva's malice, though Eva, at a loss as to how to fool Semyon, was close to despair. Then she thought of something, something as ancient as her name and as naive as Semyon, who took no notice of such punctilious details, thus further infuriating Eva, who regarded this as indifference to her and to her chastity, counterfeit though it was. As for the loss of her genuine chastity, Eva tried not to think about that.

This is why such a piece of good fortune as the purchase of a room irritates and agitates Eva – after all, the room was bought from the Smykovs! – this is why her mother's concerned advice before the marriage altar and Semyon's vagueness during the act itself enrage her and make everything gloomier, while the grassy street's snide, wait-and-see attitude, which Eva senses, hardly improves matters.

All in all, life with her husband, who is both younger, and, she thinks, stupider, even her mother and sister think so, is beginning on a somber note. The grassy street might even have accepted this union had Eva gotten pregnant and had a child, but on top of everything else she doesn't get pregnant, and she's already a walking disaster.

Meanwhile her simple-hearted husband, partially in possession of the lost connection to his past, doesn't notice her torment, though he does notice that when she comes into the room the air smells slightly and inexplicably of ammonium chloride, as she does herself, whereas when she returns from the bathhouse, where she goes once a month, small basin in hand, she smells less of ammonium chloride, but reeks of bast.

Semyon lives quietly. He goes to the factory. He carries water from the pump to the room he shares with Eva and "upstairs". He carries wood both into his room and "upstairs", but he fires the stove only in the room he shares with his wife. Every evening he reads aloud to her from the tear-off calendar, and from two pages already torn off, two vanished days in his life, he cuts out the portraits of Vladimir Ilyich Lenin and Joseph Vissarionovich Stalin with a tiny pair of scissors, then takes two saucers, puts one portrait face down in each, and covers them with plaster he has brought specially from the factory. He also places little loops woven from thin thread in the plaster and when it has set, he flips the saucers over, taps them on the bottom, and removes the molds. They turn out beautifully: from their white convex circles the leaders gaze out affectionately, and the loops for hanging are already attached.

Eva is pleased, too, and she allows Semyon to hang these beautiful things by the three-leaved mirror. And no matter who comes by, they all marvel.

Semyon reads Eva a newspaper clipping about a certain

great actor who wanted everything to be real at his performances; if his boots were supposed to be boxcalf, they should sew him boxcalf boots! If the moon was supposed to shine in the heavens, they could bring it over from the planetarium.

Semyon urges Eva to go and see the pine tree standing alone on the hillock past which he used to ride on his way to the barber's. Eva finally went, but she complained the whole way since her new pumps were chafing and, besides, it was just an ordinary tree.

Semyon, who loved his pine, was not pained, just as he was never pained by anything. The time when he would become used to being pained was still ahead of him.

He and Eva went to see the pine when it was nearly summer, in winter they went only to see friends, as well as to her parents "upstairs".

Every time they were invited out, Eva would wait until dark because it wouldn't do for the whole street to see her sealskin cloak. Many of the people on this street did that: they would steal out in their expensive cloaks after dark so as not to annoy the ones who didn't own expensive cloaks. Assuming, of course, it was winter.

Being guests at her parents' wasn't bad. Semyon always lost his head in the confusion of entering a room where people were already seated around a table laden with beautiful food. For an instant he would think, once again, that he had finally come to the last house by the church where they had tired of waiting for him, but then he would remember, though in the course of the evening something would again begin to weigh on him, something in the little amber eyes of the meat broth with beans, or in the lop-sided silver tumbler which smelled the way the goblets of darkened silver had smelled his whole life, and if they smelled that way then he must be *there*, *there* in the last house.

Though Semyon went "upstairs" several times a day, to be a guest there was another thing entirely. He noticed that guests and hosts were more demanding of each other, but in a special way, not in an everyday way. Sozilvovna would take off her bedbug-colored shawl and pin on her elephant-tooth (from a real elephant!) brooch with the two foreign letters out of the finest real gold wire.

In fact, the whole family sat there transformed, and even the yellowish water under their parchment-like skin seemed to evaporate; on the other hand, the glossy patches – after the plates of hot broth with the white beans which looked pinkish in the greenish broth and jumped easily out of their little jackets – shined brighter still.

The silent father would pour himself and Semyon each a tumbler of vodka and they would drink while Sozilvovna talked to her daughter:

"Evie, if we could buy you an apartment, we can make sure you're well fed. Give one to Semyon too! Give him a knish."

The father never said anything, although, when he brought the silver tumbler to his lips, it seemed to Semyon that he smelled that smell, too, but why this seemed so to Semyon, he couldn't tell.

The close-mouthed kerosene man always placed carefully cut out squares of plain brown wrapping paper on their chair seats to protect the upholstery. The house was full of this paper, and Eva's sister Polya didn't let it go to waste either. She would fold it into long triangles, cut out several little wedges in different places, and then unfold them: Look! Beautiful, round, lacy napkins. Semyon always asked Polya to cut something out and was about to begin folding and cutting himself, once, but Eva grabbed the paper out of his hands and screamed: "That's girls' work!" Stunned, she fell silent, turned brown, and pouted.

Eva and Raika Smykova are sitting in the empty kitchen twelve or so years ago. They've become good friends recently, especially since discovering that time of the month in their adolescent lives. Eva is sitting there with her independent and determined friend who grew up in another world, though on the same grassy street, sitting there and telling secrets. Suddenly Raika turns red and, in an unnatural voice, offers to show Eva something. She takes a piece of the plain brown paper in which Eva's father brought candles home from the store, she takes a piece of this coarse, woolly paper, quickly folds it into an oblong triangle, lifts up her skirt, sits down on the very corner of the stool and, right in front of the dimly aware Eva, shoves the strange triangle up somewhere between her thin, splayed, goose-pimply legs.

From then on Eva begins avoiding Raika Smykova, but in a week she has mastered the manipulations with the plain brown paper which become the secret meaning and curse of Eva's existence. Meanwhile she tries not to run into Raika on the street even by accident.

Being guests at her parents' was fine. Her father remained silent while Semyon announced that he and the famous Ferapont Golovaty, the first to donate all of his one hundred thousand to the state, were apparently from the same place, of which Semyon was very proud, but this made no impression at all on the kerosene man. It was either the talk of such large sums being handed over to the state, or something else, but he took no interest in this news.

Sometimes, after everyone had finished eating, Semyon would take his violin – after all, he'd brought his violin with him! – and stand up, intending to play.

We won't mind the appearance of Semyon's violin, a banal accessory in stories of this kind. It can't be helped: Semyon also played the violin. Clumsily and shakily, but he played. Various songs, for the most part. His violin had been unearthed in that same little monastery in a pile of previously under-plundered junk. No one knew to whom it had belonged – to a precentor, perhaps, or to someone else. Of course, it wasn't in good shape: something had snapped, something else had come unstuck, but Semyon wasn't a modeler for nothing – he knew how to work with panelboard and mortised wood – he fixed the violin, and, tinkling at first, it struck up, and Semyon began practicing.

Semyon played while Sozilvovna talked quietly:

"You, Evie, could have had a prince or a photographer, it's not your fault you didn't paint your lips and didn't let them touch you."

"Shhhhhhhh!" Polya hushes her, while Semyon plays on.

As we've already said, Semyon's aesthetics tended to choose what suited his unrefined sensibilities. Semyon didn't realize that his instinctive inclinations, though easily satisfied, were destroying his tranquility, just as he didn't know that he was in a state of happy tranquility. When he first took up the violin, the emanation of sound had surprised him: it was he, Semyon, who had helped this sound to emerge! When he had learned to play various songs, he was surprised not only by the fact of the sounds, but by the fact of the melody, and his ability to make this melody quiet and akin to what he felt when he smelled the darkened tumbler, or appallingly loud, like the guffaws of the girls on the boundary-strip as he was tying the ripped, stringy, shrivelled elastic over his wide trousers to keep them from falling down.

Semyon didn't play long or much for his relations – a couple of songs, and then it was time to go because Eva's father had hemorrhoids, and the kerosene man would now have to cope with the excruciating process of elimination over a chamber pot with hot water.

The water still had to be heated on the kerosene stove, then cooled, then reheated for later, before the evening victim began moaning in despair behind a curtain in a corner of the kitchen where the floorboards slanted awkwardly and uncomfortably for one's feet – but that couldn't be helped, there was no other place, one just had to dig in one's heels.

As Semyon and Eva made their way home, she listed for him – on the narrow, almost vertical staircase, and then as they were crossing the street, and again at home – different examples of his uncouth behavior at her parents'.

By now it was spring, even early summer. Home on vacation since the day before yesterday, Semyon was sitting by the open window and gazing out at the grassy street which he was seeing in all its summery splendor really for the first time.

Eva had gone to work early. Her "two degrees" had turned out to be some bookkeeping courses, and after finishing them she had worked in a cooperative sorting receipts – probably forged. Eva's undereducation, incidentally, was regarded on the grassy street as impossible commonness because the grassy street's second generation either studied nothing at all or gladdened their parents by improving the stock in institutions of higher learning.

Semyon was sitting by the window gazing out at half the grassy street, the half to the left, where the pump was, cut off from the other half by a cobbled road along the edges of which the soft dust would be ankle-deep by July. To the right, the street became mired in the senseless holdings of the Stalin Collective Farm which for some reason was still there.

Seven houses with their seven yards occupied the side of the street opposite Semyon; on Semyon's side there were six houses and yards. Across the street, by the far left-hand house, the fence was blind and good; the next house had no fence, but round the yard birch trees marched behind a strapping young poplar; next came the fence in front of Darivanna's house, whose "upstairs" Eva's parents occupied, it was also good and solid, though now in bad repair – there wasn't anyone to mend it; next was another house without a fence; then a good house with a straight wrought-iron grille instead of a fence; then a barracks with no fence; and, finally, a revolting-looking habitation whose vile fencing had been knocked together from slab boards across which someone had scrawled SCABBY in chalk.

Yesterday had been Sunday, and Eva and Semyon had gone to visit friends in Malakhovka where he had disgraced her by asking for seconds. Furious, she hadn't spoken to him the whole way home, and since he hadn't been allowed near her anyway for the past five days, he had skipped the evening reading from the tear-off calendar and simply gone to sleep, long since inured to the bodily smell of Eva's ammonium chloride.

Today Eva was supposed to go to the public baths which she did, as we know, once a month and always following the week when Semyon wasn't allowed near her. She had taken a small basin and a change of underwear and gone straight from work to Novo-Alekseyevskaya Street since the nearest baths were located there, by the Disk cinema.

Semyon gazed out at the grassy street and saw the grass, the birch trees, the sky above the birches, the white goat by the wrought-iron fence, the sprouting potatoes in the dug-up middle of the street, the tops of the apple trees behind the good fence in front of the far left-hand house, people at that same end of the street going to the pump and filling their buckets full of that wonderful water, cold, gushing and white, then carrying their buckets away, some women with yokes and slowly, so as not to spill, others, if they had one bucket, tilting to one side or, if they had two, their arms sagging down and elongated.

It was late afternoon. The cows, whose out-of-placeness somewhat spoiled Semyon's picture, were being led in from the street; some people were walking along, at the back of the fourth yard, counting from the left, two burly boys were playing a game of *rasshibalka*, in the first week of its summer season, while their younger brother burned something on the wall with a magnifying glass.

This time of day it burns worse than in the morning: the sun is weaker. But even so, this patch of sun-warmed board, painted once upon a time with a single coat of thin paint now peeling but still reddish, becomes full of detail under the magnifying glass, as if illuminated. Under the suspended lense, the brilliant light reveals a crosshatch of cracks in the scales of paint and splinters of wood festooned with a stray thread here, or a bit of last-year's dandelion fluff there, or the leg of a daddy-longlegs, or even a completely whole, if dry, grass gnat. The reflections from the swaying lense wander hither and thither over this world, deepening and amplifying it, and when these round reflections are evenly scattered, the hand draws back and on the dry-as-toast board a tiny blinding sun appears; in two seconds a wisp of smoke is curling out of the shining point, and it smells − just briefly − of warmed paint. Would you like to smell this smell again? Light the paint on an ordinary pencil with a match. But then the point-size sun seemingly fades in the smoke, leaving a scorched point on the board, and sometimes − if you overdo it − a tiny tongue of flame on the point. The smoke increases, now it's bluer, and its little plume broader; but here, holding your hand steady, you must guide the tiny sun slowly along and, if you have the patience, write something on the hot, rotten-looking old board of the hut or barn behind the last house by the church.

Semyon also sees doves in the dovecot, and though he is still bewildered by the straightness of the short grassy street, by the unaccustomed barracks, the wrought-iron fence, the oddly dressed people, and the pump with the wonderful water, the white goat, the presumable wisp of smoke under the little boy's hand, and the lonely pot-bellied man standing on the corner in his spare time, hands resting on his round paunch, all this fills Semyon's soul not with melancholy, but with loneliness.

How did he get here exactly, and yet *there*, seemingly, although you can't get *there*? And why did he get almost *there*? Almost.

The tender schoolgirl, his neighbor, walks past his window, off to see her friend in the last house on the right with the vile fencing, and − instantly − the boy with the blue accordion appears from the house opposite and haughtily begins playing Dark Night. Inspired by the familiar music, Semyon takes up his violin and, standing in the open window, accompanies the boy with the blue accordion. As soon as he hears the noble sounds, of a kind never before heard on the grassy street, the amazed and wounded boy freezes, then squeezes the distended bellows, letting the air noisily out of the exhaust valve and a torn corner of the bellows, and disappears into his house. He is a very proud boy.

But Semyon, who has never encountered pride, plays two more stanzas, and then begins *Budyonny's March*. He doesn't notice the rapid permutation of the grassy street which has never seen or heard of a man standing in the window and playing the violin.

The people on the street, such as there are, slink away home or just disappear somewhere, the boys playing *rasshi-*

balka sit down on a bench at the back of their yard, and everyone seems to feel suddenly awkward and embarrassed because of the man's ridiculous behavior. In the houses, behind the curtains, one ear cocked towards the window, women stand and are amazed: what a catch that Eva made – he even plays the violin, but a fool's a fool, just look at him standing in that open window and playing.

Semyon finishes *Budyonny's March*, and then begins his very favorite which he plays only rarely because his tranquil heart cannot bear it. He begins the song, and it turns out better than ever. Just then Tatyana Turkina, on her way somewhere and looking like an actress, appears from around the corner of the house. She stops in front of Semyon standing in the window and asks:

"What is that nice song you're playing?"

"*Oy-oy, come buy my wares!*" sings Semyon and, looking into Tatyana Turkina's beautiful eyes, he adds: "Just a song I know."

But this song he knows so thrills Semyon that he suddenly has a huge lump in his throat, the even line of houses before his eyes breaks up, the ground swells from under the houses into a hill on top of which a church is about to appear from out of a plume of smoke. In another moment, the birch trees will disappear, the little houses will huddle up the incline and turn brown, their gates will go grey, and the pot-bellied man standing on the corner will stretch into someone dark, bearded and gaunt.

"*Look, look! My feet are bare.*" sings Semyon, and the vision dims slightly because his common sense quickly takes into account the great artist's demand for truth; and Semyon, his innocent soul bruised by his bow, kicks off his shoes and goes on playing barefoot, and on the newly visible hill there appears not only the church but – Good God! – the last house, the last house – Good God in heaven! – they're still waiting, they're still waiting, they've been waiting for him all this time! And he stands there barefoot, and plays: *Look! Look! My feet are bare – Good God in heaven.*

Tatyana Turkina rests her arms on the windowsill, closes

her beautiful eyes and listens while from the direction of the Stalin Collective Farm Eva comes into view, tired after the bathhouse. She sees Tatyana Turkina at her window, and she sees Semyon standing in the window, oblivious in his visionary semiconscious state. Eva comes along with her basin from the bathhouse. She already realizes what a stupid thing that idiot is doing, playing in the open window for the whole street to see; and this fancy-schmancy girl from the People's Commissariat isn't even the problem, though she's part of it. Eva crosses the grassy street opposite her house. "*Oy-oy, come buy my wafers, / Walk up, soldiers and sailors.*" Eva is not a soldier or a sailor, but she walks up to her house, steps up onto the porch. *Oy, buy them, I'm just a girl, / All alone in this cold hard world.* Eva goes in the door, clumsily elbowing her way through with her bath sack and enamel basin behind Semyon.

"Hello, Eva! Thank you, Semyon. Goodbye!" says Tatyana, and her head disappears around the windowsill where the smoke-wreathed hill is just flying away, despite the enchantments of Semyon who would have it stay and stay.

"What's this?" Eva says when she sees Semyon standing in his bare feet by his boots. The water under her skin turns grey and brown by turns. "Barefoot in front of the whole street?" she hisses, her throat tight. "What for?" Then she takes a piece of Semyon's priceless resin from the table under the three-leaved mirror and, as it explodes in tiny crystals at his feet, barks:

"And we let crap like you into our house! Get out of here!"

Semyon sees the door slam behind Eva but, stung by her words, doesn't go after her, and instead begins picking up the tiny crystals and yellowish crumbs and putting them in an empty shoe-polish tin. It becomes harder to see them in the falling dusk so he melts the amber tear in the tin with a match. When he comes to his senses, he goes across the street to Eva's parents' "upstairs", but somebody has already brought buckets of water to the door and the door is locked. He goes back across the grass, and he − get out of here! − doesn't know what to do, he lies face down on the couch −

get out of here! – but the oil-cloth couch is slippery – go away!
– where can he go? He doesn't know what to do with his hurt
– out! – because, because this is his first hurt – they let him
into their house! – everyone knows what the first hurt is like
but him, he has only just found out – get out of here! how?
– he was about to turn the grassy street into a humpbacked
hill dotted with little houses, but now – get out of here! – he
would have let this hill go on standing, standing... standing...
and the last house by the church where they've been waiting
for him all this time. He begins to cry in the dusk. He begins
to cry, that's what. Our Semyon is crying, our Semyonchik
is crying. Don't cry, Semyonchik, or else the goat will butt
you! The goat will butt you, Semyonchik, my little boy.

He doesn't know that his orphan's tears, his incorrigible
innocence and superfluousness, his treasures in the shoe-polish tin, his love of unadulterated beauty, and his bow (the
curved sabre of his people, incapable not only of severing the
head of a Tatar from its broad shoulders, but even, after a
couple of thousand years, of sawing in two its pitiful little
violins which always stop as soon as the victim begins to moan,
torture him and drive him to tears, but never kill him off)
have already been suspended in space and time, and the banal
violinists, phantasmal brides, and grassy streets recorded. He
doesn't know about the orphan's tears of the semibanal creator
of these treasures, about whom here, on *this* grassy street,
nobody knows anything, and only the boy with the blue accordion will ever know and only if he doesn't die in his endless
hospitals and doesn't go stale reading about phantasms from
the life of Ferapont Golovaty; he doesn't know that this artist
has already wrested from himself all that is unwrestable and
indissoluble, plus himself and Semyon. This artist has cried
like an orphan, he has cried every time, but he could never
cry enough until he lay the deceased down on the grassy street
between two houses and then he sobbed freely. Our Semyon
cries and doesn't realize that the deceased has already been
foreseen and foretold by the artist, triumphantly polishing es-
planades God knows where.

ONE WARM DARK NIGHT

*P*lease, Lord, forgive me, as you forgave – if you did – the chastising of the Leningrad cat who stole from the neighbors and howled willfully rather than let me, sick and exhausted, sleep. Forgive me, too, the strange pranks, the terrible childhood inventions in which I indulged, and all the pointlessness which I couldn't have grasped then, and which no one could have made me see, had there been anyone to try, besides, those pranks amuse me even now – just a bit – or perhaps they don't amuse me, still I smile at the memory of my temerity and fun, the temerity and fun of those days, though I've long since stopped smiling at the memory of that woman's despair, her helplessness that night, her fear, and loneliness, so cruelly divined by me.

One warm summer night, the sort of summer night that doesn't exist anymore but then was rife, one warm summer night, when the grassy streets, sated with the waning day, were sinking to the bottom, and in the black depths the branches and curtains were no longer stirring – or perhaps they were still stirring gently, you couldn't tell in the murk – one warm dark night I alighted from a twinkling tram and sailed off into the darkness, to the bottom of the ocean, to that place where the branches and curtains were or were not stirring.

I stepped down onto the road alone, since I alone had been aboard the twinkling tram, and set off at a leisurely, if brisk, pace, I didn't even look where I was going, I didn't need to, I could walk that road blindfolded even now, or rather could have, because that road no longer exists, or rather it does, but not all of it, only the first three minutes where desultory streetlights once gleamed.

In their light I saw an old woman walking slowly ahead of me in the distance. It was obvious, as she trudged obtusely on, that one leg dragged. Noiselessly and without quickening my pace, I soon caught up to within fifty yards of her, a small-headed barrel of a woman on cumbersome, conical legs.

I knew everyone who lived on the grassy streets where we were then bound, so I recognized her, too, though she hadn't lived there long and lived very much alone. Now here she was alone on this warm night dragging herself home so as to be alone there, too.

"She doesn't just lock her door," my friend the shoe-maker's son told me, "she puts the chain on!" He also said that no matter how many times the boys knocked at her door and ran away, she always peeked out warily through the crack.

I remembered this when I spied the shuffling figure, I remembered the quivering face, the frightened way of speaking, the searching stare, and the coaxing look that lent a bit of bravado to the stutter, as if to say: "I'm not afraid of you, s-s-see, I'm not afraid; notice that I'm not afraid of you, and when you do, don't be h-h-hurt and don't h-h-hurt me... and don't frighten me because I'm s-s-scared to death as it is. I'm new h-h-here, and once a newcomer always a new-comer. Remember h-h-how they treated you when you were a s-s-sophomore in preparatory s-s-school... oh, what does preparatory s-s-school h-h-have to do with it! I didn't go there any more than you did!. Well, as I was s-s-saying, you probably remember that new boy s-s-sophomore year? H-h-he always was the new boy because h-h-he didn't know every-thing about you, I don't know everything about you either, but I'm not afraid. You s-s-see, I'm even looking you right in the eye. S-s-see?"

"Yes, I s-s-see!" I thought and stamped my feet, then flattened myself against the fence.

She didn't react to the sudden and absurd sound. At first, that is. She plodded on and then suddenly, as though the sound had just stamped up to her, she froze, and wheeled slowly around on her good foot. She didn't look round, she turned round so as to shield her back, the sensible reaction of any creature that can't run away. She froze, she listened, she turned round and, hugging her purse to her chest, didn't see anyone. That is, she didn't see the foot-stomper who had caught up to her.

My friend the shoemaker's son was right.

It would never have occurred to any of us to be afraid of the dark, inky streets at night. Even mothers didn't worry when their daughters came home late at night since that was the only time they could come home; the trip into the city, the endless performance — they were long in those days — and then the tedious wait for the tram brought theatergoers back to the edge of our shantytown no earlier than 11:30 and sometimes it wasn't until after midnight that one entered the God-protected precincts of that transportationless expanse and began the twenty-minute walk along dirt paths, cobbled roads, and slopes so as to reach one's stuffy burrow and eat the viscous mussel soup in the lower gloom and hear: he's/she's/they've been fooling around again: well, that's enough of that!; he's/she's/they've been wasting time again: well, not anymore! Now be quiet and go to sleep!

No one was ever hurt or robbed even during the war — even at night. And though nearly everyone broke the law in one way or another on the grassy streets, life was peaceful. The many delinquents who disappeared by turns to the antipodes for their trespasses never bothered anyone in their own neighborhood, though there were plenty of people to bother, still more to rob and frighten. Those scary-looking hoods and thieves were quiet as mice on their own turf: if they fought, then only among themselves, they liked to gang up and make a show of protecting their respective interests. Meanwhile, the old, regimented system of district police was still in force: there were always two neighborhood policemen on call as well as three pointsmen out pacing around their posts in their heroic pointed helmets. So, if anything happened, you knew where to run for help.

Nevertheless, grassy street residents did latch their doors

at night. With just metal hooks, but still. First they latched the outer door which, by the way, anyone could unlatch from the other side simply by shoving his hand through the air-hole — a secret only the family knew: robbers, it seemed, would never guess! — then they latched the door to their room and fell fast asleep. If you had to go somewhere, anywhere, you could be gone as long as you liked. You could even be evacuated during the war so long as you padlocked your door. You could even go see Uncle Yakov on Third Meshchanskaya Street, by all means, go ahead and go!

This said, things did occasionally disappear. Someone lost the laundry off their clothesline, someone else lost a hen. True, the hen could have wandered off somewhere by itself in search of a dunghill to dig in, and maybe they forgot to hang the laundry up or to wash it in the first place, or maybe the wind took it. Though that's unlikely. You could have gone looking for the laundry and the hen — and found them both.

So we won't deny it: there were thefts. Two of them.

But, as I say, anyone was allowed to walk home in the wee hours, it was completely safe.

She turned round helplessly and, clutching her purse to her chest, peered into the semidarkness but clearly couldn't make anything out while I hugged the fence and swallowed my laughter, knowing that I was about to have some real fun and, no matter who I told tomorrow, they would all whoop.

Incidentally, that's exactly what happened: they all roared when I told them; I don't remember one of them shaking their head. I felt like the hero of some awful and, as I now see it, callous composition about Tom Sawyer.

She turned round, stared, then turned back the way she was going and — on her guard now — trudged on; she probably decided that she had imagined it, that she had mistaken her own shortness of breath for that strange sound.

What she should have done was to go back and wait till dawn on Malo-Moskovskaya where the trams run, but she trudged on. True, it never would have occurred to any normal person, much less someone exhausted at night, to wait at the tram stop until morning because of something they imagined.

And if it wouldn't have occurred to any normal person, it certainly wouldn't have occurred to her: she, after all, was not all there.

But to doom herself to what was about to happen − even on that brief night journey − frankly, it wasn't worth it.

Then what, frankly, could she have done to avoid what was about to happen? Frankly, nothing. Walk faster? Run? On those legs and with that shortness of breath she'd be lucky to make it at all. That walk, twenty minutes for anyone else, would take her at least twice as long. Nor would it have made sense to wait until someone arrived on the next tram: she could hardly have imposed her hobble on a stranger, besides she didn't want people to know how frightened she was, no one would have understood her silly fears.

The best thing to do would have been to wait for Petya, had she known of Petya's existence. But how was she to know if she was usually asleep by the time Petya returned, and never went to the Dzerzhinsky amusement park to watch him play skittles?

And even if she had known Petya, it would not have been wise to wait for him: he might suddenly decide to get off at another stop, say, Alekseyevskoye Selo.

Petya generally reached his own fence well after midnight, following the performance and a friendly libation (for professional reasons) in the actors' dressing-room. Petya had a singular bass and sang in an opera choir − and was very good at it. True, there were operas where the composer's idea confined the octave to a short, stingy bellow in which case Petya's abilities were entirely wasted, and if, in addition, the bass soloist happened to be in poor voice − in those days Mikhailov was the only one in good voice − then Petya himself, as he ambled home along the dark paths, would perform the part ruined by the soloist, marvelously entering into the mood and easily surpassing anyone who ever produced a low note.

He could walk one of three ways: from the above-mentioned Malo-Moskovskaya, from the aforesaid Alekseyevskoye Selo, or from the Ostankino streets we still know nothing about. It all depended: on the arias Petya intended to sing;

on the extent of his creative disagreement with the soloist; on the friendliness of the talk in the dressing room; and, most important of all, on the state of the summer air, of the warm dark ocean on whose floor sleeping people equipped with gills lay curled up in shells or simply under rocks, while in the yards the dogs remained on chains lest they rise up to the moon.

Petya enters the sunken world and clears his throat. Immediately, from the far opposite end, a mile or more from Petya's stentorian voice, a dog starts barking. Note: the dog furthest off is the first to bark which, on the one hand, shows you what a powerful bass Petya has (and he hadn't even hit the notes yet), and, on the other, attests to the morals of dogs: the last bark first. The dogs nearest Petya see him and sense him; many even know him by face. They quietly survey Petya's enormous shape full of disturbing music, sniff the air, get ready and, just as Petya passes by, Gremin's aria on his lips, start barking their heads off, while the stupider ones lunge at their fences. Petya ignores them. He doesn't care. He saunters on, adapting a verse from Gounod's *Faust* as he goes:

> *Stop ba-a-arking, shut the he-e-ell up!*
> *Your snarling doesn't scare me-e-e-e-e!*

The singer proceeds serenely and solemnly and disturbs no one.

No one is disturbed by the fabulous voice in the night since the ones who are asleep don't hear, while the ones who aren't asleep, and are anxious, and afraid of the rustlings outside the windows, and uneasy in their souls, feel comforted, because if a man is walking along the street and singing that means everything is all right, that means there's a living soul outside the window, and since the door is hooked shut, no one can get in, not even the living soul.

For the living soul hobbling along ahead of me, however, it would have been a mistake to wait for Petya, and not because he might have gone a different way. It's just that Petya had been out sick since Sunday, because when he was playing skittles, the little Jewish novice next to him had become frightened of the leaden bat halfway through his bold, beginner's swing and let it go flying right at Petya, just then taking aim at the remains of that difficult figure known as a sickle. The terrible bat with its tin-plated tip, terrible even in the hands of that little Jewish boy, rammed Petya right in the back, and the singer hadn't sung a note for a week for fear of the blood-spitting that ruined Maxim Gorky and many other revolutionaries.

Well, she hobbled on towards her home, towards her horror, that is, then froze again, turned round, peered into the blackness, listened, then again turned back the way she was going and set off – quietly, quietly – only to suddenly begin bustling and waddling vigorously: she had decided to pick up her pace, she evidently thought she could. But after only fifteen steps or so, she stopped dragging her legs in that determined way, started hobbling again, and tried to catch her breath.

I went on hugging the fence. I wanted to let her get round the corner. Round the corner, the road would turn to the right, then go on straight – almost to the end – and down into a broad depression at the bottom of which ran a little river, the Kopytovka, spanned by a first-rate log bridge.

When she got to the corner, I came out of the shadows, again stomped my feet, and again flattened myself against the fence. She rushed round the corner. She disappeared and – just as I was about to come out of the shadows again – peeked out and nearly caught me. Oh, you sneak! Oh, Aunt Polly! Then she peeked out again – she did it so furtively – and ducked back. Over and over, she peeked out and ducked back, studying her fear, while I – in the pauses between those clownish peeks – took little leaps along the fence towards the corner. Intention's greater inspiration was in my favor: she didn't notice me. And soon she stopped peeking out.

By the time I reach the corner and peek round, she is forty yards ahead of me and hobbling on. Still hidden by the corner, I start stamping my feet with all my might, like someone running headlong down a mountain, while she – hah! –

cowers, turns round with a jerk, and helplessly holds her hands up in the air with that crappy purse.

Again she sees that there is no one behind her.

She goes on standing there like an idiot with her hands thrown up, then puts them down, glances in her purse, and clutches at her heart. I somehow sense that she is doing this for effect: to show that she is sick, that she has a bad heart, and that it would be mean to hurt her. She may even think that whoever it is only wants to play with her, and so is letting them know that they shouldn't go too far, otherwise her heart could give out.

Just as I thought: she claps her left hand to her collarbone in a picturesque display and, catching her breath with audible effort, scrutinizes the darkness by the fence.

Again spying no one, she turns away and trudges on, more heavily than before. She goes slowly now, ready to stop short and turn round at any moment and, out of her mind with fright, lumbers right past the dark, saving barracks with its one light burning in a ground floor window outside which she have could screamed for help.

But she missed the barracks round the corner on the right and realized only afterwards that she really was being followed, by which time I, hugging the blind fence (it seems there was a kindergarten on the other side, but I can't say exactly), had rounded the corner and found myself by the barracks with the yellow window. She was long gone with nothing to look forward to now but a lonely wooden structure jammed down on a little hill just before the bridge, on the far side of which empty expanses veiled the vale of the Kopytovka, seeping along the bottom of the obscurity. There would be exactly two streetlights, both beyond the bridge, and until the bridge there would be only darkness, begloomed by those greasy blots gleaming in the distance.

Overlooked by her, the barracks suddenly attracts me. It is home to the thick-ankled girl in my drama group. As it happens, the ground-floor light is on in her room, I could try whistling: she might look out or even come out. My body tenses. So what if it's late. Though I hardly know this girl, at our last rehearsal she stumbled as she was climbing up onto the stage and grabbed me, standing on the edge of the apron, by the front of my pants to keep from falling. I was so stunned I couldn't even react properly to her hand (it must have been the unexpectedness and her nails), whereas she, when she had regained her balance, let go of me and went calmly on to rehearse a scene from the life of Young Pioneers in Rozov's inane play.

This is why I'm all choked up over the idea of whistling. I've already been by once, when her mother was home, to copy down my part. Now, impelled by the spawning instinct, I am about to veer towards the yellow window with the white bolting-cloth curtain, I've already decided that she didn't grab me by accident, and I've imagined all sorts of sizzling continuations including our winding up on a desert island together so that I can grab my thick-ankled girl back and feel under her school pinafore with the tucks.

But I don't stop and I don't whistle. I don't give in to the greatest of the shantytown's temptations, for now I am a light-footed beast in pursuit, bent on running to earth the sure prey on the path ahead of me.

My prey is so defenseless that she readily mistakes even a false sense of security, even a false hope of salvation for the real thing. In her bleak existence, hope of anything is such a rarity that she jumps at any chance to believe in the possibility. Otherwise why would she calm down all of a sudden and start walking normally? She can't have gotten a grip on herself. In her panic, she must have decided that her pursuers have either lost her or lost interest. Perhaps the soft, warm air, too, deceived her instinct, as if to say: the night is balmy so everything will be all right. After all, if I had hung around by the yellow window with the white curtain, her Calvary would have ended then and there, and she would have felt easier as she went, though she still had a long way to go and it was still scary, but then there wouldn't have been those horrible foot stompings, those inexplicable bangs, the truth about which only the accomplice-night knows.

One can assume all this now, but then.

But then she stood by the fence in front of the lonely wooden house jammed down on the rise by the river. The house was so Godforsaken that one could fill it with anything one liked: with emptiness and darkness where the finger that pierces the thick, dusty spider web lands in a cold sticky blob of black sour cream; with shaggy phantoms running up and down the walls; with someone buried alive a century ago and stashed behind the door-jamb to gather dust, a decayed corpse which, when you step into the dark, will tumble out whimpering and then, softly smacking its lips, clamp onto your neck with its round mouth. Beneath the round mouth with the drooping Gogolesque moustache, your jugular vein swells and starts spurting blood.

To call out to someone from that house for help would only rile its midnight existence, its deafness, and desolation.

Actually, it only seems that way: the house is simply sleeping, but again it only seems to be sleeping; with my keen, shantytown-front-garden eyesight, I immediately spotted the silently writhing couple on the bench by the wall behind the elder bushes. Even before I came along they had quieted for fear of being caught by the house's occupants: what if his mother is asleep, what if hers isn't (there are no fathers in places like this), but as soon as they hear, and then see, the approaching silhouette, they freeze, cease their manic manipulations, and press their knocking knees to the bench.

She doesn't see them because she doesn't notice that sort of thing, she missed her chance at it long ago, or perhaps she never had the chance, or perhaps she was married off posthaste before she had ever been kissed on the carried earth, or embraced on a bench, or driven to distraction in the bushes. If she had noticed those two and asked them for help, they – no matter who they were – would have helped. The ravisher would have gotten up and sullenly sidled out sideways, keeping his protuberant pants in the shadows; a minute later the one ravished would have pulled herself together and peeped out of the darkness, damp and praying for another unsnapping of snaps and unbuttoning of buttons and unhooking of recalcitrant hooks, and mounting, and – oy!– conquering of every inch of her bashful but concupiscent surfaces by that hot importunate palm.

My victim, however, doesn't see those two, the dark house makes her tremble, she has eyes in the back of her head, her brow glows white with fear, her right eyelid quivers, her cheek, I suspect, twitches, and her throat can't possibly make the "h-h-h" sound in "Help!".

Nevertheless she turns towards the h-h-house, as if she means to appeal to the buried alive singer of the psychopathic Taras Bulba, or to the fleet and fidgety phantoms. She peers at the small, dark structure but can't make up her mind to call out: her discretion and tact outweigh her survival instinct (this must be why there are so few well-brought-up people left, soon there won't be any at all). She stands there peering tentatively at the house, or perhaps she is just resting, just catching her breath and gathering her courage for the road ahead.

This suits me since now I need to pass her so I can hide under the bridge she is about to cross. The bridge, as I've said, spans a little river which, in the thousand years of Russian statehood, has bored a broad ravine with steepish sides.

We are walking along a high embankment which I will use for cover when I steal up to the bridge by a little side path. This path is a bit eerie, and I have always been afraid of the night and the dark. Shadowy bushes and dark rooms scare me, and I won't go to bed with my window open on the ground floor for anything, though I do walk along the road at night, though I do sleep out in the garden on a canvas camp bed when it's sultry – the spit and image of the white deceased – and sleep like a baby. Why is that? Probably because walking along a man-made road means feeling protected by the sensible shoulder, by the cleared expanse, by the cobbled foot-path; while sleeping in the garden because it's hot means sleeping in the garden because it's hot. But to fight one's way through the bushes and burdocks by the side of the road (bushes, as we know, are denser and higher at night, while the paths are more narrowing and harrowing, and in the bushes there is murk, and in the murk there is matter, black to the touch and determined to merge with the murk in you, moreover, it can get at you through your eyes, ears, and nose, while your only protection is that thin, whitish skin being scratched by prickles and burrs), that is eerie and unnatural.

I'm not afraid now, though, for I have *her*, my prey. *She* protects *me* from my fears. If not for the figure tottering by the Godforsaken house, if not for the randy pair behind the elder bushes in the little front garden, I would never ever have snuck under the bridge. All three give me the courage to disappear into the burdocks and crouch down on a log in such a way that, when she comes along, I will see her but she won't see me.

I crawled into the moldering darkness, something rustled and rained down into my eyes and collar, but I, as I say, was not afraid: I had her, while she had no one.

Armed with a big stick I had picked up on the embankment, and conveniently seated on the end of a log to one side of the bridge (anyone who has ever seen a bridge like this knows that its piers are jumbles of logs intersecting willy-nilly, and by conveniently seated I mean that the road and the wooden bridge were at eye level), I began to scrutinize the darkling figure some thirty yards off by the house on the hill.

I sat quietly. The figure stood quietly, too; she seemed to have caught her breath. But all was not quiet in the front garden. Either he began to snort or she thrust her lust out so far she hit her head on the wall, whatever it was my object suddenly started, and, glancing anxiously round, plunged toward the bridge... the bridge... the bridge... Come on, come on, get me away from that Godforsaken house with its spirits and resounding desolation.

She must have decided that she had finally discovered the source of her fear – and then bolted. Look at her go! She was falling all over herself, but she was going; despite her big, broad steps, she kept pitching forward. She even picked up speed at the bottom of the hill. She was wheezing. I can still see her white face, her slightly crooked mouth, her cloth bag, flat with a bulge at the bottom – either a rutabaga or a roll. Since my eyes are level with the road, I especially notice her huge, swollen, sourdough legs spilling over the tops of white socks. She heaves ahead, she doesn't look where she's going, and she doesn't look back: she doesn't have the coordination, she is rolling from leg to leg as it is, while her upper torso careens every which way because she doesn't know, doesn't know – as if she never learned! – how to walk fast. Needless to say, she doesn't notice the ruts in which roads that run into bridges have always ended, everyone knows they're there, but she doesn't.

I see how her veiny, knotty, blotchy leg turns, how she stumbles, cries out, and nearly falls – she is saved from falling by her fear, her hysterical, panicky fear. The unexpected rut breaks her forward motion and she steps – slowly – onto the bridge. Listen to her breathe! Breathing in always sounds different from breathing out, but with her it all sounds the same, like a pump pumping in one direction: *hiss, hiss, hiss.* She takes one step, then another, and another, while I, sitting on the butt-end of a log do here's what: just as she is about to take a fourth step, I thwack the bridge from below with my big stick.

Thwack!

"What?!" Hiss, hiss, hiss, hiss. "What's that? What-what-what?" she squeaks, nearly stops, but goes on, blindly now, and in a daze.

I'm doubled up laughing, dying laughing, shaking, hugging my knees, and gagging, collapsed against a dry, upright log. To keep from laughing out loud, I breathe in musty air from the bridge's floorboards through my nose.

Snorting and choking with mirth and my future damnation, a mixture of sweat (it's stuffy under the bridge), dust and dryrot dribbling down my face, I knock on the bridge in time to her staggering step, then stop. The knocks turn out just right – dull and distant – because the boards are moldering and spongy underneath.

These coincident sounds so flabbergast her that she stops – the knocks stop – and suddenly I hear laughter. And sobs. Has she gone mad? Then she pulls off her sloppy, lopsided shoes – these I spied as she dragged herself onto the bridge – and her white socks. She really is insane... no, she's sane! She has decided that *that* was the sound of her own shoes. She wants to check. She does have hope, after all. She thinks that in her fright she imagined the whole thing.

All right, let her think that if she wants, I won't knock any more. She walks the rest of the way barefoot, obviously enjoying it: everything is quiet, isn't it. At the end of the bridge she stops: thank God, thank God, she figured that out, now she can think about her poor feet! What if she were to keep on going barefoot? On the one hand, the noiselessness of bare soles does not prevent one from listening to one's fear, on the other hand, it's easier on the feet. But to hold one's purse in one hand and one's shoes in the other seems sort of silly.

She is apparently deciding to put her shoes back on. Exactly. She has gone over to the railing, put both shoes down, bent over and, grasping the railing, begun to raise one foot. She is gripping her purse straps between chest and chin while her stiff, sockless foot is just about to go into the waiting shoe when I bang my stick with all my might. Not on the moldering underside this time, but on the dry upright log.

How do you like that! "Don't!" she screams and plows ahead barefoot, somehow grabbing her stuff as she goes, though one shoe remains on the bridge. "Don't do that!" she screams. She screams, but in a strange way: she screams as hard as she can, but softly. So that her persecutor will hear, but not the rest: she doesn't want to impose on the rest of the world, doesn't want to prevent the rest of the world from moving its gills, as if there were a rest of the world on this embankment. There are mice and spiders in the burdocks. Sparrows are nestled in the taller bushes sleeping. But the mice, sparrows, and spiders won't come running, or crawling, they won't bother; as for the people, they are buried on the bottom in thick drifts of sleep, and the nearest dogs are far away, while the furthest ones don't hear the quiet wails: they are sniffing the waning moon which, as it turns out, has been in the sky all along, only you couldn't make it out because of the streetlights. Still, there is a moon, and its being on the wane only makes the night more shadowy and dangerous.

She runs screaming, runs whimpering, mutely wailing, while I'm laughing so hard I can't see a thing, I can only imagine what happened next. I'll imagine it for you now.

This, I think, is what happened:

Having lurched off barefoot, she wobbled on a short way, but by then people had already begun to foul the ground, and along the dusty roadside to which her pudgy soles naturally clung, she stepped on some small nails, or a rusty jigsaw blade, or a piece of barbed wire. She cut herself on something, or bruised herself, because she cried out like a bird, the way people do when they hurt themselves, she stopped, pressed one leg against the other and stared back at the shoe abandoned on the bridge.

Whimpering, or perhaps sobbing, she slowly puts on the shoe she has, hesitates a moment, then takes a step towards the bridge. Then she stops. I keep quiet. She stands there. Then she takes another little step. I keep quiet. Then she freezes. Then she takes another step. She is crying quietly. I can hear this because I am keeping quiet. No, I misheard. She is whispering something. Pleading. She is pleading and whispering here's what: "Don't, don't, please stop it." I keep quiet as can be. Then she takes yet another step. I've decided not to bang any more. Zip: she jerks her shoe back, and I keep quiet. I'm tired of laughing on the end of that log, I want to go home.

Now she was probably putting on her other shoe − I couldn't see well. But I could hear: first there was silence, then muttering, silence, muttering, and finally − hiss, hiss, hiss − she pushed off.

Let her go. Let her go far away. I need to get out onto the road so I can go on with my story.

The scene has shifted to somewhere beyond the bridge and looks like this: a cobbled road, sparkling with the bits of glass and mica in the cobbles, runs along the embankment and straight up the hill (for a quarter of a mile or so), then levels off and continues straight. Just beyond the embankment, on the left, a huge school building – it's really only four stories – looms. Huge by night because of its dark silhouette, and by day because of the surrounding tumbledown sheds and shanties where the grassy streets begin. The road goes past the school, and keeps straight along the right side of the rectangle formed by the block of grassy streets.

Imagine that the page in front of you is that block. The road goes from bottom to top along the right-hand margin, the school is located perpendicular to the road along the bottom of the page, she and I both live along the left-hand margin: she lower down and I further up. But so far neither of us has reached the school, the bottom right-hand corner of the page, that is, and we – in our journey and our story – have gotten somewhat ahead of ourselves.

She had already gone fairly far beyond the bridge or, rather, dragged herself fairly far, thanks to her hurt foot she was now limping, too. (You couldn't tell which leg limped, the one that dragged or the one that didn't.) She lumbers on and doesn't look back. The moon is shining. I come out from under the bridge, creep along the railing, and wait for her to reach the first streetlight, the one that looked like a distant greasy blot when – remember? – I rounded the corner.

She had barely made it to the streetlight when I let out a loud, resounding gulp. An eerily mysterious guttural sound. Like someone swallowing. Oo-ootp. Inexplicable. Again she shuddered, again she turned round, then I came out of hiding – so what if she saw me – bent down and bounded across the road into the tall weeds on the other side. Pause. She stared but didn't move. I ran back across the road into more tall weeds from which I let out another loud gulp, rumbling and terrible under the moon. Oo-ootp.

Now she finally sees her persecutor or, rather, persecutors – *they* are running back and forth across the road. But what can she do? Get down on her knees? Beg for mercy? From whom? She still doesn't know who her persecutors are, and they're too far away. Get down on her knees on the cobblestones? In a dark place? That would be silly: they wouldn't see her. And under the streetlight, although they would see her, it would be strange and scary. Perhaps she should sit down? She badly wanted to sit down. She was so tired I think she wanted to lie down. Lie down and die. You can't die standing up, after all: you'd fall down and hurt yourself.

It's at this point that I see the thing I won't tell anyone about afterwards. Because it would be too hard and too boring and therefore not funny. On the other hand, in my then reptilian mind, instinctively waiting for the Decalogue without ever having heard of it, perhaps something was beginning to dawn, and perhaps not.

She, meanwhile, is standing under the streetlight, she sees many persecutors zigzagging back and forth across the road with short oblique bounds and lying in wait along either side, and then something happens to her that I hadn't counted on at all, and that, I have to admit, I did not grasp that night, which is why the Lord let me see *that* again.

Many years later I was living in Leningrad, in a communal apartment. I was living in half a room, and not alone. There was a large orange cat. Not a Persian, but enormous and unforgettable. To say that I love cats would be an understatement: I melt at the mere sight of those impressive characters and cannot take my eyes off them.

The large orange cat stole from the neighbors. Not for food, just for fun. Then he would hide. Then there would be a scene. Then the cat's distressed mistress would go looking for him, in among the firewood, say, stacked up in the endless corridor, and whack him with her bedroom slipper because she could have broken her hand hitting that huge cat who, in response to the less than merciless slipper, would flatten his ears, crouch down, and generally seem to suffer, yet by the way the slipper bounced back it was obvious that the thief would not be reformed by such pats on the back.

The cat's mistress had gone away somewhere, and the cat (who ordinarily slept at the foot of her bed on a local Leningrad newspaper, and would rise with his mistress at six, then issue into the fetid, lampblack corridor to his sawdust or to his morning saucer) – the cat took to yowling at night as if he absolutely had to go out. Stupid with sleeping pills,

I let the cat out to his sawdust (which meant I would have to chase him back in again in my semiconscious state to keep him from prowling among the pots and pans), but when I went to find him, he was hiding under his mistress's low bed and there was no getting him out, even with the poker. He, it seems, was having his fun. I went back to bed and the whole business started all over again. It was three o'clock in the morning and I, in a state of torment (I won't go into why), was finally succumbing to my fourth barbiturate.

This went on for several nights. The cat yowled, I got up, the cat hid, and so forth. Finally I had the idea of sealing the bed off with suitcases. That night, when the meowing began, I got up and watched him as he tried in vain to wriggle under the barricaded bed.

Then, to teach the cat a lesson, I resorted to the most terrifying thing he had ever seen in his life: the vacuum cleaner. I turned the machine on and slowly approached that defenseless beast (whom I adored in the extra-soporific world) with the snaking hose. The cat arched his back, fluffed up his tail, and began retreating, inch by solemn inch, into the corner where the hose was forcing him. We both knew it was the end. Finally I had him cornered, the yowling hose near his ear. Then he rose up on his hind legs, sat back on them, and, forgetting all dignity, wedged his back into the unforgiving corner. The whistling hose crawled up the wall after him but then the doomed cat's muscles suddenly gave way: he began twitching and hiccupping and heaving violently as if wanted to throw up but couldn't. He didn't narrow his eyes, he shut them, and shook, maybe his little orange heart had swollen in his veins and arteries and was leaping up into his throat and trying to get out, but my simple-hearted fellow lodger shuddered, half standing with one useless and not at all proud paw suspended in mid-air.

I turned off the vacuum cleaner and slept off the pills.

That is how I came to see *that* a second time. In the cat. And I'll never forget it. I pray to God that my good cat in his cat's paradise isn't holding a grudge against me and has forgotten the whole thing.

I saw *that* for the first time under the streetlight. Perhaps it was the shudder of the oncoming nausea, or the tenfold hiccups, or the heart's thumping in the veins.

She stood under the streetlight, lifted up her face, and began to shudder and twitch and heave. Her crookedish mouth showed black against her white face, her purse and socks dangled from her limp hands, her sweater sagged down over her flat chest and protruding stomach. She was fairly tall, her skirt hung down well below her knees, while her dropsied legs spilled out of her shoes like so much leavened dough. She twitched more and more violently. I stopped darting across the road. I guess I was sick of it.

And then what happened. She didn't die any more than the cat did; she walked on, and I walked after her. Just walked at a distance. When she stopped, I stopped. She rarely looked round. Now I know why she stopped. Her shins kept filling with leaden fluid to the point where she could not bear to take another step. I don't know the cause, maybe an intermittent lameness, maybe a muscle spasm, but now the same thing happens to me, too, and I have to stop.

Pacing ourselves that way we reached the corner where, perpendicular to the road, the school loomed, eclipsing the moon. She could either go round the school to the left, but then she would have to walk in the school's sinister shadow, or round the school to the right, along the bullies' back alley between the moon and the grassy street's squalid, miasmal sheds which she, being more dead than alive already, could not bring herself to do, though that was the shortest way home.

She, as I've said, lived (if the block is this page) lower down the left-hand margin and I lived further up. The road ran straight up the right-hand margin between sleeping houses and streetlights, and she now followed it, preferring to walk counter-clockwise round the block (or page) and a good half-mile out of her way rather than brave either side of the dreadful school. Then again, the long way round would take her past my house.

I turned left, passed quickly through the black back alley

and in a few minutes was sitting by my house, in the bushes, on the warm, crumbly carried earth. Not a dog was barking, not a branch was stirring — much less a curtain.

I had to wait quite a while. Finally, hiss-hiss-hiss, the tall, obscure figure with the small head materialized. Occasionally she would stop, then trudge on, muttering to herself. When she reached my house she noticed the bench outside the fence and sat down. Her hands bobbed in her lap. I couldn't see her face since I was behind her and a little to one side, but presumably her cheeks were, as Turgenev used to say, twitching to beat the band. She kept whispering to herself, while I sat stock-still on the carried earth.

"What was that?" she whispered. "What-what, what-what-what... h-h-how *could* h-h-he... wh-h-ho was h-h-he... and I don't h-h-have any more drops... pres-s-scription... what, h-h-how... where are you Georgie? George where are you? no more tablets either... but where are you... Lord, what is wrong with you... I don't know what's wrong with you... I'm the one who's alone... hiss-hiss-hiss... all alone, George... h-h-how could you? s-s-such h-h-horrors... all my life... were you really like that... s-s-such a nightmare... George, George... you waltzed... hiss-hiss-hiss... twenty drops, Georgie... and I'll be fine... where *are* you, *where*... and all because you're not here..."

The next day the boys and I would have such a laugh about all this. I got up, as usual, at one in the afternoon, and spied her walking past my window, looking straight ahead, seemingly, but also to the side. It was hot so I went out and sat down on the bench by the gate. She reappeared carrying water from the pump, and I noticed the semitransparent, cambric handkerchief wound round her big toe sticking out of an enormous oilskin sandal.

She stopped — as if by chance, as if to catch her breath — right by my bench.

"Excuse m-m-me!" she said suddenly, thinking herself brave as she stared at the ground. "Excuse m-m-me, was that you s-s-sneaking up on m-m-me last night? If it was, then why? I'm not easily s-s-scared, you know, but I'm going to h-h-have to talk to your m-m-mother..." She glanced bravely and despairingly at me, ready to jump back from her bucket at any moment.

"Me? What do you mean? I listen to the radio every night. Last night, for example, they read letters from workers. To Comrade Stalin. Then they played *Carmen*, the opera, by Bizet, the composer." I stared shamelessly at her twitching, swollen face. "Bizet, you know... Georges Bizet..."

"Oh, s-s-so that's it!" she sputtered and turned white. "I usually do t-t-too... letters, you s-s-say... from comrade workers... and m-m-music... very nice talking to you... Do you like Brahms?" she said suddenly (as if she'd just remembered something), despairingly, but helplessly. "Do you like Brahms? I do," she said, running far ahead into a future life, yours and mine, that she would never see. Now that life so far in the future has become my past, my distant past, and life has gone on still farther, but for some reason both she and her mutterings are in my life again.

If you would like to know what I think about all this now, go back to the beginning and reread my bold and rambling prayer.

It's just that I don't know for whom to pray to God: you see, I don't know what her name was, I never did know, and now there's no one left to ask.

TWO TOBITS

*O*ld man Nikitin washed and dried the cow's hindquarters, tail, and the rest, but the cow again fouled herself, and his efforts were wasted. Old man Nikitin did not curse, however, he merely narrowed his terrible colorless eyes. Again he bathed the cow and rubbed her dry, convinced that while grazing she had licked the *alatyr* stone harmful to cattle.

"Missed the boat!" he said.

Old man Nikitin tallied his taxes, but spelled the word "Total" the old way by mistake: with a hard sign. He had to start all over again. Still, old man Nikitin did not curse.

"Missed the boat!" he repeated.

Old woman Nikitina set a bowl of food before him and he, having said a prayer and crossed himself imperceptibly, fell to, but just then a man came strolling down the summer street smoking and the smell of tobacco wafted into the room. Old woman Nikitina slammed the shutters shut, while old man Nikitin again narrowed his terrible colorless eyes and said softly:

"Missed the boat!"

Old man Nikitin took a tome full of hard signs from its hiding place, sat down away from the window which the old woman had again opened, and began reading without any glasses. He became lost in thought, however, and, having narrowed his terrible colorless eyes to a slit, he again did not curse, but concluded wistfully:

"Missed the bo-o-oat!"

Then came the muffled sound of a double shot way away in the distance. It rang out over the Leningrad Highway, then veered toward Khimki, flew over the left bank of the Moscow River, and over Petrovsko-Razumovskoye, then splintered into scattering echoes and finally reached our grass-grown street.

Old man Nikitin un-narrowed his terrible eyes, got up and straightened his shirt. Old woman Nikitina got up, too. They glanced at each other and crossed themselves imperceptibly. Once again old man Nikitin did not curse, but said simply and with satisfaction:

"Missed the boat!"

He exclaimed the first time because the cow had been left untended; the second time because those who had once treasured the hard sign hadn't even noticed when this letter had been taken away from them; the third time because of the window being unbarred against sin; while the fourth exclamation was a wistful sigh over the forfeited priesthood from Jesus Christ which the Old Believers — too busy counting Nikonians' fingers, being brutalized, and suffering over trivialities — had forgotten to foster when they lost their lawful prelates and churches.

The last exclamation was in response to the two distant shots.

They were shooting near Khimki. The Germans were marching on Moscow. The capital, too, had been left untended and on the grassy streets all the landlords and landladies couldn't wait for the Germans to come.

To make the time go faster, old man Nikitin decided to read the Book of Tobit, while old woman Nikitina, also without glasses, set to scraping the wooden dish for bread and salt.

"...I Tobit have walked all the dayes of my life in the way of trueth... Then all my goods were forcibly taken away, neither was there any thing left me, besides my wife Anna, and my sonne Tobias... and I slept by the wall of my court yard... and mine eyes being open, the Sparrowes muted warme doung into mine eyes, and a whiteness came in mine eyes..."

Suddenly everything fell into place. He was Tobit whose

eyes had been sullied by the sparrow (the godless regime), but the angel Raphael would bring his son home to him (Kolka Nikitin was in jail for petty theft) and with a cure, and the scales would fall from his eyes which, though seeing, were still confused by the hard sign, although that hard sign would be saved, and in Moldavia – or maybe even in Germany! – a bishop of the true faith would be found.

With the bishop, old man Nikitin's splendid mood was suddenly spoiled. No, a bishop would not be found! Would not be fo-o-ound! And the one to blame for this, terrible to say, was the holy archpriest! Just think of it! How could he have?

"Missed the bo-o-oat!" old man Nikitin said in a terrible voice, his terrible colorless eyes narrowing terribly.

He was right, you might say, about everything, except Tobit. Tobit was – or rather would be – Hymie who lived across the road behind the water pump which you can't really use right now since it's slathered with mustard.

Mustard? What is this nonsense? Hymie, the cow, Tobit, the priesthood from the God-Man, and a pump slathered with mustard? No, this isn't nonsense. This is how – naturally, if oddly – Great Events are transubstantiated on the little streets overgrown with grass, in the lives of ordinary people, in other words. But not only, not only! Even if you're somebody, you're never very far from the cow, between her udder and your cup your morning milk goes through three, maybe four pairs of hands at most; whether you're Tobit, or an Old Believer martyr, or a dictator, you often have to fetch your own water – from the pump or the spring – yourself; you keep mustard on the table whether you're something or nothing; and no matter where, when, or who you are, the verb "to slather" is part of your vocabulary: the sparrow's "warme doung" slathered your eyes in the Holy Land; the cow's hindquarters are slathered with mud; and the veal cutlets, when Molotov dines with Hitler, are slathered with mustard.

People everywhere live essentially the same lives, though they consider them different. And even if they are different, the difference is only superficial, for the mustard-slathered cutlet and the mustard-slathered pump are participial, strangely enough, to one and the same thing, while for the action of slathering there is, thank God, a verb!

Have you ever thrown anything, reader? "I have!" say you. What's the best thing for throwing, what's the worst? I'll tell you:

Brick shards make bad missiles: the big ones are awkward, the little ones lack the necessary weight. Brown bottle slivers fly no better, while slinging stolen crab apples, dry clods of earth, last year's pocked potatoes, and loose-handled axes is no fun at all. Little balls of damp putty are good to throw, as are smooth, round, flat stones from the seashore (should anyone have brought you some), regular-size green garden tomatoes, the small slippery cobbles made of flint found in Moscow soil, small alatyr stones, copper two-ounce weights, and various other things.

Those are the best things to either throw at a target or just plain throw. Of course, it's more satisfying to throw at something: the splat of a tomato sends any hen into a panic; the perfect stone knocks the pane right out of a dormer window; rounded Biblical basalts hit the harlot's sweet body hard, yet softly and dully.

But a small jar of mustard hurtling at the pump: there's nothing better! It has the necessary weight, yet fits snugly in a child's hand, while the viscosity of the contents sends it somersaulting through the air before exploding in a delicious succession of four discrete sounds: the tinkling of the glass, the cast-iron drone of the pump, and next − if the lid is carbolated − the crackle, as if someone had stepped on a large beetle or a gramophone record, followed by the clang. And then the smack of the mustard's impact: soft yet hard, as if the pump were a harlot's body, or juicy, like blancmange in a film comic's face. In addition to which the mustard, though the color of diarrhea, which in itself is hilarious, smells good and sharp, and − most interesting of all! − you can throw it all day long and the grown-ups won't stop you. Have as many jars as you like.

But where does the mustard come from?

From the food stall by the pump.

What do you mean?

Just that. The only thing left in the stall is mustard.

Where did everything else go?

The vendors took it.

Why don't the grown-ups stop the boys throwing mustard?

Because they're too busy doing the same thing, grabbing whatever they can.

The food stall, incidentally, would never have any more food, but would be pulled apart for firewood; meanwhile, stores would be piled high for the next four years with sumptuous stacks of canned crab bearing the foreign label CHATKA that no one would buy. They would go hungry, but they would not be issued any crabmeat; they would force themselves to eat potatoes turned sickeningly sweet by frost, but they would not be issued the crab. It wouldn't occur to them to add the crab to the potatoes and make a Salade Olivier since sophistication in such matters would come only much later, somewhere between the cosmopolitans and the cosmonauts; they were still stuck in the time before the zampolitans, though that era would dawn immediately after the events described in this story.

But where are the ones they call zampolitans?

Not around.

And the police?

Also not around.

What do you mean not around?

I mean not around.

Where are the police, where are the people who are supposed to stop boys from pelting pumps with pilfered pots of mustard?

Nobody's around.

One fine day, one day in particular, please note, the grown-ups could not be bothered. That day, or two, or three − I don't remember − came to be known as the panic. What prompted it? What was it all about? I don't know. But I can attest to the hurling of small jars of mustard. I hurled some myself and often hit the target since, as we've said, the missile-like perfection of those jars exceeded even that of the Biblical stone in David's sling.

Now, however, as I look back on that strange pastime, smelling of mustard and crisp autumn days, my sense is that the grown-ups didn't stop the children because there were no grown-ups around: some were away in the war, others had been evacuated, still others couldn't be bothered – they, too, were grabbing whatever they could. So then does that mean that the proper grown-ups, so to speak, never stopped them either? Where had they disappeared to? And what about the ones who were even more grown-up? Where had they gone? And the ones who were even more grown-up than that and were supposed to keep an eye on the merely more grown-up? Do you mean to say that none of them were around either? They, of course, did not steal from the food stalls and store-houses, but they could easily have slipped away. Then what were the very most grown-up thinking? Can it be that they, too..? But in that case why didn't the most grown-up of all do anything? Unbelievable?! And the highest of the high? Where was he?

Here the logical chain breaks and clatters to the ground. And well it should, although every time I start wondering where – damn it all! – the junior-most grown-ups went without chasing us kids away, my silly thought again ascends the scaffold of cognition, especially since – just now! only yesterday! – the usual, impeccable order reigned, and on the grassy streets that order was so established that a couple of local cops could deal with whatever and whomever in no time flat, but now here we are throwing things and nobody even bats an eye!

Night and day single shots rang out from Khimki, I can also attest.

One of the grown-ups who didn't stop us – he, incidentally, could see the pump from his stoop where he sat out every day and babbled at whoever came for the white, gushing water – was Hymie, not yet Tobit because he still had his health and gruntingly hauled two enormous sacks he had swiped from the little canteen at Calibre – the famous defense plant! – all the way home. One sack contained unsweetened pink gelatin, the other sugar.

That was all Uncle Hymie had and with what he was content, thus dooming himself to the awful consequences, for there was a war on and you had to grab whatever you could, but he grabbed some gelatin! True, he grabbed some sugar, too. But Hymie was stupid and lazy so the sugar wouldn't help him, especially when the landladies on the grassy street were already modelling their shawls and glass beads in anticipation of the Germans, while the Smykovs had gone so far as to mend their antique magic lantern with views of the Tikhonov Hermitage and Carlsbad for the amusement of their future lodgers – now when you turned the little mother-of-pearl wheel on its straight brass spindle, the marvelous lantern's brass cylinder moved dully and irreproachably along the impeccable rack and pinion of the past.

Still, you mustn't think that anticipation was the rule. On the contrary, it was the exception. But exceptions were all that remained on the grassy street since everyone else who was registered there had disappeared: some had evacuated on their own, while others had been evacuated with their factories, so that mostly only those landlords who hadn't abandoned their houses were left – almost all the houses on the grassy street were privately owned and each householder lived with a multitude of tenants. So then, only the landlords were left, and some of their tenants. Hymie, for example. And the family that lived opposite Hymie, and some others, but not many.

The family opposite Hymie, and Hymie himself for that matter, really should have left, but the man of the family opposite (who, like Hymie, was much too old to be drafted) couldn't make up his mind, and when his grown daughter broke down in tears for fear of what the approaching Germans would do to her, and he had all but decided to leave, a large boil appeared on his foot and they missed their chance. The girl is still sobbing, shots are echoing, and the air raids are driving us out to the trench we dug in the apple orchard where the now brazen landladies don't want to let us in and never let us near the warm stove – the nights have grown cold. The landladies try as hard as they can to keep us out, then finally let us in and go right on talking about a German leaflet that no one has actually seen but that supposedly says:

> *Oh, little Moscow ladies, dear,*
> *Don't you hide in your little lairs,*
> *For our little tanks will appear,*
> *And they'll bury your little lairs.*

Some say, "And they'll flatten your little lairs," others say, "And they'll wall up your little lairs," but that doesn't change the gist.

The gist is that they're shooting night and day near Khimki, meanwhile boys are pelting the pump with little jars of mustard. So any day now. They say the Germans have already named the day. And planned a ceremonial parade. Slow and unhurried. For the appointed day... For now they don't want to get here one whit faster. That was the Germans' mistake, say some historians today. I don't know, I'm not well-versed in these matters and I won't speak out of turn.

But that they tried to keep us out of the trench, I can attest. And when the mother of the sobbing girl asked her landlady Lyubov Alekseyevna (not an invented name) to sign the so-called standard forms you needed to get food coupons, Lyubov Alekseyevna first shouted: "Get down on your knees, 'cause soon you'll be dead!" – and then, when the mother threatened her back, she signed the forms after all and stamped them with her round seal on which the address was spelled with hard signs and which read in the middle: "Shuvalov, Landlord" (not an invented seal).

While poet-Captain Wolfgang Amadeus Gelderling of the German propaganda division composes new leaflets in his flawless Russian, while major turning points occur in the war, and while the sobbing girl begins writing to the front on postcards showing two little children on tiptoes struggling to drop their letter into a mailbox next to the inscription: "Papa, kill that German!" – while all of this is going on, the first winter of the war goes by, cold, early, unexpected, with air raids, trenches, alerts, and malnutrition, for which Hymie compensates with sugar, mixed with a little dry gelatin.

By spring he is reeling from this pink pabulum, especially since the sugar is running out faster than expected, and soon he'll have to figure out a way to eat up the pink powder by itself.

The whole street is eating it up. They are boiling sour pink aspics out of it (saccharine has yet to appear, and no one has enough sugar left), and sprinkling it in their tea, barely sweetened with the tiniest bit of rationed sugar which they spoon onto their tongues and suck.

I wish I could say that they were using the gelatin to make mousses and blancmange, to roast kebabs and shape Kalmyk dumplings, but no one on the grassy street knows anything about anything like that, just as no one suspects that it might make sense to go to Kazanka (the log hut housing the only store in the district) and be issued some of that crabmeat canned for export, instead of those rock-hard sweetmeats, and so turn the grueling great patriotic existence into regular feasts like the ones served up in the world's best restaurants; just as no one suspects that Roosevelt is dying for some crabmeat, but in America crabs are as scarce as hen's teeth and it never occurs to him to send Ambassador Harriman to Kazanka in the Willis, besides the ambassador is in love with that ballerina, Lepeshinskaya, and she's working with Lemeshev, that tenor whose naive chest voice booms from the black loudspeaker every day: "Oh, Nastasia! Oh, Nastasia! Open the gates! Open the gates and meet your swain!"

The last cow doesn't have much longer to go on the grassy street, and one can already say with confidence that this street has ceased to flow with milk. True, there is a little honey left, or rather gelatin, but Hymie's is powdered. And day after day he sprawls on his sun-baked stoop, his stomach ballooning from malnutrition. A worthless old man with the face of a chimpanzee. That's right! He looks just like a chimp! The stoop is hot, but he goes on lying there, he wants to eat, but he doesn't want to move, others go in search of food, but he's too lazy to bother.

He hasn't planted potatoes in the middle of the street or dug a kitchen garden. True, the room he has rented from Lymarev since long before the war is such a bad deal it doesn't include even a square foot of earth for a kitchen garden; the stoop abuts a fence – or rather, used to – for that fence, like all the fences, as well as the aforementioned food stall – everything wooden and unoccupied, in other words – was pulled apart for firewood the first winter of the war.

So now there's nothing left between Hymie and the pump, not even the old food stall. Incidentally, the difference between a stall and a store seems to be that customers come up to a stall from the street and buy – or rather, bought – whatever, while the vendors and the goods are located inside; whereas in a store everything is inside: the buyers, the sellers, and the pyramids of canned crab, only the extra provisions are stashed behind a partition where, while the line squabbles, the saleswoman dashes all winter and tinkles into the vat of pickled cabbage. There's nowhere else to go: the outhouse behind the store has also been stolen for firewood. So while the line for cabbage keeps getting longer – people haven't learned to pickle their own yet, and where else can she go? nowhere! – she keeps dashing back to the vat because she caught a chill diddling a soldier standing up – it's bitter cold out!

As soon as the stall was gone, grass grew up on the empty patch and some ancient paths reappeared. The ground had evidently been busy with its own grassy, pathy, and gnatty affairs irrespective of whether the stall was standing, or bullets were flying, or Hymie was staggering from malnutrition. But when the cow began grazing the new place, the ground was glad and kept throwing up quantities of lush grass from out of which, warned by the cow's warm breath, ants and gnats scattered, disappearing into pin-size burrows or revving the sure-fire engines of their tiny flying machines.

On the grassy street, besides Nikitin's cow, there were two others. The Krivoborskys' and the Lymarevs'. But right after Molotov's speech, they both mooed their last, so that now only Nikitin's cow remained. At the moment, she was preventing Hymie, lolling on the stoop, from seeing his interlocutor, sitting out on the mound of warm earth by the house opposite.

"I think I'll plant some potatoes!" says Hymie.

The mound-sitter, screened by the cow, quietly tries not to smile because besides Hymie, only the Stalin Collective Farm, locally located at the other end of the street behind an enormous dump, would think to start a potato-planting program in August.

"Or maybe you think carrots? You don't think?"

"I do think!"

"See how bad my right leg is already?"

"I do see, but only part of it. The cow's in the way."

"Get the hell outta here, you mother!" Hymie suddenly yells with all his might the way that man on the train yelled at that woman on the train that time when Hymie was on his way to propose to Gita, who has now been evacuated from her factory to Yangi-Yul along with their son and daughter, while he has to lie here with not enough to eat.

"Don't you yell at that cow, you lug!" old woman Nikitina sticks her head out the window, but then old man Nikitin's terrible voice commands her from inside:

"Drive her in and milk her or you'll miss the boat!"

"Well! Have you heard? Such a war going on all over the world, people's blood being spilt, and we're supposed to put up with those kulaks' henchmen! And they have milk and eggs..."

What eggs have to do with it is anyone's guess. The Nikitins don't keep chickens, and will soon lead the cow away. When the cow shambles across the cobbled road, her udder swinging from side to side, old woman Nikitina strides after her in low felt boots with double-thick soles. She has bad legs.

Well, and what of it? Hymie's legs are swollen, too! You'll laugh but Roosevelt, he has bad legs, too, and what hasn't he tried for those legs of his, but Stalin, he said he won't let Doctor Burdenko see him until America opens a second front.

From the depths of the goosefoot behind the house in

front of which the mound-sitter is sunning, a siren screams: an air-raid warning. Though the sound dies away, like that of a real siren, the screaming is obviously being done by some little boys in the goosefoot. Nevertheless, the landlady peeks out the door and then, her face ashen, quickly slams it shut. Just what the boys in the goosefoot wanted. Lyubov Alekseyevna gets diarrhea every time there's an alert, and she's the last one into the trench. Now she's closeted with another attack, we'll think of it as revenge for those so-called standard forms − remember, when they were shooting near Khimki?

The scientific term for what happens to Lyubov Alekseyevna is "butterflies", but no one on the deserted grassy street knows this, then again everyone who's left will soon learn the ancient name of another ancient sickness.

Here's how it started.

Early one spring, or rather, one fine day in early spring, or to put it more precisely, one fine evening, everything went black before Hymie's eyes. Until then Hymie had thought of the expression "everything went black before my eyes" as one of those national, or rather, national-emotional embellishments. When he had thought of it at all.

But now, at the end of the day, something was happening to him himself and that something could only be described as "everything going black", or at least blackish. Otherwise he felt fine, he still wanted to eat, he still wanted to sleep. And so long as it was light out he wanted to read the paper.

But how can he tell if it's light out when everything is black before his eyes? And yet he's not in any pain, even if his legs are somewhat swollen. Oy, those legs! But his heart isn't palpitating, he's not spitting blood! And now that it's so much warmer out, his room is finally warm, he just wishes he could make out what's written on those three bread coupons for workers; a lady neighbor gave them to him in exchange for a little of the dry gelatin − her soldier lover and his commander are coming to dinner today and she wants to make a mousse (they've learned how!) out of semolina (he brought some!) and saccharine (now you can get it!).

But then night fell and Hymie lit the oil lamp, that

indisputable symbol and visible sign of absolute darkness. Now he had no way of knowing whether the blackness was before his eyes or because of the oil lamp. And no matter how he tried that evening, no matter how he scrutinized the plywood walls of his hutch, no matter how he paced with that little square piece of paper in his hand, he could not manage to make out a single bedbug. And he so liked to corner the fleeing bugs, force them onto his little piece of paper, and fling them out the door, as he said, "onto the cold" or, if it was spring, into a mud puddle, and in summer into a barrel of standing water, reeking like the raggedy shreds of food extracted from a rotten tooth.

The next day, also towards evening, everything again went black before Hymie's eyes, but, you know, only for a second! Then his eyes were fine for two weeks, and he forgot all about both incidents what with the bombs dropping, the anti-aircraft guns firing, and the searchlights combing the sky.

A dirigible went up every evening from the yard of school No. 271, its floppy forked tail drooping at first, then gradually filling with hydrogen till it resembled a stuffed chicken neck — if you took a little chicken skin, filled it with lot of flour, and let it swell up in some broth.

Actually the dirigible looked more like a huge beached bomb; or an elongated poppy pod in the milk stage when it is a bluish grey with quilted soles along its poppy meridians; or a seed cucumber, grown dark and moldy out of brine, dragging its dill-stalk of a cable up into the sky where only a yellow sunset could turn this dreary vegetable into a golden Yangi-Yul melon.

The dirigible didn't look like much of anything to Hymie — not even a chicken neck. Yet as he gazed at it, it did occur to him that he had seen something like it somewhere before, just what and where he couldn't think, though his primate's brow was furrowed and his forehead as wrinkled as need be for him to remain anonymous among a bunch of chimps, when one is threading a needle; another is inspecting what it has picked out of its nose on the hard nail of a shameless finger; a third is trying to count its extremities; and a fourth is pursing its lips from exertion because it is amazed by something, or relieving itself, or thinking.

Then everything went completely and permanently black before Hymie's eyes. Soon he couldn't see at all in the evening. Of course, he told everyone about this, but no one believed him: you see, the only people left on the grassy street were the ones who didn't especially believe anyone, while the ones who had begun straggling back from the front minus an arm, or a leg, or a pecker, couldn't be bothered just then with Hymie's tales.

No one believed Hymie because he didn't inspire any trust, he ate only his ration, he had a dependent's ration rather than a worker's ration because he didn't go to work, just as he didn't sew the buttons back on his fly, while his pants were bunched under a belt that kept sliding down under his belly like the second-from-the-bottom hoop on a barrel. And just as the hoop, when it slid down, left a whitish stripe flecked with little balls of dust stuck to the staves' splinters and spurs, so Hymie's belt, when it slid down, exposed a rumpled, unfastened fly in whose dim recesses flickered bits of lint, mold, rot, and a limp chicken skin only loosely filled with all manner of male junk.

No one ever would have believed Hymie, but then one night, when the searchlights were rushing about the sky, and a small plane caught in their beams was trying frantically to get away, and the anti-aircraft guns were jumping up and down like dogs that had chased a cat up a tree, in the midst of an air raid in other words, someone noticed that Hymie, instead of urinating against the side of the house and hustling into the trench, had urinated the other way – into the street – and tottered off, arms outstretched uncertainly before him, towards the Stalin Collective Farm.

When they struck from three directions at once, he stumbled and, arms waving, fell into a ditch from out of which had to be pulled after the All-Clear. While the raid was still going on, however, the consensus in the trench was that Hymie had been hit by shrapnel. It was Lyubov Alekseyena, by the way, who brought the news, having been waylaid at home by the usual emergency, and now shaking like a pitiful leaf.

Fished out of the ditch, Hymie, too, was pitiful, but most pitiful of all was the poor pilot of the downed bomber as the cabin began to fill with smoke from the burning tail, and the aeroplane began to somersault, not as well as, say, a little jar of mustard, but as badly as an empty cigarette box. When it turned out that Hymie hadn't been wounded everyone was happy, though not nearly so happy as the ones who had knocked that little cardboard box of a plane out of the sky.

Now everyone believed there was something wrong with Hymie's eyes.

But what? But what?

By day the man sees out of both eyes, he even reads the paper without glasses. If he's not lazing on the stoop and basking in the sun, then he's going about his business and, say, borrowing the aforementioned newspaper from his neighbor across the way. But at night his eyes are shrouded in darkness. How is he supposed to catch any bedbugs? He can't even see to take his socks off, for that matter his over-shoes may still be on. He keeps missing the little jar where he puts his false teeth.

Why don't you go to the doctor, Hymie? How am I supposed to go to the doctor when the doctor doesn't come to the wooden clinic over the post office until five o'clock in the afternoon and sees patients for two hours, and I'll have to walk home alone in the dark? All right, I'll walk you there and the boys will walk you back!

You bet they'd walk him back! – you can imagine how all those urchins loved to play tricks on anthropoid Hymie.

The boy taking Hymie home from the clinic felt a little shy at first, but when his classmate came sidling out of a side alley, the boy made a monkey face like Hymie's, and calmly walked the night blind man into a lamppost.

"What are you doing?" screamed Hymie, hugging the log pole like a long-lost son. "I could crack my head open!"

"Let go! It's high voltage! It'll kill you!" the boy screamed in desperation, while his classmate tickled Hymie's hand

with some sort of nonsensical wire. "Ick!" Hymie fell back
screeching and would have lost his balance entirely if not for
the palms of both boys kindly propping him up. "That's it, I
gotta go," said one, once they had steadied the stunned fool,
while the other continued on with Hymie, and both nearly
died laughing over the chalk-white poem on Hymie's back:
"BIG DICK BIG DICK". Their four saving palms, inscribed
ahead of time with the letters, only in reverse order, had
printed the words on Hymie's worn, crumpled, ill-fitting
jacket. Still, the boys' haste showed: in both cases the "K"
had come out backwards.

"I was so frightened!" Hymie told his guide, who blamed
the lamppost on his friend's sudden appearance. "I was so
frightened! After all, I can't see a thing! So you know what
she said, that doctor? That I need vitamins and iron. And
what is it called my sickness?

"Night blindness."

"Run find out! Where can I get some iron?"

"I'll bring you some from the airplane dump. We'll file
it with a little file and you can mix it with some gelatin! Only
it has to be 100-percent pure."

"Now I know you're a good boy, not like those bullies.
Shake hands!" says Hymie amiably, unaware that he would
have been stuck with the nickname "Hymie Big Dick" if not
for the gathering gloom preventing passers-by from making
out the chalky cuneiform on his raggedy jacket.

The grassy street, too, learned the diagnosis. Night blindness! Just imagine! We never had that before! Tuberculosis,
yes! Consumption, yes! Blood-spitting, yes! But you have...
What did you say you have?

"It's Svetochka, that fat doctor, who said! Night blindness!"

"Where did you get it? Oh, Lord! Another alert! Come
on, I'll walk you to the trench."

It's warm. It's hot. It's simply wonderful to lie out on
the stoop in the sun and swell up from hunger. No matter
who comes by, the conversation is always the same: "Well,
what do you know! Night blindness! Who would have thought
it! And you're considered blind? Only at night? Well that's

good! What's good? But whatever you do, don't let them register you or they'll give you a dog you'll have to feed and it will definitely give you worms. And then where will you get any santonin, I'd like to know?"

Every time he went to get water, especially in the evening when he had to haul some forty buckets for the kitchen garden — the Nikitins had replaced their cow with a kitchen garden (now they're allowed, kitchen gardens are allowed on the grassy street!) — old man Nikitin would overhear these conversations by the pump. Everyone in line for water felt compelled to speak to the sufferer reclining on the stoop and with every exchange old man Nikitin narrowed his terrible eyes and pursed his lips. And once, when only he and his fellow believer were at the pump, he said to Yeremei, but so that Hymie would hear:

"That used to happen a lot to people during Lent, remember, Yeremei? The world became unsightly..."

"Happened to my Pa. 'Course I remember!"

"It'd be so dark you couldn't pray your way out. Then suddenly it'd be gone! When they slaughtered the calves. And you ate some liver..." Nikitin enunciates. "Liver, I say, half a pound is all, and you can see again. You watered your carrots yet? I'm nearly done mine..."

Hymie hears every word. And indeed... The doctor, she told him: vitamins, iron, some calf's liver would be good, but he, he was so upset by the name of his ailment, he forgot to listen.

"Where can I get some liver, where?"

"Well? Have you asked around?

"Why not stew a cow's udder?"

"They have liver on First Meshchanskaya Street sometimes, but it's pork."

"Wait a minute! Wait a minute! Who's registered on First Meshchanskaya, let me think..."

"They say that someone brought you some liver yesterday and you refused it, is that true?"

The whole street was racking its brains trying to think where Hymie could get hold of some liver.

Anyone who was at all nosy was obsessed with the idea and every time the helpless Hymie was carried feet first into the trench, someone would invariably sigh: "Oy, what you need is a good piece of liver!"

Hymie, meanwhile, had begun seeing color spots during the day. Say a man was approaching the pump, Hymie would hear steps and peer in their direction, but instead of a man he would see a spot on the bright street.

Nikitin was a red spot. And he, to be honest, was not Tobit because — now it's obvious why — the verily unseeing Hymie had become Tobit; and a little sparrow was not to blame, the culprit was a small plane-bird whose time of passage was called "the war" and was dragging on an awfully long time, though occasionally a bird did turn up on the airplane dump from which the boy said he would bring Hymie some 100-percent pure iron.

So old man Nikitin was a bony red spot, complicated by the yoke sticking out on either side and the zinc-coated buckets attached.

"Listen, Nikitin, your Papa, did he really cure himself with liver?"'

The red spot doesn't even answer. Instead, it narrows its terrible eyes.

"Listen, Nikitin, why did you send your cow to slaughter? Without a cow you're not a man. A man like you is not a man without a cow!"

The red spot by the pump lifts its wispy grey beard up to the sky, narrows its eyes as always against the still bright sun, and sets off home without a word.

"Comrade Nikitin, if I bought some liver from you I would pay you well. Why won't you say anything? You're a Soviet man, after all! You have to have a cow! Well! For a man to not have a cow!"

The red spot turns round suddenly, then turns slowly away and recedes, buckets swinging.

"Comrade Nikitin, let's do this: I'll get you some gelatin, only dry, and you ask the other milk-sellers.

"What did it ever bother you, having that cow around?

She didn't bother me! Once I even gave her some gelatin. A whole fistful. You should have seen how she ate it up! And now, without a cow, you're not a man... Are you a Soviet man, comrade Nikitin? I gave her some gelatin, honest to God, a whole fistful."

"W-what?" the spot sputters, turning orange around the edges. "W-what? You gave her gelatin! And I thought we missed the boat! But we missed you... You! All swollen up! Can't see! Blind bum! Gel-latin!" old man Nikitin is in a hurry, someone in the distance is coming towards the pump. "But I have a c-c-calf... Near Vostryakovo, where they bury your kind... It's in Vostryakovo..." Hymie is hearing this strange name for the first time; later it will be all too familiar, but about that another time, not here. "The old woman and I are taking the calf to slaughter tomorrow or the day after. The calf's at our son's godfather's. The godfather's a clean man. And there'll be liver... Fresh liver... It'll cure you, Hymie!" says Nikitin, suddenly amiable and merry. "You're doing the right thing, neighbor. It's an a-a-ancient remedy!" – the one come from the distance chimes in. "Got to go and water those carrots... Oh-ho-ho!" and Nikitin walks off, eyes narrowed, muttering: "Lord! May his blood turn black. He missed the bo-o-oat."

The next day there's no Nikitin. And the day after that, and the day after that, no Nikitin and no old woman, neither one comes to the pump, that is. Then again it's raining so there isn't much point in watering the kitchen garden.

As for Hymie, he doesn't lie out on the stoop when it's raining. He dons his raggedy jacket and peaked cap and hobbles to Kazanka, and a couple of days later he notices what seems to be a red spot shining in Nikitin's window: old man Nikitin is sitting there for some reason and, or so it appears to Hymie, counting and re-counting something.

Hymie drags himself home from Kazanka and mixes the cocoa he has been issued with the remains of the gelatin, and then there's that piece of herring somebody gave him: so he sits and eats. And when he falls asleep, he sees nothing but dirigibles in his dreams, dirigibles streaming out from under medical red spots and racing headlong to Kazanka, all to Kazanka, only one is climbing the wall.

A few days later Hymie is shuffling past Nikitin's house at dusk when he hears an alert. Everything starts to blur. But the house is right there: just three puddles away. After the unpleasantness with that other alert – remember? – Hymie isn't afraid of air raids, and the Nikitins never go into the trench because if there's a fire – those incendiary Old Believers were used to burning – they have to carry certain things out and not miss the boat.

Alerts really don't frighten anyone anymore. First they announce them, then comes the All-Clear. You almost never see those small planes, and even when you do, they rarely fire.

Hymie's vision is slightly blurred, but that's all. Not bad at all, you might even say. But now the greatly debilitated Hymie, still blind as a post come evening, suddenly starts making things out: the summer vitamins in the beet leaves that are sustaining him along with the hope of some liver must be having their effect. He even makes out the Nikitins' fence of brush and wire, which is why he pauses by their window. The window is open – the evening is still fine and warm – and, hidden by the fence, Hymie overhears someone reading. Old man Nikitin, unafraid of passers-by because of the alert, is reading in a kind voice full of emotion here's what:

"...neither turne thy face from any poore... Because that almes doth deliver from death, and suffereth not to come into darkness."

Hymie listens carefully.

"...and according to thine abundance give almes, and let not thine eye be envious."

Oy, how carefully Hymie listens!

"Then Tobias saide... to what use is the heart, and the liver, and the gall of the fish? And Raphael said unto him... As for the gall *it is good* to anoint a man that hathe whitenesse in his eyes and he shalbe healed."

Hymie purses his lips in amazement.

"...I am Raphael one of the seven holy Angels, which

present the prayers of the Saints, and which go in and out before the glory of the Holy one..."

It is almost pitch dark. The street is quiet and deserted. Hymie stands there in his raggedy jacket and doesn't budge from the fence. All of a sudden searchlights shoot up into the sky and – more surprising still – anti-aircraft guns start firing nearby: that's the battery they installed last week at the Stalin Collective Farm. The salvo startles even the calm Nikitin. The old woman goes to the window intending to close the rattling shutters but then she sees Hymie, crouching by the fence for fear of another volley, and yells:

"What're you hidin' there for! Come to steal, you devil!"

Old man Nikitin appears from behind her, but his eyes are neither narrowed nor terrible, they are even somehow warm. He looks up at the sky alive with searchlights, crosses himself in full view of Hymie, and says:

"The godfather and I gave the liver to the police to keep'm quiet. For it says: 'And the third, I gave unto them to whom it was meet...'"

He stands there smiling. And again he crosses himself with a sweeping gesture.

"I hope those three fingers you just crossed yourself with dry up and drop off, you mother!"

"W-what? W-what? Me? With three? With three fingers? Old woman! Old woman... give me that, give me that, give it here!"

An average-size hammer (a very handy contrivance, incidentally, for throwing) comes somersaulting through the evening air at Hymie.

Bang! Bang! Bang!: anti-aircraft salvoes from the Stalin Collective Farm drown out this desperate scene.

Hymie dodged the hammer. He was seeing better, after all. Hymie went home. Quietly, and on his own. He truly was seeing better. He lit the oil lamp. He took a little square of paper. He furrowed his brow and began to write:

"Kulaks' henchmen are again activating already and spreading jimson from the ambo like under the tsar-father. I being an invalid, with blind eyes..."

You know the rest, reader. You know *what* – with the best intentions – they write in denunciations. You've written them yourself... You haven't? Yes you have! Every one of those applications explaining the circumstances, every petition, every request, was in essence a denunciation denouncing those very circumstances, your relatives. With the best intentions, of course.

Hymie, too, is writing with the best intentions. This is not revenge. He is truly indignant. The secret slaughter of livestock. The hammer. The insults for no reason.

But where is the angel Raphael?

Why didn't he deflect the hand of Tobit in whom resentment had overcome the usual sloth, why didn't he deflect his hand from those terrible words on paper out of which old man Nikitin may never have been able to pray his way.

Why didn't he quell the rage and the spite in Nikitin (say what you like, he, too, is a Tobit!), why didn't he inspire a meek love for his wretched neighbor the blind man whose son, Tobias, is now trying to teach his sister how to milk a male donkey dry in Yangi-Yul?

Why, why didn't the angel fly to them through the midnight sky?

Perhaps he didn't think he could manage two Tobits at once without a second Tobias to gladden the bestial ringleader in the labor colony with his young body. Or perhaps not even the most beneficent of angels would have flown to them for fear of hitting the cable attached to the dirigible? What if the cable were to cut his dove-like wing, heaven help us, and bleed him of all his ethereal substance? Or worse, what if he were to become caught in the searchlights' crisscrossing beams and to shine, like that small plane, in the dark blue summer night sky?

He will shine, the angel of the Lord. The radiant angel Raphael.

JULY

*I*n July when the sides of the cobbled road are ankle-deep in dust, soft and hot, like some exotic cure, and the cobbles' grainy skulls are hard even to the eye, and the blades of grass that poked up between the stones in spring have withered and are sticking out of bits of broken glass or out of the coarse-grained sand, then the horses, far more common here than three-ton trucks, abandon the cobbles and − pshhh-pshhh − sink their hardened dray hooves into the downy roadside dust, two wheels continue to clatter along the cobbles, while the other two are hushed by the sand, the cart's progress becomes partly muffled, but the bucket hanging on the back begins to jangle − with Newtonian persistence the vertical vessel insists on the earth's gravity and so clatters against something under the cart against which it wouldn't clatter were the cart still level.

But the horse knows better. To that animal shambling through the outskirt, this cobbled road − known as Third Novo-Ostankinskaya, and the only paved street − is a welcome respite before the exhausting ruts and huge pits in the dirt road onto which it will have to turn sooner (by the arboretum) or later (at Vladykino). It is also a respite from the horse flies who know this road has always been within the city limits, and so off-limits to horse flies − bane of the fields and the peaceful countryside.

The first horse fly will greet you by the brick Church of the Holy Trinity, a model of Moscow baroque, though baroque has so far never been heard of by anyone here, much less by the horse, who will be forced by the first buzzing tormentor to make the sign of the cross with its tail and appeal for mercy to the equine saints Flor and Lavr.

As for the driver, he is just hot. He wiggles the toes on his bare feet hanging down from the cart. His feet are large and festooned with a multitude of toes with thick nails, some of them crusty and yellowish. He isn't guiding the horse, or even threatening it, though his horse responds to Russian, and that is something to be grateful for because those trophy horses that have turned up here and there won't eat rotten hay, shy at shaft-bows, and understand only German, meaning you have to keep hold of the reins the whole time and can never sit back.

July was always sultry, it seemed as if the earth would crack; once it did and nothing good came of it: people knocked themselves out lugging evening buckets of water from the pump to the kitchen gardens without which they could not have survived.

Multitudes of green flies flew up out of the cesspits and settled on your food in July, just as horse flies settled on horses, and house flies on people, though house flies and green dung flies bothered horses, too. But then no one on the grassy streets kept horses, and the cobbled road that wandered through the settlement was, as we've said, even a respite. Towards evening the mosquitoes would come out and, though there weren't many of them and they didn't last long, the arms and legs of every child would be covered with bites. Come dawn the sleeping children – damp from the night heat and sweating from the morning sun slanting through the window in a dusty beam – would have to pull the lace day-pillow covers up over their faces to keep the flies off.

When your children are grown and gone, the flies harass you instead, hence the glass trap standing in the middle of the oil-cloth-covered dinner table: a natural invention from the serene nineteenth century when the multiple deaths of whatever (in this case flies) did not put one in mind of anything in particular (in this case the multiple deaths of, say, people).

The trap appears to have been made by a master glassblower. Blown from thin clear glass, like a chemical retort, it is − in terms of its form and meaning − a finished work of art.

Imagine a glass bulb the size of a small saucepan on three stubby − half an inch or so high − glass legs. Underneath, where the garden bulb sports a stubble of old roots, the glass bulb has a large round opening, whose edges curve up inside the empty retort. On top, where shoots would sprout from the garden bulb, the glass one is crowned with a perfectly ordinary bottleneck.

That's what the trap looks like.

Now pour some water into the neck. Rather than running out at the bottom, the water will cascade down the walls, filling the glass moat formed by the bulb's curled-up edges. Next add a little milk or whey: the water will turn an ugly whitish color. Finally, cork the bottleneck and place a small lump of sugar on the oil cloth under the opening at the bulb's base. Now watch the fly run under the three-legged trap, nibble the sugar for a while, then fly up only to be forced down by glass dome.

Trapped, the fly either falls into the cloudy drink immediately; or it tumbles in after a struggle, after fighting and buzzing, but dully (since the retort contains the sound); or, which hardly ever happens, it flies back down to the sugar from which it inevitably flies up again and, clinging the glass wall, considers tasting the delicious sun-warmed water, only to fall in instead.

The fly may flounder about for a bit but in the end it will grow torpid and float motionless in the white murk in its black kapote, sometimes with its stiff legs up, in which case they appear dry and brittle, other times on its stomach, with its legs hanging down, in which case they swell slightly and look wet and hairy, while the implausibly fine film on the water's surface bisects the fly's half-submerged eyes which, were they alive, would spy the cork in the glass dome far above and, far below, the sugar crag − made monstrous by the water and the curve of the glass − on whose sweet crystals two flies, limp from mating, are now feasting.

When the water is covered with sour sodden flies, uncork the vessel, pour the flies and water out, then repeat the whole process. Once a day, or once every three days: as needed.

During meals the retort, of course, remains on the table because meals only make for more flies, more flies buzzing dully and then showing up black in the milky moat.

Flypaper is worse. You can almost never find any, your hair gets caught in it, and the drone of the half-stuck fly – especially if it's a green flesh fly – is always despairing.

It's hot. Especially to a newcomer. Indoors it's stuffy. And you are tired of sitting at the table – with your arms crossed on the oil cloth and your chin on your arms – watching flies meet their deaths. You can't sit like that for long anyway because your shirt sleeves are rolled up and your damp skin will get stuck to the oil cloth and when it comes to getting it unstuck, the sticky oil cloth will pull slightly at your skin and your sticky skin at the oil cloth.

It's hot and everyone goes bathing in the pond. It's a strange sight to see: droves of swimmers – to whom the pond seems ample, if not capacious – fill the swimming hole up to its sandy edges. With a "Hands up!" gesture, the men peel off their fishnet T-shirts, pull off their boxers or coarse cotton drawers, and stride naked into the water, then fall on it (the water barely splashes) and, turning their heads this way and that, start swimming the crawl, that strange stroke that always suggests the swimmer, glancing constantly and energetically back over his shoulder, is swimming away for fear of the Tatar arrow about to be released from the shore where he himself was just praying to the blinding sun, but then heard the buzzing of horse flies, harbingers of the infidels' invasion, and plunged into the saving water.

Most of the women don't swim so much as squat down in the shallows in their large brassieres and white calico pants which the water turns transparent. Others are in rayon (stretchy here, baggy there) pants; of these a few can do the dog-paddle, then the air inside the wet rayon turns their buttocks into pink billows as they creep through the water like sickly skater bugs.

The children neither scream nor play. The water doesn't splash, so it doesn't sparkle. But the sun sparkles over all, including the pale, lifeless bodies of the grown-ups; beneath the men's stomachs is blackness, and in the blackness a white member dangles.

Even if you never go bathing, you will still go by the pond around which and in which people are sitting, some wriggling to save their lives. But the proximity of this small body of water does not refresh, and even if you happen to be wearing your white foreign-made trousers with the black pinthread and a white shirt with the sleeves rolled up − after all, you can't go around like the locals in a fishnet T-shirt over your hairy chest and a handkerchief knotted at the corners on your head − and even if just ahead you can see tall white birches topping the fence of the open-air summer cinema, and a flickering, fine-leafed shade seems to beckon, even so it is unbearably hot, and you aren't used to such heat, and you can't stay indoors: you'll suffocate. The night, too, will be sweltering since that strange and unaccustomed wooden house is tempered all day under the frying-pan lid of its iron roof, and you lie there under a sheet, soon to be in knots, and breathe the way people breathe in July, when the earth is about to crack.

There is nothing left to do but touch solitary objects in the dark: your glasses on the chair pulled up to the bed, the convex face of your pocket watch, its open lid and heavy chain. The watch is ticking − tock-tick, tock-tick − beating out the rhythm you never could get when you were giving oxygen to your dying daughter: you couldn't keep in time with her frantic breathing, you kept pressing the oxygen pillow when you shouldn't have. It should be: *now* air, *now* air, *now* air, but somehow it always came out: wheeze *wheeze*, wheeze *wheeze*, wheeze *wheeze*.

The pillow, like so much before it, quickly came to an end, having finally managed to banish her panicky breathing which also soon came to an end. Then everything came to an end. And there was no one left.

No one ever wants to look at the person rushing home

with an oxygen pillow under his arm. It's hard to say why. The ones carrying the oxygen pillows feel awkward because of it. Awkward because of everything: because the pillow is large, yet there isn't much air in it, because they are in a rush, yet their feet drag (and they have to move fast!), because this is the last resort (then why bother?), because it won't save the one gasping for air (then what is it for?). It is always painful to see the oxygen pillow with which a man gets on, say, the tram, and the tram still stops at every stop. The pillow is a painful sight because it is an accomplice to the asphyxia. To think about asphyxia is unbearable. No one wants to think about it. Having saved yourself and your daughter from one attack of asphyxia, she dies from another, and now the room is so stuffy you can't fall asleep.

Some people, or rather many people, carry camp beds out into the small front gardens and sleep in the midst of the night, their white forms stretching almost into the street, but it's hardly pleasant. Go out to the outhouse and you will see more cots set up in the backyards. The sleepers snore; occasionally two or three of them jump up and start chasing after one or two others. They run noiselessly so as not to wake anyone else up. The runners are lanky, taller than the fences, they are running after the person or persons caught throwing pebbles at the sleepers. People run after each other like that at night, showing up white on the run against the grey dawn. This, too, is strange and unpleasant. Because somehow it is noiseless. They run noiselessly.

The next day, while taking the measurements of a mountainous lady customer (they are all like that around here), you glance out the window and see a horse (pshhh-pshhh), a tipping cart, and somebody's feet hanging down with a multitude of toes, the horse's horsy smell wafts in the window, and suddenly you notice the sweat streaming down from the lady customer's armpits, and when your tape measure brushes against her brassiere she lowers her eyes, those big eyes you will never see again because when her short, enormous legs are set apart to reveal her damp, shaggy groin, she throws a pillow cover over her face and, sliding your organ into her slippery orifice, you see not her face but the braid on the pillow cover, and when it becomes altogether slippery, she begins gasping for air under the pillow cover, then leaves without raising her eyes. So you don't see her eyes: once she lowers them, you never see them again.

July is also when the sense that you are alone is strongest – even if you really do have no one and are alone. Friends or relations mean get-togethers and it's hard to imagine getting together with anyone in this stifling heat: why get together to drink tepid water? You can't serve them your sour clotted milk – the heat has left you with quantities of sour milk – you can't very well serve the sour clotted milk standing on the window-sill with cheesecloth over it and a crust of black bread in it to make it sour even faster, can you?

No man has any relatives in July: he is alone. The sleeping cat lies sprawled on the arid earth by an enormous dusty goosefoot. And though the dust and the cat's fur have long since coalesced, the cat is not dead: there are no beetles on or about its body. Only the skater bug feels fine: surrounded by other skater bugs, it skims across the pond's molten surface, kicking up the water with its tiny heels, etching quick, short lines in all directions. If the skater bug decides to dash in a straight line, then it makes the evenest stitches on the surface of the smoothest muslin and there's no need to wedge a strip of rough newspaper under the leg of the sewing machine.

Towards evening it may – just possibly – cool off slightly, the heat may abate somewhat, and the black gloom and gloaming may deliver us, at least in part, from the stuffiness. And though there is absolutely nowhere to go to get away from the heat if it doesn't abate, you don your canvas shoes and white trousers and abandon the low-ceilinged room for the pond by which you stand awhile trying for the thousandth time to breathe in time to the never-mastered rhythm of the useless oxygen pillow – *now* air, *now* air, *now* air – which only compounded the asphyxia. After all, you kept pumping fresh air in just as she was trying to breathe her own suffocating air out.

It's so dark, the pond water no longer feels warm and

there seems to be more of it, the pond looks enormous in the dark, but its edge is so innocuous that you step right over it in your canvas shoes, now like cooling sponges, and wade easily along the boggy bottom. Your wet trousers, too, cool you: it is so much hotter above water than below! Your shirt, for instance, isn't wet yet, and it is warm, but now it is wet, you are already up to your neck in the water, and when the water comes level with your mouth, the coolness is complete and even pleasant, you open your mouth and the water flows in as if into a funnel, you drink it in, breathe it in, and a sleeping skater bug − master of the even stitch over muslin − flows in with it; the insect and the poplar down that slipped in on the muslin make your throat feel scratchy and your insides feel queasy, you shudder three times and cough the skater bug back up into your throat, the insect skitters into your larynx and winds up behind your tongue. And since the only thing you can do properly is sew, since you can't swim, breathe, save yourself, save others, spit up skater bugs, or do the dog-paddle, then you can at least recall the address − 19 Grodskaya Street, Lublin, General Governorship − later, just as you have made up your mind to pull yourself out of the water, you make a false step forward in canvas shoe... and sink down.

That's it. You drowned yourself. Come morning you will be found floating with your cool face down in the water, your body hunched and half standing, your cold arms dangling. A sparrow fresh from its bath in the soft, warm dust will stare at you in disbelief, but soon some children covered with mosquito bites will come along and catch it, having put salt on its tail.

INASMUCH AND INSOFAR AS

*E*very body is either at rest or in a state of uniform rectilinear motion *inasmuch and insofar as* it...

The physics teacher's body was at rest and simultaneously in a state of uniform rectilinear motion since the earth, as usual, was revolving around the sun. But since the sun was not up yet, the earth was proceeding blindly along its crooked path which may be considered rectilinear *inasmuch and insofar as* you and I are thinking in terms of approximate grammar-school wisdom.

The body of Samson Yeseich, who lay flat on his back, was at rest *inasmuch as* he was under a cotton blanket minus the blanket cover, and *insofar as* he was asleep, barely kneading his flat pillow in its dimly discernible pillowcase.

In the daylight, too, the pillowcase is almost impossible to make out, not because it's dirty – it's clean and even very! – but because it is made of coarse calico. That says it all.

Coarse calico occupies a special place in the visible part of the spectrum. Thanks to the stout threads, tangled knots, bits of horse hair, chaff, and other odds and ends skillfully woven into the fabric, it looks yellowish to one person and greyish to another.

The sleeper's feet were encased in something dimly glinting and manifestly zinc. By this I do not mean that the teacher had two feet in something inevitable, as in, say, a zinc – God forbid! – coffin. No! This thing is smaller and – look closely! – shaped like a truncated cone. Perhaps it's a bucket? Yes. A zinc one. But Samson Yeseich, God bless him, is asleep, and in the course of our story may nothing sepulchral, such as gangrene, creep up from the soles of his feet to his splendid curly head, thus turning the bucket into a zinc-plated sheath of death.

As for the bucket, it is filled with soft oakum in which the pedagogue's very warm toes are now buried.

But that is not the only use to be squeezed out of a bucket in bed.

At the appointed hour, according to his old Baku habit, the sleeper will roll over (this happens once a night and always towards morning), and the bucket will roll with him, banging against the iron bar of the bedstead.

Is that clear?

The clatter will wake the sleeper and he will spring out of bed, having first taken care to extract his feet from the bucket lest it send him crashing to the floor.

At night, of course, one could just as well warm one's feet against other feet, dear to one's heart, but Samson Yeseich is a bachelor and his bed devoid of steadfast comfort. "Fine!" you say. "He doesn't need women. But he doesn't need the bucket either. He should build an oblong box (not zinc-plated!) the width of the bed!" "But the box won't roll," say I. "Well, all right!" you persist. "He could stuff a coarse calico pillowcase with oakum and put his feet in that!" "But it won't bang!" say I, and that says it all, especially since the sleeper has just turned over causing the bucket to bang and awaken the sleeper who, having pulled his toes out of the oakum, is now on his feet.

He is stark naked except for a cloth cap with earflaps which we hadn't noticed against the enigmatic coarse calico. He removes the now superfluous cap, and in the pale morning light we see a strong, stocky man; all that we see of him is vigorous and weighty.

Look up at his face: the nose is a little too large, the lips a little too thick, while the eyes bulge slightly. Samson Yeseich looks Armenian but by birth he is a Tat. Tats are a Caucasian people who profess Moses' Pentateuch and whose features, if they are genuine Tats, are not aquiline and dry, but fleshy and large; because of this their faces, though proud, are kind, while the big whites of their brown eyes are moist and bulging with little red veins.

By the way, about Tats. They aroused suspicion at every passport office. Since abbreviations were not allowed in personal documents, much less in internal passports, Tat citizens were always accused of trying to dodge the question of nationality, and told to write theirs out in full: Tatar, and that's that! It took a lot of patience to get the accusers to turn their attention to the multicolored map of the multinational USSR pinned on the wall behind them.

Samson Yeseich, however, was a genuine Tat. And though some, whose nation also weeps over Moses's Pentateuch, suspected him of having converted to Tatism and thus committed sacrilege, this was untrue, and everyone, truth to tell, knew it. Besides, Samson Yeseich did not avoid his brothers-in-doctrine. If anything he sought them out, though they had moved a long way from their common traditions, as indeed had he.

But enough about Tats: space and time are short, especially since our hero is presently to receive a new acquaintance by the name of Tata.

Yet where did Samson Yeseich live? Where did he wake up so as to go on living and teaching physics in a school for adults plus moonlighting at a certain business (about which later)?

He lived on the ground floor of a barracks known as the Pushkin student dorm (hymned in literature heretofore, so those interested may look it up). As for teaching physics, it was just a job; in actuality, Samson Yeseich was a seer, a hygienist, and a genius.

Is that a joke? A nice turn of phrase? No, it's not a joke. Though it is a nice turn of phrase. Now you'll see why.

If one thinks of life in the barracks as the Stone Age, relatively speaking (though it was absolutely), then solitary Samson Yeseich was a creature of the Bronze Age, a lone forerunner of future civilization.

Single-handedly he would sail to Colchis for the Golden

Fleece; deceive the Minotaur; compose *The Iliad* while supposedly blind; sit and cry by the rivers of Babylon; build the pyramids; expose the queen of Sheba and her hairy legs; write the brilliant *Anabasis* using the pseudonym Xenophon; drink hemlock; teach the Phoenicians to live on the Mediterranean the way the Odessans live on the Black Sea; observe that everything is in a constant state of flux; sculpt Nefertiti, having discovered her brain to be a cube; classify Greek fire as so secret that in future no intelligence service would guess *what* it was the Greeks were burning; paint Faiyum portraits; invent first- and second-order levers; condemn certain people for generations. All this he would do on his own, all on his own. All except the Archimedes' screw which he would create from nothing with the help of the Koptevsky flea market.

Is that an exaggeration? No! In the first place, anyone could create an Archimedes' screw from nothing with Koptevsky's help, otherwise they wouldn't have shut the market down. In the second place, Samson Yeseich played an even neater trick: he built something truly amazing and made it work. And this in the Stone Age! With his own bare hands – not counting, of course, the hand of fate.

For though Samson Yeseich was all alone in the world, he did not lack companionship. Besides Tata, who, as we've said, shall appear shortly, and besides old Aunt Dusya who cooked for him, he had been befriended by a bright youth who, for friendship's sake, gladly shared his fresh ingenuity and thus freed Samson Yeseich's brain for Bronze Age service.

It was to this youth – then in earnest mourning along with everyone else and shocked by the boldness of such a prophecy – that Samson Yeseich said: "Well, he's dead, but you wait! Soon they'll be kicking him in the moustache and out of his tomb!" The youth would not believe Samson Yeseich. But he should have. Always believe the one whose pen-knife is bronze, if yours is only flint.

In other respects, the youth displayed real brilliance of imagination. He was the one who had the idea, unheard-of for that era and that neighborhood, of calling photography shops in Leningrad (having extracted the numbers from intercity information), finding out what they had, leaving that evening for Leningrad on the train, arriving the next morning, buying a return ticket at the station first thing, stocking up on 16 x 20 photographic paper (mat, regular, No. 3), catching a glimpse of your wrought-iron railings, revolutionary cruiser, and Klodt's stallions, leaving that evening for Moscow, and arriving the next morning.

Samson Yeseich covered all expenses including a per diem of one chervonets (three rubles in today's money). The plan was so unprecedented that even the youth's mother, who had hysterics every time he ran away to the Uranium cinema on Sretenka Street, could only throw up her hands.

This was an Iron Age tour de force since the railroad was involved. The youth, however, would never have thought of it; as for his older friend, who sanctioned the mad plan, he had his suspicions but didn't bother to define them, being once again disturbed by the state of his hygiene, about which later, when the subject comes up.

Why the subject of 16 x 20 paper came up is this:

If you, the reader, would like to have a portrait of yourself blown up from the only photograph ever taken of you − which happens to be of you in your coffin − then we, the creators of this portrait, must have 16 x 20 paper (mat, regular, No. 3). The rest is easy: we can airbrush the coffin and open up those dark eyes of yours to boot.

You see them skulking around everywhere, nondescript men in cowls and enormous felt boots encased in patchwork galoshes glued together from bits of old tires and inner tubes. To these total strangers from God knows where, people entrust their dearest possession: faded, perhaps, or ripped, or fly-blown, or brown, but always their only photograph. Of a person who died, or disappeared, or went missing, or was knifed on the post road; of themselves the way they used to look, of themselves in the company of others not themselves, of themselves the way they no longer look; and, of course, of prodigal sons, to say nothing of transient cavalry officers.

Everyone risks what is dearest to them in the name of its promised and truly precious transformation. As for the itinerant scoundrels who burst in the door wreathed in icy steam, their job is to collect the worn photographs and deliver the enlarged portraits.

Their fast talk repels, their familiarity offends, but they are the unwitting hawkers of happiness in these desolate huts in the irrigated steppe and the staid wild fields where each portrait will be promptly hung in the most conspicuous place for all time, its retouched Byzantine eyes boring into those not yet portraits.

The men from the cold aimed to take as many extra orders as they could – over and above the plan – using fake receipts. All the extras went straight to the airbrushers, and from them to the lab assistants who rephotographed the original snapshot to produce a faint, barely discernible print on 16 x 20 paper (mat, regular, No. 3) which they passed on to the retouchers who completed the whole criminal process.

Then the itinerant scoundrels spirited the portraits away and returned with the cash. Meanwhile, the plan was the plan, and the rest was the rest, for in our land of the Soviets we overfulfilled the plan.

In this illicit hierarchy of cottage artisans everyone got his share, while people living in the middle of nowhere, miles from anywhere, and even on the Yamal peninsula, became the proud and astounded owners of likenesses as perfect as they were flattering.

The customer who had always been ashamed of his padded jacket would appear in tweeds, his bad eye replaced with a new one, while the switchwoman at that halt in the hinterlands who had been jilted in her youth would triumph retroactively over that sad event in a montage of herself wearing a wedding veil and her cad wearing a tie, his caddish temple tilted towards her dear little head.

The humble airbrushers, without a word to the retouchers (whom they did not know, in case of problems with the police), would remove anything superfluous that was superfluous, while the masterful retouchers would add anything superfluous that they deemed not superfluous.

Your war medals could be pinned on a photograph taken

before the war, and a Guards badge (not yours) thrown in illegally; pursed lips could be made to smile, while a smile could be crimped to match an unblinking Faiyum-like gaze. Those merry and munificent artists lavished gold earrings and pendants (guaranteed 93-carat) and little hippopotamus pins on those who had none; put fountain pens in the pockets of pigherds; shaved the unshaven; clapped velour hats on prisoners' shorn heads; and even adjusted the thickness of your eyeglasses. They did everything a customer could ask for and, when he didn't have the wit, they used their own judgment.

Occasionally a photograph was so faded that even the subject's sex could not be guessed (and the man who took the order could not help). In this case, two portraits were prepared — one male and one female — to which the cunning retoucher would add the features of some famous person. *Inasmuch and insofar as* everyone knew who the most famous people were, the retoucher would pick one of them — excluding, of course, the two most famous of all. The anxious customer would invariably nod when it was suggested that he or she whose portrait it was looked a lot like so-and-so or such and such.

That is the sort of inspired work it was, and with what wonderful results! What's more, our Portraits with the Unblinking Gaze were easily as good as the ones done in Faiyum. The Faiyum portraits were also done by fly-by-night artisans, and so what if that was the Bronze Age.

Why have I told you all this? Because Samson Yeseich was in the secret business of producing faint 16 x 20 images to be retouched; it was risky, but he had to supplement his teacher's salary somehow, otherwise the seer, the hygienist, and the genius combined in him would never have had enough to eat or drink — and drinking was one of his chief pleasures in life.

He loved cooling drinks. This passion and his memory of pitch-covered roofs (his father had been a "pitcher" — a person who covered roofs with a special tar made from oil-industry waste) were all that remained to him of his native Baku which he left for a technical college in the Soviet capital.

Fortunately, you can almost always find something to drink in Moscow; take, say, yesterday's tea with lemon. But how can you cool it? You need ice. But where can you get ice? What do you mean, Where? You can get it at the Pushkin market!

There was an iceberg at the Pushkin market, or rather the visible part of one, towering up from the cracked pavement and protected from the summer sun by a thick layer of sawdust (some people say the sawdust should be mixed with peat, but at the Pushkin market the sawdust was pure − pure pine).

This great mountain was called the visible part of the iceberg because the invisible work that went into putting it there was still greater. As soon as the first frosts set in, a long black hose would be hooked up to a water main and left running. The water would wash over the asphalt, cool and lunar to the touch, the way all asphalt is come December, as opposed to July when it is soft and hot and the consistency of pitch. But about July later: for now the frigid water is spilling over the frigid asphalt, its transparent molecules freezing to the grey molecules and coating the pavement with a glass of oblivion in which the detritus of summer life has become frozen, litter raised to the level of art object. The water runs and runs, new ice accumulates on the old ice, and the once lucid glass of oblivion turns gradually dusky.

But what about the hose? They probably forgot about it and it froze into the first ice! No, it didn't. The invisible but skillful hand of a certain person at the Pushkin market uses a thick rope to hitch the hose up onto special poles, letting it hang down just far enough so that the ice can form in layers, otherwise − if the water goes on gushing indiscriminately − it will be harder to apply the sawdust.

The water runs all winter, and all winter the ice mountain grows. In February it is still a lusterless hulk, dulled by the dry snow wedged between the frozen whorls, but about the middle of March our diamond mountain suddenly begins to sparkle under the sun's rays. The water is still running and still freezing, but as soon as the sun begins making mischief and turning the bottom of the ice castle into a moat of melted ice and snow, dark against the bare pavement, then you run and shut the water off! Quick! Grab a hack, shut your wife's trap, and carve steps into the mountain. Climb the steps in those special waffle galoshes and dress warmly, that means padded pants, y'hear, otherwise your balls'll freeze; when you get to the top, pull up the bucket your old lady has been filling with sawdust and sprinkle it as fast as you can – thinly at first, then every day make the layer thicker – and have your old lady do the same around the foot of the mountain.

That's how this gigantic mountain of ice the size of an ancient glacier is created. But Nature spent hundreds of thousands of years on hers, whereas this one was made in a matter of months by the market man.

Our glacier will loom like a mountain glacier, and like a mountain glacier it will drip slightly. The name of its creator and keeper, incidentally, is Fedchenko, and the name of the first fizzy water man to push his soda cart up to the shaggy iceberg will be Riceberg. Fedchenko will sweep away the sawdust on the north slope and chop off a chunk of ice with a crowbar for his first taker and from then on this patch will remain bare and, chunk by chunk, the breach will increase to reveal bluish white geological layers. The dark moat of melted ice and snow that first appeared in March will also widen. By July rivulets of water will be snaking away from the south slope and trickling under the market sellers' sacks of seed, slim shadows of the passionate stream from December's hose. As for the first –- remember? – wet herring-bone tracks left by Riceberg's two-wheel cart, they will never dry, even though it's summer, even though it's July.

"You can get it at the Pushkin market!" we exclaimed two pages ago, meaning the ice. But how are you going to carry it home? There aren't any polyethylene bags: polyethylene hasn't been invented yet – and won't be until those American spy balloons made out of it start flying to East Germany. You could, of course, wrap the ice in, say, oilpaper. Or oilcloth. But the ice would still melt, and by the time you got home there would only be a few pieces left, speckled with dust and crumbs from the bottom of your cloth bag, and to put those dingy remains of the former brilliance into a glass of homemade lemonade would be discouraging.

Especially to someone as fastidious as our hero. Of course, when he sent Aunt Dusya to get ice he could have supplied her with a Dewar vessel on loan from the physics lab. But even if Aunt Dusya didn't drop the priceless vessel on the way, its narrow mouth meant that the ice would first have to be chopped up into small pieces. Where? Right there on the asphalt. How? With a chopper, or a chisel; and every shard would probably be handled ten times over by Fedchenko, or by Aunt Dusya, on top of which Aunt Dusya might not be able to set the vessel on its stand – this thing (a vacuum flask, simply put, though one of particular perfection) will not stand upright, after all, but will fall on its side. So we have been wasting our breath on the Dewar vessel while Aunt Dusya has gone on lugging ice back in a leaky oilcloth bag or in an apothecary jar.

Oy, it was so unhygienic! The fastidious Samson Yeseich washed each piece of ice in manganese before dropping the now rose-colored lump into his cooling drink.

"All he needs is a refrigerator!" say you, the reader.

And you're right, but with the rightness of a descendant, the rightness of a consumer, for our hero is stranded in the Stone Age and it's not a refrigerator – not a refrigerator! – that he needs, but the Bronze Age! He needs a human genius, and we know who that is. We watched him getting out of bed this morning hand in hand with the hygienist and the seer.

Because of something the seer foresaw, the hygienist put work aside for a while and got the genius to create a cooling system. For the genius (even before the war) had read in *Young Engineers* magazine about capitalist mercenaries overseas rigging up chests for capitalist sharks in their capitalist villas to store their hamburgers in: apparently, it was as cold in those chests as in the arctic city of Obdorsk. Apparently, Rockefeller Sr. had acquired one of those hamburger chests for an astronomical sum and now his wife could grind her hamburger meat a week ahead – it wouldn't go bad in that diabolical box . What's more, while still a student, the genius had happened to notice in his textbook – on a page that hadn't been assigned – the diagram of a cooling system, and his marvelous mind had memorized it and never forgotten it.

Now the genius betook himself to Koptevsky market (a place we won't bother to describe: many people know it so let one of them knock himself out evoking that Field sown with dead parts and odd components) – to Koptevsky market, I repeat, where a lame war veteran sold him a white trophy icebox *with the door still on.* You could see right through the door – since it wouldn't shut and the icebox had no back – and see clearly the next crook practically giving away a section of rusty rail nailed to six perfectly good ties reeking of creosote and passengers; the front left leg of a bentwood chair; the original manuscript of *The Tale of Igor's Campaign* bound together with the pamphlet "Work Fast Each Day the Stakhanov Way"; a little pile of printer's type composed entirely of the tsarist letter "yat"; a pound of decorative eggplants made out of papier-mache; a hopelessly crooked billiard cue (but with the chalk!); and a 36-pound rivet lifted from the Crimea Bridge to the distress of the City Council.

You are prevented from seeing the rest by a serpentine pipe dangling from the roof of the icebox, and by the veteran who is swearing that until Victory Day capitalist Krupp kept his sauerkraut and his dog's body in this fucker and you better take what's left of it because the fucker had loads of parts – been sellin' them off for the last month now – there was a double-phase motor and when he broke it open that pipe in there started leakin' pus like it had the clap (at this Samson Yeseich winced), and there was cotton battin' in the walls but the women they all grabbed it, and all the other crap's gone, too, so I'd take it if I was you because when that clap stuff stops drippin' (Samson Yeseich winced again) that pipe'll be worth its weight in gold for makin' moonshine, and I already got one Jew who wants the box, wants to turn it into a dacha in Malakhovka and rent it out to the Comintern kindergarten for June, July, and August.

Samson Yeseich bought the box because he knew *what* he was buying. And by listening carefully to the veteran's

nonsense, he contrived to supplement his magazine and technical college knowledge of this billionaire whim.

Now that he had his frame, he rewound the coil of some
compatible motor, sharpened the crucial thing that needed
sharpening, created countless parts to replace the ones that
vile veteran had spent a month unloading, adjusted the stop
to turn on automatically (during the war stops had been
attached to every meter in every house, assuming, of course,
the house had electricity), soldered the jagged holes in the
coil pipe and then introduced under pressure (my God, how
did he do it?) the very thing the veteran had taken for a
gonorrhea-like secretion (Samson Yeseich winced again, remember?), it was called Freon (Lord only knows how he knew
or where on earth he got it). He fitted the icebox with a large
square can that had once contained American condensed milk
(that's right, a freezer! for the ice!), reattached the door with
good barn hinges, and riveted a pair of lugs for the padlock
(the unit would have to stand outside his door in the corridor);
the one thing he could not manage was the cotton batting.
Here the genius in him lost heart, while the seer merely
grinned – bitterly and sarcastically.

No, he could not find any cotton anywhere! And he
needed it for the insulation. He didn't want to raid his bucket
of oakum. But then the genius who had lost heart took heart
and lined the inside of his cooling system with aspen slab
boards, and stuffed the space between the white wall and the
slab boards with... of course, pine sawdust!

The Jew, by the way, would have done exactly the same
thing had he turned the white box into a dacha. But we
won't look to Moses's Pentateuch to explain this similarity of
approach; besides, if cotton had existed, the solutions of these
co-religionists would very likely have diverged since the Jew
would never have paid good money to insulate a dacha already
made over to his son-in-law.

Now the only thing still to do was to plug the Stone Age
into the Bronze Age socket.

Samson Yeseich did this composedly while the whole
corridor stood by, gawking at the white fucker: first the fuses

burned out, but they fixed them with some wire, then, while everyone turned to stare at the fuses, someone wrote to the police here's what: "So-and-so is making fires with the fuses. We protest. (Signed:) the hole barracks."

Meanwhile Samson Yeseich's creation started up and began cooling whatever you put in it. Inside, it had the sweet familiar smell of a barn, of musty aspen bark. The genius kept glasses with a little bit of water in them in the freezer: the water froze and then all you had to do was pour in some blancmange, when you felt like it, or some fruit-flavored mineral water or yesterday's tea with lemon. The icebox was forever chuckling exultantly – ha-ha-ha! – because whenever the motor turned off automatically – ha-ha-ha! – the lack of two shock-absorbing springs – ha-ha-ha! – mattress springs would have been too large and rifle springs too tight – ha-ha-ha! – caused the sides of the icebox to thump and, arms akimbo, it would shake its white belly and chuckle – ha-ha-ha! – chuckle exultantly: it took the Ice Age a hundred thousand years, and Fedchenko the market man a whole winter, to do what it did – ha-ha-ha!– in little more than an hour.

Someone wrote to the police here's what: "So-and-so has put an epileptic chest in the corridor. We protest. (Signed:) the hole barracks."

Now do you see why Samson Yeseich was a genius? We already know why he was a seer. And as for why he was a hygienist, we're getting to that.

Well, for one thing, he slept naked. The cap with ear-flaps doesn't count. For another thing, he was fastidious – remember the ice from the market? And for a third, he was cleanly: he was the only one on the whole corridor who kept a washstand in his room.

So what if the room was a mess, so what if there was a joiner's bench, and rusty tools, and not rusty tools, and pupils' copybooks, and soot-filled radio valves jumbled together with all kinds of scrap iron in a shabby trunk, and three nails sticking out of the wall in place of a wardrobe, and a zinc bucket in the bed, and several dog-eared reference books on the whatnot along with a second pair of boots, and a small

vat of salt in the corner (that's not salt, that's hyposulphite!),
and corkscrew strips of withered film hanging from raggedy
ropes; but... the strips of film were interspersed with sticky
strips of flypaper, for Samson Yeseich, the only one of us to
have ever seen a fly's leg under a microscope, was shocked
by the impunity of the merry bacteria on the hairy extremity,
and came to loathe flies; but... by the washstand there was
a cake of nice pink soap, a bottle of eau de Cologne, a test
tube of manganese, a nailbrush, and some other marvelous
thing, just what I can't recall.

Clean sheets, clean food, cooling drinks, sound sleep, and
disinfectants galore: everything would have been all right if
not for one little annoyance. Samson Yeseich winced twice,
remember?

No, not gonorrhea. Just an inflammation, a hangover from
his student days – nothing really! – but it did make our hero
miserable at times. As a young man he hadn't paid it any
attention until it was too late, and now. And now he had only
to eat, say, a sprat, or to drink, say, some red wine, or to
catch cold – threading his way between the snowbanks along
the ash-sprinkled paths of the settlement streets – and his
old ailment would make itself quietly felt.

When it made itself not-so-quietly felt was when the life
line on Samson Yeseich's large palm intersected the love line
on the small palm of some sweet person. At first everything
would be fine, but within three days Samson Yeseich would
spy signs of something ominous on his person, and go, poor
fellow, to the doctor. The doctor would shake his head, and
Samson Yeseich would start to fret and to hate the sweet
person, though she was not to blame and though he knew
what was. But anyone would fret, even you, the male reader,
would fret and accuse the innocent female reader. You might
even break off with her, as Samson Yeseich always did, though
with a heavy heart and a sad look in his kind eyes. His kind
eyes were the kind you could depend on, and women like it
when they can depend on the look in a man's eyes.

But what does a hygienist need when observing his organism during an acute condition? He needs a nice little room

in which to perform his ablutions and his toilet, and he needs his glasses in case his eyes give out due to nerves. But not only during an acute condition! The hygienist always needs a place for his ablutions and his toilet, as does the non-hygienist.

The Pushkin student dorm's communal latrines did not satisfy this requirement since they did not satisfy any requirement at all. Samson Yeseich, of course, used the school's facilities as much as possible, but he spent only the evenings there since his days went to producing 16 x 20 portraits (incidentally, where was he to get rid of the water and the used solutions given that his business had to be kept under wraps?), or toiling at his workbench, or paying calls on nearby acquaintances, on the youth, say, or listening to Beethoven's Kreutzer Sonata performed by the violinist Miron Polyakin.

Haven't you ever heard of him, reader?

Samson Yeseich loved this musician, for he did not limit himself to the standards of the age (the Stone Age!) during which you, the reader, missed the violinist Miron Polyakin, who went unremarked in the era of leaderism when every branch of industry had its own leaders, including the musification branch, where, as elsewhere, the leaders were anointed for all time (though, unlike in other dioceses, they weren't bad!). But that's not the point, the point is that the ones who never became leaders began to play erratically, to feel anxious and fearful, and to be excluded from gala concerts, they became second class musicians *insofar as* the first class ones had been singled out for all time. So we'll rosin our bows for our friends, family, and the small hall where these friends and family will come, and if we're lucky the understudy for our State's first violinist may even look in on us for a second.

Play, Miron Polyakin, play like God, but only for your acquaintances. Then take a sedative, become a misanthrope, give up or hang yourself, *inasmuch and insofar as* that is how your life turned out. Then die, glorious violinist. But, my God, where is your grave? Did you really exist? Was that really you playing on Samson Yeseich's phonograph records of the Kreutzer Sonata?

Pioneers! I appeal to you, my friends! Please find the grave of the violinist Miron Polyakin, otherwise I'll always think I just imagined those records.

O, fate, unkind to the violinist, you showed great kindness to our hero when you caused that precious little screw to fall through a crack in the floor. Others would have − I don't know what they would have done! They would have gone to the Koptevsky flea market. But that advocate of sensible solutions Samson Yeseich immediately took the floor apart, or rather pried two boards loose with the help of a first-order lever, felt around under a third board and found both the screw and something utterly unexpected.

Sticking up amidst the plump spools of feathery dust was a funnel-shaped opening. Anyone would have known what it was, but Samson Yeseich was somehow confused. He tapped it with his pliers. Cast-iron. He took a deep breath and − all at once − dumped a pint of delicious compote down the funnel. The compote disappeared − obviously to some faraway place. Then the Metol developer disappeared, followed by a large used bottle of fixing solution from which Samson Yeseich had been planning to extract pure silver by means of electrolysis. Next to be sacrificed to the cast-iron hole was a bottle of violet ink. It, too, disappeared. Only when Samson Yeseich grabbed a container of that horrible etching acid did he come to his senses, put the devilish solution away, approach the orifice, and... (the female reader will please leave the room, or turn her back, while you, the male reader, and I, if we wish, may join our hero).

Even that disappeared.

Now Samson Yeseich knew what it was. He knew it even before running those experiments of his. It was a sewage pipe, located in the exact center of the room.

How about that! Apparently the barracks' planners, too, had been yearning to enter the Bronze Age, and Samson Yeseich's room was to have been the barracks' lavatory until someone went and denounced those Trotskyite architects as squanderers of living space, and the communal cesspool won out.

And to think that the funnel was sticking up in the geometrical center of the room! This did not bother Samson Yeseich, for the hygienist worshipped the genius, and the seer seconded the hygienist. Meanwhile the genius got down to work: a post from floor to ceiling: one! Three more posts along the corners of an imaginary four-foot square: two! Bars connecting the posts at the top, the bottom, and in the middle so as to create a frame in the shape of a paralleliped to be covered with netting: three!

A cage? In the middle of the room?

"Yeseich, you gon'en decided to keep parrots in yer room? Or doves maybe?" asked a neighbor who kept doves and knew about parrots from *Krokodil*, a satirical magazine in which the then U.N. Secretary-General Trygve Lie, Marshal Iosip Bros Tito, and other world-class yappers were portrayed as parrots.

"Yeseich, you cookin' up cement in there?" another curious neighbor inquired. The work had indeed been wet and messy. Samson Yeseich had to mix the cement in a wash-tub, then tamp it into the mold with a bronze pestle.

"Yeseich, that a booth I see in yer room? Fat chance they'll ever give you a public telephone!"

"My dream is to become an amateur photographer. I need darkness."

"Yeah, well, if I was you I'd give the window three coatsa tar varnish. I got varnish, and I gotta tarbrush, too!" yet another neighbor volunteered, forgetting, the idiot, that if you varnish the window the room will always be dark, even before and after the negative and positive processes.

In the center of Samson Yeseich's room (10 feet x 15 feet, with a seven-foot ceiling) there now stood a thin-walled, square-section, cement column. Or, to put it more precisely, a pylon. So far this pylon is of no particular order for it is nothing but the rudiments of a functional design. Inside these rudiments, however, is a little tile floor sloping slightly down from the walls to a splendid round orifice, neatly covered with a home-made balloon-rubber mat. There is also a little light in the little square ceiling. No, no, not an 8-watt bulb, but a bright, bright light, like in an operating room! And you can even lock yourself in with a type-setting bolt.

Soon the police receive a document dark with meaning: "So-and-so don't piss where everyone else does. We protest. (Signed:) the hole barracks."

Meanwhile Samson Yeseich knocks together a table around the pylon, as if it were the trunk of a shady tree in a southern courtyard. This table is nothing if not convenient: you can tin wires in one corner, correct copybooks in another, and work on 16 x 20 portraits in a third; there is no fourth corner because the pylon door is there.

Winter, by the way, is over: Samson Yeseich has stopped sleeping in his cap with the ear-flaps, his feet buried in a bucket of oakum. Now it's summer and a certain Tata has turned up. His life line intersected her love line in the agonizing recesses of the bushes beyond the Kamenka river the day before yesterday. And − miracle of miracles! − here it was the third day and he felt fine. For the first time he wasn't suffering, which circumstance was beginning to threaten Tata with marriage. Then again why should it threaten? Even before that intoxicating encounter in the bushes, she had come to depend entirely on the kind look in Samson Yeseich's eyes.

Yesterday, instead of going to the street meeting at which neighborhood policemen Kolyshev and Vorobyov had urged residents to turn in their weapons, and everyone had just stood there staring at Vorobyov and Kolyshev, who didn't get it either, but orders was orders and their orders was to tell everyone to turn in their weapons − so then yesterday, instead of going to the meeting, Samson Yeseich had gone boating with Tata on the pond in Ostankino Park and so had not heard the cops informing residents that *inasmuch and insofar as* everyone was turning in their weapons voluntarily... and so on.

The police received another written complaint: "So-and-so didn't go turn in no weapons, unregistered people are sleepin' over. We protest. (Signed:) the hole barracks." Now, finally, the flatfoots decided they better do something and that evening Kolyshev was dispatched to check out the complaint.

For his part, Samson Yeseich was expecting a visit from Tata that evening – most likely her last since one couldn't very well visit oneself at home.

The pylon table, over which he had taken great care, was spread with all sorts of fish and sausage, and even some caviar (Baku folks really know how to do things!); the beets-and-pickle salad had been dressed with mayonnaise by the seer, the only one buying mayonnaise at the time since everyone else thought it was tainted butter being palmed off in small jars that then would be impossible to return. He set out a crystal bowl full of punch; tidied up the room; replaced the clothes scattered about on the three nails; stacked the dusty chaos of Kreutzer records in a pile; put out two little shot glasses and two wine glasses; insinuated a bottle of champagne into the freezer; and filled the bottoms of the champagne glasses with water for ice. In case the electricity went off, which happened in those days, and the ice in the jolly white fellow wouldn't freeze, Samson Yeseich had gotten hold of some liquid oxygen and brought it home from school in the famous Dewar vessel with the intention, if need be, of oxygenating the champagne and the punch. Replaced on its stand by a most skillful hand, the Dewar vessel sparkled at one end of the table, reflecting in its mirror-like, in its samovar-like surface the ardent little lights shining all around the nice, bright room. Meanwhile Samson Yeseich kept disappearing into the pylon – manganese, clyster, and magnifying glass in hand – to check himself one more time, but could find no cause for alarm.

Then Tata arrived. She already felt at home in the room. She knew just where which bottle of what acid stood, she had been warned against dipping teaspoons into the liquid oxygen, and the electricity didn't go off. They ate and they drank. Several times the courtly Samson Yeseich, who also felt at home, said: "Excuse me, I'll just be a minute!" – and vanished into the pylon for yet another searching self-examination while Miron Polyakin produced his finest pizzicato. Samson Yeseich had been leading up to something and was just about to come to the point when he exclaimed: "And now let us go on to dessert!" – and on they went. They rose and removed to the opposite side of the pylon where dessert was served. Samson Yeseich stepped out into the corridor to fetch the surprise – ice cream – and noticed Kolyshev crouching by the icebox. "Samson, just the man I wanna see!" said Kolyshev springing up. "We gotta complaint! Gotta check ya out!" He followed Samson Yeseich with his ice cream into the room. Tata, who had taken advantage of Samson Yeseich's absence to slip into the pylon herself, was nowhere to be seen.

"How come you didn't go turn in no weapons?" asked Kolyshev, blinking in the bright, non-barracks light. "Don't have nothin' to turn in, that it?" "What do you mean I don't? I do!" In the corridor – ha-ha-ha! – the icebox, free at last of the ice cream, snickered. Ha-ha-ha! – Kolyshev jumped back and grabbed his holster.

But his holster was empty.

It was empty not because not every policeman had a gun in those days, though every one wore a holster. And not because of the generally bizarre way in which the police were armed: every railroad policeman, for example, carried a cavalry sword – effective on horseback, but useless on foot. Long and cumbersome, the sword was forever knocking into the railroad policeman's left boot and tripping him up as he, in his black uniform with the raspberry piping and aiguillette, struggled along the tracks. It was almost impossible to walk as it was – what with the high rails, the loose stones flying up from underfoot, and the ties fouling up one's stride – without always having to catch up one's cavalry sword to keep it from banging against the rails and the switches.

Worst of all was the having to rush helter-skelter (especially at the sorting stations with many tracks) when two empty locomotives came racing along the first (secret) track – headed either to or from the south – followed by a train bearing our best beloved, followed by two more empty ones.

Aha! So that's it! That's why the cavalry swords and the black uniforms with raspberry piping. To make them look like tsarist police. So our best beloved could relive his heroic escapes from Siberian exile all over again, though from a different perspective – watching through a special window as the clumsy, cowardly police, big boots flailing, scrambled out of the way of our hurtling locomotive, while an armored train, also ours, waited on a sidetrack.

It looked just like a scene from a movie about life before the Revolution.

Kolyshev's holster was empty because, to give the illusion of plenitude, it had been packed first thing with a stewed turnip sandwich, long since devoured by the ravenous policeman in the course of his wanderings about the grassy streets.

When someone burst out laughing behind his back, and his holster turned out to be empty, Kolyshev funked, jumped out of the way, and asked, looking round:

"Anybody else livin' here?"

"No!"

Here a door squeaked, not the door to the corridor, but some door he couldn't figure out. The policeman leapt back and stared in astonishment as a woman emerged from the cement wardrobe in the middle of the room. "You said there weren't nobody else here, Samsoska!" Kolyshev bellowed but promptly shut up when he realized that Tata was the daughter of those well-to-do people who bought his godchild's mother's shed and turned it into a house. He was just collecting his flatfoot's wits when that person began guffawing again behind his back, causing Kolyshev to completely lose his head and cry out in a quavery voice:

"What's goin' on here, you Armenian you?! Why ain't you turned in no weapons?"

"I am a Tat, and here is my weapon," said Samson Yeseich, smiling proudly and triumphantly as he took a tattered physics text from the whatnot. "Why don't you join us, Mokei Petrovich, since you've come. You know Tata, I mean citizen Raskina. And as for where she's registered, you know that too!"

"But who was that laughin' at me?"

"Why don't you sit down and I'll tell you!"

"Not so fast! First I gotta see who you got hidin' in that closet!" said Kolyshev and thought uneasily to himself: "Geez!

What if them Jews are diggin' tunnels to the Armenians and they're runnin' back n' forth? She didn't come over here to eat no cabbage stalks!" he reasoned, not without effort, knowing that women like Raskin's daughter didn't fool around.

"Go ahead and look! Go on, don't be afraid!" said Samson Yeseich, clapping an arm round his guest's shoulder and squeezing into the pylon with him. A minute later the genius came out, closed the door tight behind him, put *Splashes of Champagne* on the gramophone, and removed an untimely strip of film from the line where it had been put to dry.

Kolyshev lingered awhile in the pylon, what with one thing and another, then made his grand entrance only to be shown casually to the washstand by Samson Yeseich, on his way to the icebox, and handed a waffle-cloth towel by the hygienist. Next Kolyshev inspected that joker of a safe or whatever it was — looked like a corn-bin — and admired the padlock. Then they all three sat down to the table around the pylon and Samson Yeseich explained the Carnot cycle or how refrigeration works. After that they all drank champagne with ice while Samson Yeseich discoursed on the Dewar vessel and plunged a peeled carrot, by way of example, into his vessel full of liquid oxygen, then pulled it out and tapped it with a spoon: the carrot disintegrated into countless tiny crystals before the eyes of the astounded Tata and the flabbergasted cop, while the icebox exploded in more peals of laughter, though by now no one noticed. The genius and Tata had more champagne, but not the cop. The champagne was making him burp up his turnips so he switched to the rubbing alcohol Samson Yeseich used to clean the lenses of his enlarger and all minor skin cuts (just in case!) And after that, Kolyshev began complimenting Tata to Samson Yeseich for some reason, and Tata felt suddenly shy, while the grateful Samson Yeseich gave forth on the advantages of radio and the role it would play some day not only in our lives, but in police work. In all likelihood the police would soon need miniature two-way devices so as to be able to whisper instructions on the sly, as if into their pockets. Tata and the cop listened and marvelled. "And they'll need tiny microphones to catch saboteurs!" the

seer prophesied. "And what about fast-moving all-terrain ve-
hicles with searchlights at both ends, or light-weight
waterproof coats the color of graphite?" Tata and Kolyshev
listened to this as to a fairy tale, but when Samson Yeseich
got to the boots with waterproof polish, the self-polishing buttons, and the fog-penetrating binoculars, lamenting that
inasmuch and insofar as, Kolyshev lost the thread and reluc-
tantly stuffed two of the fishloaf sandwiches brought by Tata
into his holster as he got up to leave, wishing them both, if
and when it came to that, every happiness.

He ambled along the little streets, dark as the inside of
a boot polished with permanent polish, through the alleys and
fenceless plots; he would have known his way blindfolded.
He was dreaming that he was a policeman of the future and
imagining that he and, say, Vorobyov – who he never really
liked – were shadowing Berenboim, a big-time schemer who
happened to be in cahoots with the local police chief so that
casing his place on Third Road was out of the question. But
they aren't policemen of the future for nothing! They are
equipped with SI-235 wireless receivers (the size, say, of a
beige ankle boot) and indelible binoculars.

"This is Volga! I'm on his trail! The suspect just got off
the No. 39 tram. Now hc's takin' the long way around to his
house, No. 38. He's wearin' felt boots. Over!"

"This is Rotgut!" the disagreeable Vorobyov whispers into
his radio. "I'm waitin' for the suspect. I'm hidin' by the
Crooked-woods dump. Say your password. Over!"

"This is Volga! This is Volga! I'm headed for the kerosene
store, 'bout to go under that streetlight. Password: Forget your
beets, now hit the streets!" our cop snaps, then climbs onto
his noiseless bicycle of the future and races off into the night
without moving a muscle. No one sees him, but he sees everything because in the beam of his searchlight the night
disintegrates into countless tiny crystals, like a carrot.

"This is Rotgut! This is Rotgut! This is Rotgut!" comes
Vorobyov's hoarse whisper from somewhere in the future,
while Kolyshev – in the present and, as luck would have it,
right outside Berenboim's house – considers knocking on Saul

Moiseich's door, even though it's late, and puttin' up a sorta smokescreen about tomorrow's sorta search. To which, as always, Saul Moiseich will say: "Oy, come in, come in! I have nothing to hide!" and give him a glass of vodka and, despite the late hour, will have a glass himself, too, by the way. Then he'll pour them more vodka and Kolyshev will scoop the sandwiches out of his holster and Saul Moiseich will be amazed that the policeman's wife makes such a good fishloaf, and he'll pour them each another drop.

"You take good care of yourself, comrade Kolyshev, Mokei Petrovich!"

"Yeah and don't you get sick neither, comrade Berenboim, Saul Moiseich!"

Inasmuch and insofar as...

SORRY LOT

*T*he great Czech educator Komensky championed enlightened teaching and the abolition of corporal punishment, but then he mainly had to do with neat Czech children, meek and well-behaved.

The great Russian educator Ushinsky campaigned for progressive teaching and practical schools, and succeeded in all his efforts thanks to the quiet and socially intimidated, if somewhat naughty, scholars in his charge.

The great Soviet educator Makarenko packed a pistol and used it to perform simple confidence tricks. The children with whom he dealt were considered major mischief-makers, but you mustn't forget about the pistol.

She had only a milk-can.

She brought it to drawing class empty and took it away full of children's warm urine.

A milk-can is a cylindrical object and so a superlative model for anyone wishing to master the fundamentals of applying shadows. No matter how, where, or when we scrutinize the solitary milk-can — so long as the light is from the left — its surface will be a patchwork of light, highlights, light, half-shadows, shadows, and reflections. Shade a flat sheet of paper with intersecting vertical bands of the right width and you will have the likeness of a convex surface; use the same method to depict the smaller cylinder of the milk-can's neck. Now all you have to do is the handle.

But if you grab that hopelessly bent-out-of-shape, thick wire handle, and swipe the milk-can from the teacher's desk, and pass it around the class, you can easily fill it: just think of all the children who are afraid to use the school latrines.

I hate to bring up such extra-literary subjects and harp on circumstances traditionally amusing to the easily-amused Germans, but, for the sake of being true to life, I cannot not mention these important, daily, or rather hourly, if not half-hourly, matters: these are children, after all. One has caught cold; another has drunk his tea with saccharine, or rather always drinks it with saccharine; a third is sick with some ticklish children's complaint and would better be cared for in a warm, cozy apartment, given extracts and warm drinks, wrapped in warm Turkish towels, and bathed in a warm bath under a bright chandelier by a beautiful Mama and a kind Nanny, while Papa pores over his stamp album in the sitting room and waits impatiently to hold Mama, defenseless and a little tired, in his pajama-clad embrace.

Yes, but how do the children manage to swipe the milk-can off the desk? (As for why some are afraid to use the latrines, that comes later.)

They manage to swipe the milk-can because the drawing teacher happens to be in desperate straits. Just how desperate, I can't say, I don't remember. She seems to be staring dumb-founded at the slogan on the board where she was about to depict the play of light: *Maria Ivanovna is a kuntt*; or maybe she wants to catch that crazed back-row boy in the act of slamming his desktop down (remember, there are forty other boys in this class, none of them fence-sitters). Or maybe ("It didn't!" you say in horror), or maybe, I repeat, the soggy blackboard rag hit her smack in her grey bun; well, all right, it didn't! In that case, she must be looking around for the chalk that was just there a minute ago, but now is gone for good; or perhaps she is darting between the desks so as to dodge a certain little boy (while the other forty, minus the ones engaged in filling the milk-can, whoop with glee, naughty boys!) – a certain little boy who is running after her with a fat, pale pink helminth squeezed between two capable fingers. An earthworm, you say? No, this is no earthworm. Earthworms belong to summer when school is out. Helminths abound year round, and this little rascal has come late to class on purpose with one: he has helminths all the time.

Why doesn't she walk out of the classroom and let the children face certain disciplinary action? Because two desks have been shoved against the door and if she goes near them she will face sadistic helminthological action.

From all the dark corners they come out to that tango and she comes out... a slender little girl... she comes out and comes toward me... all this is born of the darkness, of my mood, of the spasm in my throat.

How did all those children wind up in that school? Are they special? Is the school special? No, the school is an ordinary elementary school. The children are ordinary children, except for a few gifted ones. The writer of these words, for instance. You must agree that a schoolboy who would ever engage in the written word could only be called particularly gifted.

They all got there quite simply. In winter they motored to school in felt boots. In spring they dragged themselves there from various grassy streets and out-of-the-way places. Some came in bare feet. One would catch flies along the way and eat them to make his friends laugh; another would swallow the chalk as soon as he came into class; a third wouldn't come at all, preferring to rout around the airplane dump (it was worth it!), or to buy some oil-cake (that was worth it, too), or to wander off somewhere else (also worth it).

They motored to school in felt boots (incidentally, one very sad poet, who has now died, dreamed of motoring to school in felt boots even as a child, and I understand him) — in felt boots, then, and not only in felt boots: they might be in kersey boots, or they might be on skates fastened to the galoshes pulled over their felt boots or fastened to their kersey boots with a homemade tourniquet (a twig in a string that made the shiny galoshes sag down in front like pouting lower lips), and so, in their motley footwear, they would motor to school by hooking onto the back of the occasional one-and-a-half-ton truck. Though those one-and-a-half-ton trucks didn't come through often, their technology looked mighty impressive. They didn't run on gasoline, they ran on wood, or rather birch or alder chocks. These blocks of wood were loaded into two large cylinders (which you can now picture) towering behind the cab. The chocks burned and gases were formed, thus setting this second- or third-generation Soviet truck in motion along with all the little boys, big boys, and full-grown joes who hitched rides using long ropes attached to big hooks.

The boys would lie in wait at a turn in the road for as long as it took and then fall on the unsuspecting truck from either side, from both snowy banks, until finally the truck began to look like a wolf trying to outrun a pack of wolfhounds.

Indeed, as soon as the leader had thrown his hook — an S-shaped cramp iron — over the side, he passed the rope to one of the hounds panting alongside, who passed it on, and in a trice the whole pack had grabbed hold, and over the bumpy, very bumpy ice-covered road, studded with manure and wisps of hay, little boys, big boys, and full-grown joes would race to school or to their heart's content. Some would squat down (the ones at the end, usually) only to be thrown up in the air going over the bumps and pits; others would bend their legs up-down, up-down, up-down and — look! what an incredible invention human legs are! — absorb the shock in their knee joints. These days that quality of suspension is associated strictly with Mercedes Benz, whereas in those days boys came by it instinctively while hurtling over rock-hard manure, or losing their skid on a patch of frozen hay: in response to the sudden jerk, their legs would begin to mince, bow, and then bend again — up-down, up-down, up-down — like the supersuspension on a Mercedes Benz.

Benz! The boys bang into school. The afternoon session. They are wearing their felt boots so it's winter! So it will get dark early! Benz! A boy who has been held back too many times kicks the light switch! Smashes it to smithereens! His is a crude and unpopular method. Not that he doesn't know a better way, he's just impatient, though smashed light switches enrage the principal. But today — benz! — the hysteria is out of control. Now there won't be any light, or classes either. Still, the better way is this: calmly unscrew the only three light bulbs there are and stuff the sockets with urine-soaked blotting paper, then screw the bulbs back in again. As the blotting paper begins to dry in the warm socket, the light will begin to dim until finally, when the paper is bone dry, there won't be any light at all. What's more, there won't be any uproar, and school will be called off for a few days at least because such sophisticated technology is very hard to divine.

I take it back! This is no ordinary school.

You were told it was nothing special! Just an ordinary, four-story, red-brick school in the vestibule of which hangs a letter − framed and under glass − thanking pupils and teachers for collecting one hundred and fifty rubles (fifteen rubles in today's money) for the defense fund, and bearing the humble signature: J. Stalin.

In the latrines (there are two on each floor, one for boys and one for girls; but there are no girls because J. Stalin prefers separate education, so now both bathrooms are for boys) − in the latrines there isn't any light at all, there aren't even any bulbs in the sockets so that it's pitch dark except for the red glow of cigarette ends, while the slop on the floor soaks the coarse felt soles of your coarse felt boots, yet the porcelain toilets are all intact, then again there isn't a single handle. There is only darkness and cigarette ends, just what you'd expect.

Come on in, those of you in desperate need, come on! Come in and feel your felt boots squelch, feel the heat of the smouldering gleams against your cheeks and, while you fumble with the shrivelled elastic on your wide flannelet trousers and wrestle with the intractable knots, feel yourself completely coated, defiled, desecrated. Actually, you'd better just rip the elastic, fast, but don't let go of the ends, hold on to them, you hear me, now go ahead and go, but hold on to the ends, then run back to class cursing the indelible memory of that merry latrines, only hold on to the ends! If you don't get called on, you can tie the ends together, you'll find the moment.

"There is in early autumn... in Ostankino's hushed arbors... a lorn palace, sad and solemn... wherein... a bewitched count wanders... Sheremetev... the stone goddess... Pomona tastes her sweet first kiss... and on the bench she eclipses... someone has scrawled... "Kiss my ass!"

You'll be sorry! Better not do that or you'll be sorry! Look out, or you'll be sorry! People so often frighten people, people so often threaten people with punishment, humiliation, pain.

"Gimme your baranka, or you'll be sorry!"

"Pig! Bastard! They'll kick you out, you'll be sorry!"

"If you go out that door, you'll be sorry!"

"If you don't tell, you'll be sorry!"

"If you tell, you'll be sorry!"

"You'll be fuckin' sorry!"

Yet how could life be any sorrier? Take, for instance, the games. They sweep through the school in great waves all year long. One scourge after another, one more energetic and graphic than the next. But none deters the ebb and flow of that truly dashing and devil-may-care pastime, of that truly daring and valiant sport dating back to the dawn of our native education.

Say the old soldier who fought in Galicia has gone down the hall tinkling his bell. It's recess. The classroom doors fly open and the hall fills with brutality. "Kokyn did it! Kokyn shit!" a gang of miscreants thunders. "Kokyn" is a nickname, I don't know what it means; shit should be taken to mean farted, made a bad smell. Not hard to do as a child, especially if you happen to be gnawing on oil-cake, not the kind with sunflower seeds, but the kind with split peas, as Kokyn was doing, sucking the mustard-colored cake and biting into the hard, fibrous crumbs resembling fossilized Polovtsian halva.

Here he comes now tearing down the hall, he knows just what that shriek means: "Kokyn shit!"

Tradition is a great thing, it is the basis of all that is truly Russian, pre-Petrine, and native. Indeed, there are those who now trace Kokyn's nickname to that celebrated and mysterious line in *Zadonshchina*: *Oko kynul knyaz* (The prince cast his eye). Some surmise a scribe's mistake and claim this line should in fact read *Okokynel knyaz* (The prince was struck dumb); others attribute the confusion to that mischievous Vasily Lvovich Pushkin, the day he stopped by Musin-Pushkin's to buy six serf architects for resale and play a game of *svaika*.

But even if you blame the scribe, the expression *okokynel knyaz* still doesn't explain the word *kokyn*, not that it matters. What matters is that this word existed and exists. So the tradition exists, and the exponent of this tradition, that hungry half pint Kokyn, makes off while he can, but he won't make it, despite being an exponent of the tradition, because the exponents of that traditional seminarians' game are g-g-gaining on him with their shriek: "Kokyn did it! Kokyn shit!", and... folklorists, write this down! What follows is a playful adage of old:

> *Fight-fight, fight-fight, fighters, fight!*
> *Hangmen all are out tonight!*
> *He who does not join the fray,*
> *He will have to pay, yes, pay!*
> *Sheath or flame or poppy seed:*
> *Pick or choose one of the three!*

A four-foot trochee, the traditional folk meter. And a good beat, too, for beating up even a little person in the ensuing chaos. This is what is going on in the hall right now. But notice how clever it all is, here you have the rudiments of collective responsibility: "He who does not join the fray, he will have to pay, yes, pay!" And no one is fool enough to stay out of it. *Everyone* joins in. But now here are the rudiments of collective irresponsibility, for to put *everyone* on such a piddling job is stupid. Besides which, you can't even get at the object of the fistfight, so the bungling hall mob is stamping its feet and waving its fists in vain. But we won't incite tradition. It bears no responsibility for the post-Petrine period.

Instead let's scan the adage for other rudiments. Rudiments of justice, this time. Notice, by the way, how easily and aptly the incongruous and complex concept of "hangmen" is introduced into this playful verse! But we digress.

The object of the fistfight has, as we know, *shit*, that is he has fouled the air with a gratuitous stench for which he must be punished. Yes! Lynch law! But it is swift and *just*, for Kokyn may decide his fate. He has a choice! "Sheath or flame or poppy seed: pick or choose one of the three!" Kokyn knows *what* this choice means, as do his tormentors, but a game is a game and always new, and a choice means at least a let-up in the beatings and a glimmer of hope, however vain – it's a choice, after all!

Depending on the situation you must pick one thing.

Let's consider the three possibilities (the fourth doesn't count since everyone joined in, otherwise Kokyn could have shouted: "Hey, they didn't join the fray! They're sitting it out in Tashkent!" and so diverted attention away from himself):

First comes "sheath!"

"Sock in the teeth!" screams the horde, and each one socks you in the teeth. If you happen to be losing your baby teeth and one of them is wiggly, it will be knocked out, and the one that eventually replaces it will come in crooked and yellower than the rest. I can prove it.

"Poppy seed!"

"Done's the deed!" the crowd howls. "And it cannot be undone, which takes you back to square one! Fight-fight, fight-fight, fighters, fight! Hangmen all are out tonight! He who does not join the fray, he will have to pay, yes, pay! Sheath or flame or poppy seed: pick or choose one of the three!"

So then, what we have here are the rudiments of a sort of appellate court. If Kokyn shouts: "Flame!", the gang will howl: "Who's to blame?" – in this we detect the rudiments of openness and tireless civil zeal. No secret denunciations here! Word and deed. I will testify openly against another; let the devil who made me make that stink get him over there, then we can all practice our swift justice on him. Then on someone else and on someone else after that, and we'll all suffer, we'll all suffer. *One* shit, but *all* suffer: it's an ancient idea, ecumenical and endemic.

It's only an idea, though, and Kokyn must say who's to blame. Meanwhile, the bruisers nearest him are the biggest and the dumbest, and if he points to one of them there will be hell to pay, and the real shame won't be his swollen black eye, the real shame will be the failure to apply the great, compassionate, and redemptive idea of universal repentance.

But Kokyn can't see anyone suitable, his tears are in the way, and then he remembers: "Rozya!" He instinctively finds that little runt to blame. "Rozya! Rozya! Rozya's to blame!" everyone wails. "Where is he? Where's Rozya? I know! I know! He didn't join the fray! He's hiding! Rozya!" the hall erupts.

Rozya really is hiding. Rozya always sits rounds of this violent game out in the cupboard where the maps are kept or under one of desks in the back row because he knows that all the same he will always be the one to blame. This, too, is an ancient idea. Deep-seated, true, and definitely pre-Petrine.

When the cadging of *barankas* (rationed at the rate of one per day per boy) makes no sense because none were delivered, or when it's very cold, or dark, or everyone feels somehow frightened, or anxious at heart (this happens, thus fulfilling the transcendental prophecy "you'll be sorry"), then the above-described game is transubstantiated into its folkloric mutation. But here I request folklorists and all those interested in the Russian heritage to rise to the occasion of the communication below.

Specifically, I ask that you not use fountain-pens, ballpoint pens, or pencils – all legacies of Peter's assemblies and that accursed Lefort. You must write either with quills and cinnabar or with a sharp object. Either, or. And not on paper. You may use parchment, or paste, or, those of you who don't have any, birch-bark.

Ready?

Now let's play the tape back. No, tape is out of place here, too! Never mind. We can trust Kokyn to foul the air again, he'll manage. Smell that? Now our job is to fall on him and scream. Write this down! Scratch it out! This is an original seminarians' text, I'll prove it:

> *Chichiroo-chichiroo,*
> *Your mother she taught you:*

Don't shit,
Don't break wind.
Choose you copper or tin?

What strikes one first about this verse is the heartwarming "your mother she taught you", you can just see it: the log hut, the gentle peasant mother, or the devout Old Believer boyar's wife who, in the name of a healthful climate, is teaching her progeny not to shit or break wind. Simple women, an unhurried way of life, the ancient maternal principle. Otherwise, just imagine how much shitting and breaking of wind Ilya Muromets would have done sitting on that stove for thirty-three years if his mother hadn't taught him!

"Copper!" Kokyn yelps.

"Three smacks in the kisser!" the second-year boys and the rest decide. Oh, no!

"Tin!" says Kokyn.

"Again begin!" the second-year boys and the rest decree and again begin drumming: "Chichiroo-chichiroo, your mother she taught you!" Oh, no!

Did you notice? There is no third choice, no chance to transfer the blame. No idea of collective repentance. The brothers in suffering have disappeared. This time-honored text reveals *new* wicked attributes. Foreign influences. But what's it all about?

It's all about "chichiroo-chichiroo". It's Latin. *Cicero* (pronounced chichero) means pea. And this pea (or, in Kokyn's case, split-pea oil-cake) has always given people gas, eat too many peas you'll act as if the peas had overeaten. Latin! Why can't we just speak plainly: "You eaters of peas, contain yourselves please!"? But no, you can't do that: it's Latin! By Latinist priests. From the West. "The Roman harlot," as the archpriest Avvakum used to say. So it's the seminary. This text is akin to one quoted by Pomyalovsky and he's at least one hundred years old. Simple folk forgot themselves when they played this daring game, despite its foreign reek. That reek is what led to the seminarians' brutality and, echoes of kindness ("mother taught you") notwithstanding, to two no-win situations instead of three indulgences. After all, "Copper: three smacks in the kisser!" (here "kisser" means face or head) and "Sheath: sock in the teeth!" are entirely different things. You may say, to hell with your head, but you still need it to think your thoughts, whereas your teeth you can do without – you can always soften your oil-cake with spit. "Tin: again begin!" and "Poppy seed: done's the deed!" is another comparison that does not favor the former alternative. Meanwhile the impossibility of shifting the blame onto a Rozya points to the insidious machinations of you know who. They certainly know how to ingratiate themselves: your mother, they say, she taught you...

From all the dark corners they come out... and she comes out... a slender girl... "I'll meet you," she says... where... by the statue behind the museum... which one... the one in the blouse... we both blush... that implies the others have nothing on... we blush and tears well up... I feel a lump in my throat... all this is born of the darkness... of my mood... of a fading echo now washed away...

"Fight-fight, fighters, fight" gives way to an epidemic of finger slingshots bearing no relation to normal slingshots with their thick, square bands of elastic, leather holders, and y-shaped sticks. Finger slingshots are compact, easy to make, easy to hide, and less conspicuous when in use, if short-range (you can't hit a bird), but even so, if the shot is metal, made out of a bent nail, say, or out of copper, aluminum, or iron wire, it can do terrible damage. Hit someone in the eye with that and the eye is as good as gone, which is why these savage shots are rarely used and then almost always from behind.

Finger slingshots are mostly made out of a thin bit of elastic excised from one's underwear, and fitted with a tiny paper tube folded in half. A good hit with that shot will make the victim cry, while a direct hit, again, could cost him an eye. But I don't remember anyone ever losing an eye: we all went on having two thanks to the skill of the shooters.

"Sit down, I said! Sit *down*! On your desks! You *pigs*, on your desks! I mean *at* your desks! Yevmentsev, give that back! Give me back my grade book, Yevmentsev! You pig, you rat, you numskull! Are you going to give it back or not? I can*not* take this anymore! I have *had* it! O-o-ow! Who shot that! You bastards! Ba-a-a-stards! Aa-ah!!! What's that? What have you put on my chair! Well, what is it? Su-et? Why suet? What is this filthy piece of suet doing here? What's the meaning of this? What's the meaning of this you give me my grade book back this minute Yevmentsev! Stop it! I will *not* tolerate this! Ow-w! That hurts! Stop it! I am not Maria Ivanovna... This is not drawing class! This is... Stop it! I won't stand for it! Take that! And that! And that! That's my grade book for you, you pig, you numskull, you rat! Class mon-i-to-o-or! He! He! He hit me in the chest! You! You! Better bring your mother with you next time, or else! Next time you bring your mother... Do you hear me, you louse, do you hear me, you numskull?! You bring her with you, got it!"

"Got it! The fuck I will!" fifth grader Stenyushkin sasses Maria Pavlovna, his Ancient History teacher, and doesn't even duck the slab of grey suet flying his way since the crazed woman slings it predictably wide.

Here the jingle of the wounded veteran's bell breaks in and puts an end to the class in which one might have read out loud, say, this: "And Xenophon said: 'I have heard that there are Rodhosians in your army many of whom shoot from slings, and that their projectiles fly twice as far as those of Persian shooters. The Persians use stones the size of your fist so they can't shoot far, whereas the Rodhosians also know how to shoot lead ingots.'"

Come to think of it, had this passage been read it might have made for a more accurate slinging of the suet or a rejection of suetslinging altogether... As for extra homework, Maria Pavlovna was prevented by the bell from assigning any in the textbook by Zhdanov, Kirov, and Stalin (the same Stalin whose letter is hanging in the vestibule).

Incidentally, about Yevmentsev. He's actually Yumyanov: that's his real last name. But for some reason he also answers to Yevmentsev. No, that's not his stepfather's name, or his mother's maiden name. Yevmentsev doesn't have anything to do with Yumanov. Nevertheless, he went by that name through the fourth grade. It seems that during his first ever roll-call his first ever teacher called out: "Yevmentsev!" She must have stared at him because he was the only one who hadn't answered yet and she was at the end of the list. Then the whole class stared at him and he blurted: "Here!" His real name had probably been written incorrectly or illegibly. The teacher even fixed something in her grade book, and he must have decided, the way an adopted dog decides, that he would have to answer to this new name and so − with all eyes fixed on him − he did.

Or it may be that on that wonderfully festive first day of school when he first entered first grade (he would enter it again the following year) he simply forgot his last name or maybe he didn't know there was such a thing, maybe he was as naive as that other boy who kept telling the whole class (his listeners were also naive) that since the Klimovs' mother (a very risque woman) had two children that meant that she had already *frucked* twice in her life. He insisted on this though he slept with his mother on a government-issue trestle-bed in a room measuring 12 square feet at the Marfino State Farm and welcomed Uncle Vitya's arrival in said bed every night and described different methods of coitus − quick, long-drawn-out, multiple − very well. His innocence evidently prevented him from making sense of his experience, hence his suspicions about the Klimovs' mother.

As for the Klimov boy, he had no reliable information of his own on that score and so could neither confirm nor deny the assertions of the Marfino know-it-all.

From all the dark corners they come out... and she comes out, too... the round pocket watch I took from home says she's two hours late... she comes slowly toward me... in the birch grove by the veterinary clinic a sick horse neighs softly... without touching... three feet apart... we walk along skipping pebbles... all this is born of the grass... of the summer... of a place the gentle horse glimpsed... of the pebbles I've long since stopped skipping...

The drawing teacher quit to become a postwoman. Sometimes she would appear at the gate − a mannish form with the flabby, barren face of an old revolutionary and a lumpy, porous nose, her skirt hanging off her hips at odd lengths, her stale cotton cardigan drooping every which way, lugging her bag of other people's communications – so as to some day never reappear.

"The moon, boys, came out... Of its locket! He drew a knife, boys, from his pocket. I will cut you, boys, I will hit. All the same now you are 'it'!" he says, striding into the classroom for the first time and suddenly pointing at one of the boys standing stock-still by his desk.

"I've already done class duty!"

"To hell with your class duty! You're 'it'! Go to the board!"

"Wow!" another little boy stares, stunned. "What a ball-breaker!"

"Ball them all, you're riding for a fall," the geometry teacher replies. "So I suggest you stay seated. And keep it down. I will cut you. I will hit..."

"I will fuck your mother's slit!" several boys intone, quietly but in unison, without moving their lips.

"No-o-ow! See, I used to be a homeless kid like the ones in *The Republic of SHKID* and that *Pedagogical Poem*. So-o-o," says the teacher going up to the boy he wants, taking the boy by the nose, gripping the boy's nose between his index and middle fingers, gripping hard and, seemingly oblivious, pacing up and down and all around the room, trailed by the writhing boy. The boy doesn't try to break free though, that would only hurt more. Besides, there's the teacher's authority. So far the boy can bear it, so he keeps walking, head first, after the new teacher, while the rest of the class watches intently, and the one who's "it" goes on standing at the board with a wooden triangle and piece of chalk.

"Well!"

"I'm erecting a perpendicular!" comes the nonsensical suggestion from the boy at the board.

"To what? To your butt?" the teacher clowns. "What's his name, kiddies?" he asks the class, now spellbound and wondering what the new teacher intends to do with his left hand given that his right is still gripping the boy he wants' nose.

"Osip!" the spellbound class choruses.

"Osip, you're a nut! Understand?"

"I understand!"

"Why'd the dog roll in the sand?" the once homeless teacher concludes to the kiddies' delight. "Sit down, Osip. You'll make a poor student. And what's your name?"

"Tutudashef..." the nose-boy says through crimped nostrils.

"Are you a Tatar?"

"Dno. Moundain Shodian..."

"You're lying. Don't you dare be ashamed of your people. Go wash your snout, Shorian..."

We loved geometry in spite of ourselves. We learned everything there was to learn, we grasped the magic meaning of the indisputable assumptions and the proud proofs, everything, only to forget it all in the course of life. Nose-pulling became popular practice among all those who could afford to indulge with respect to those who could not. True, when the latter grew up they managed to forget even this, though that humiliating helplessness seemed to them the greatest sadness of their "childhood", and they made up for it with the happiness of pulling other people's noses, the noses of the utterly weak, the utterly helpless, of those with respect to whom they could afford it.

The road to school goes through a firing range. The firing range consists of five separate wooden stands resembling pagodas surrounded by a bizarre landscape: an endless, pinkish desert, a mosaic of countless flat piles of pink ballast and earth extracted by metro builders from Moscow's Cambrian depths and dumped here for years and years.

At the firing range hunters fire from double-barreled guns at clay pigeons hurled into the air without warning, smashing them in flight. The sharpshooters' contests are judged by Vasily Stalin, son of the man who sent that letter and came up with the idea of teaching boys and girls separately. I don't know what the girls learned, but the boys learned all sorts of vileness. We, however, are not much interested in the firing range right now, though to see the clay pigeons fly up at odd angles from out of nowhere and be shot to smithereens, like small crested birds, does have tremendous appeal.

Yet neither the shots, nor the explosions can distract the big, school-bound boys from that chief and unbearable vision. But first about the firing.

Next to the school there was an airplane dump, so-called, where you could find anything you wanted. Most likely, the dump consisted of all sorts of military equipment, or perhaps it was just airplane parts; whatever, we hauled away fantastic quantities of the most indispensable and always fascinating things. Section aluminum, wiring, camouflage-colored rivets, catches, and stateless components – all of which was ingeniously adapted for perfidies, pranks, and nice tricks like this:

Apparently they were engine valves. The size and shape of small, three-pound dumb-bells, they had thin, even cross bars, as opposed to pudgy, sloppily cast ones. On the ends – in place of the balls – were flat polished disks just like the buffers on railroad cars. But saw the disks and cross bar in half and you had a trove of metallic sodium.

Metallic sodium is a soft substance the consistency of very thick white honey. Little chunks of it would be picked out with a piece of scrap iron and deposited in, say, an ink-well: the sodium would begin to run and run, run and run over the surface, growing hotter and hotter until it had destroyed itself and the ink with it. Then again, if you struck the ink towards the end of the heating process with, say, a nail – and not even hard – it would start madly spraying tiny, terrible, boiling drops that burned through clothes and skin.

Those were basic experiments involving the oxidation of an unstable metal in air or in liquid, but if you were to leave the sawed off dumb-bell in a toilet bowl, immersed in the standing water, then you could go calmly off to class with everyone else, including the ones spending the day in the latrine so their mothers would think they were in school and their teachers would think they didn't give a damn about school.

Even they abandon the latrine and head for the classroom where, furious at not being allowed to smoke, they distract themselves by, say, decoloring the ink with carbide. Once the carbide is in the ink-well, the ink begins to froth and foam, and the air to stink stubbornly of hydrogen sulfide, you'd like to *chichiroo* the atmosphere itself, meanwhile the ink is almost colorless and refuses to stay on the pen, leaving pages of copy-books etched with the barely visible shadows of the great language's great lines, say, "There is in early autumn...", but we've already quoted that one.

Or else the class comers may duck under the desks in the back row and stretch out on a relief map or a political map of the Motherland. Needless to say, the political map is preferable since the rivers, mountains, and valleys on the relief map make a hard and knobby berth for anyone but the Prince of Death; the political map, on the other hand, resembles the patchwork quilt that every boy knows from home, and lounging on it makes him feel as if he had never left.

The loungers lounge quietly, but only in those classes where the teacher doesn't dare leave the board. Lounging placidly, the loungers torture the sitters (also troublemakers: they've been sent to the back row, after all), slashing their sodden, post-latrine trouser bottoms to shreds and quietly lighting anything they can with lighters, while the sitters sit there stewing, squirming, cheeping, but never betraying the loungers, for...

Bang-bang! Bang-bang-bang! Those are real explosions. The sound is real, and so is the force. That's the soft-as-thick-white-honey metallic sodium going off in the last three toilets left on the floor. All the doors on the hall fly open and boys tumble out screaming and jumping for joy! The teachers who know what's wrong are livid with rage. The ones who don't are pale with fright. Euphoria, exaltation, whoops, shards of toilet bowls and − a-a-ah! − not a single porcelain bowl on the entire floor. There aren't even any in storage. There aren't any anywhere. They may manage to scrounge a few by next September, but the airplane dump isn't going anywhere, so we'll get those bowls, too.

For now there is pandemonium in the packed corridor, the loungers are getting ready for when the boys who ran out come back. First they lock the classroom door by shoving a chair leg through the handle, then they begin paying puny pathetic Kondrashka back for something.

Kondrashka has been stripped naked and smeared with pale inky blobs. The synthetic blobs combine with the natural dirt on his body to make the hapless, helpless fellow an altogether pathetic and painful sight. He's so sorry-looking, he'd be better off locked up in the cupboard where those patchwork political maps are kept. The cupboard isn't very big but Kondrashka's a shrimp, he should fit... and in he goes.

Now Kondrashka's anointers and exposers begin tearing around the room: lying under those desks made them stiff! The door is still locked. Out in the hall people are worried and looking into the matter: it's bedlam out there. And it's bedlam in here: the noisy numskulls don't realize that all the classes have gone back, except for one class that can't because the door is barred with a chair. Luckily there's a hole in the door – from the English lock that used to be there before someone ripped it off – and the teacher is trying to peep through it. But she catches only glimpses of the numskulls galumphing past and can't identify them thanks to the boys shoving outside the door and purposely knocking into her, she finally gives up and goes to get the dean, leaving the hall boys to whisper through the hole: "She's gone to get the dean!" But the galumphers go on galumphing round and round the room and, as they go by the hole, either shove pen tips through it, or take aim and spit, so that when the strict, straight, grey dean peers in, she gets a huge gob right in the eye. Silence in the hall. In the classroom, too. The half-blind dean is led away by the teacher, tears flowing from her left eye, like an Amazon's (because according to a legend that only I know, the Amazons, who burned off their right breasts the better to draw their bows at full tilt, shed maidenly tears not from their right eye over the breast cauterized for martial purposes, but from their left).

Thus the dean disappears, tears streaming from her one,

unpolluted eye; in the meantime the hall morons let the loungers scram, then go back to their seats and are sitting quietly when the teacher returns with the principal. No one has any idea that that shrimp Kondrashka is curled up, as if in the womb, in the cupboard with the maps: he kept quiet through all the running around, hoping his concerned captors would forget about him. But now that order has been restored, the little fool starts wriggling; teacher and principal both make a beeline for the cupboard — oh, they think, now we've got the ones who got the dean. "Come out of there, you rats, come out this minute!" But out comes the lilac-colored, stark naked Kondrashka with a hop and a jump and — "Ha-ha-ha!" the whole class howls, "Ha-ha-ha!" — bounds off like a scared rabbit, and teach after him, whacking the air with her grade book, he's too quick and small, he darts between the desks and over them, the boys try to trip him and spank him, but he, the rat, is impossible to get — there's so little of him — though naturally they do get him once, in the balls, in his small balls. These are fifth graders, after all. They found a way...

From all the dark corners they come out to that tango... and she comes out... I couldn't meet you, she says... you were with someone, remember ... nobody was with me, don't lie... I was on my bicycle I saw you... you shouldn't follow me around like that... this all comes of such regret... such hopelessness... such confusion...

Straggling through the firing range, we are distracted by the shooting from double-barreled guns at clay pigeons. But the dense thickets of small trees circling the range — hawthorn or guelder-rose — beckon. In their gnarled tops, in their whittled leaves (not so large and perfect as maple or oak leaves, but rather small and irregularly shaped as if carved by some clumsy country hand trying to copy those masterpieces) — in their flickering leaves stand stout, sweaty girls from the pointless state farms that existed for some inexplicable reason nearby, girls gathering hawthorn or guelder-rose nobody knew why.

It's an old story. It's Indian summer. Sunny and clear.

Berries are still on the trees. And girls. Girls from the farm. The girls stand with legs apart, one leg on one branch and one on another, and you stand down below, craning your neck, while up above in those hazy recesses, pink from her translucent skirt, such a complicated sight unfolds, a kaleidoscope of soft thighs, flannelette drawers, patched or not patched, creases of flesh spilling over elastics, bands of flesh spilling over garters – it's only now one can piece the bits together, for then it was all an indistinguishable, indefinable tangle – perhaps it was the blouse that confused everything, perhaps it was tucked into her tattered drawers and those were its coarse calico tails sticking out the bottom and making her thighs look winged... I don't know. I don't remember. I can't say. Then the girl squeezes her legs together, go away, for shame! And you threaten: I'm coming up. You just try, she taunts, so small and thick, never seen a big dick. Oh and you have, well I'm coming up. You'll slip and fall and bust your balls. No I won't, see, I didn't slip, gonna get you now. Getcher hands off or I'll push you off... Their blouses are full to bursting, their smoldering flannelette drawers overflowing with soft flesh and fleshy pulp, and if you perch on a branch beside her, you may have the luck to brush against her, the shaky treetops rustle and hiss as the lusty girls, feeling safe, indulge the boys, or seem to, then burst out laughing as the boys slide down the trunks, crushing their ripe knobs against the knobby bark and skinning their poor palms fresh from what is softest in the world. The boys are on their way to the afternoon session at school. "Come'n paw us again tomorra," the merry girls call after them, "only don't furget to ask yer mas!"

"I can't stand it any longer, they're monsters!"

"There are no bad pupils, only bad teachers!"

"I'd like to do to them what we did to the Germans – from a grenade!"

"Well said: from a grenade..."

"Comrades, it is our duty, I repeat, our duty to educate our pupils in the spirit..."

"But they aren't even human!"

"What about Makarenko. He had it mu-u-uch harder!"

"No, I can't stand it! I walk into that classroom and I'm already in tears. And, you know, they... they hurt me... physically..."

"But that's shameless!"

"Stalin, Kirov, and Zhdanov say..."

"I know, I know. Before the Revolution they didn't know how to teach. But they used canes then!"

"Canes clear brains..."

"I can't, I can't, I ca-a-an't! Recess is almost over... I can't, I'm not going back, give me a cigarette... I can't, don't push me, I won't tell you what they wanted me to see..."

"Ha-aa-a... You saw but you didn't die... Come on, there's the bell. Let's go..."

"I can't, I can't, and I won't!"

"Come on, stop crying, you're the one who's always saying you weren't raised in a convent! A teacher in hysterics is all we need! Now pull yourself..."

A suppressed sob is heard. Then the sound of someone drinking a restorative glass of water...

In the spring we all liked to play a game called "starting line". Where we came from there were three ways of jumping over a person. The oldest, merriest, and most venerable was, of course, leap-frog. An almost Chekhovian pastime. Papa, Mama, little boys in knee socks, and guests in raw silk suits leaping nimbly over one another along the path from, say, the cherry orchard to, say, the spring torrents. Or to the tablecloth spread out on the grass. They leap and fool. A meadow. Bees drone. Butterflies hang in the air. Pollen is everywhere. A smile on a face. A young lady in a mobcap. A tiny tear on the end... of her eyelash. From laughter! From happy laughter...

That's leap-frog. But in another setting it makes no sense: you won't come across any spring torrents, only a fence or, if you are playing in the schoolyard, a pile of coal. And where are you to find young ladies, mobcaps, widowers, fathers and sons? There aren't any. The essence of the game is lost. So there's no point in playing.

The second way of jumping is called "goat". One person bends over, puts his hands on his knees, and stands perpendicular to the jumpers: he's the "goat" and has the right to throw the jumpers who must perform various difficult tricks in flight. "*Barankas* for the goat" means digging your fists into the goat's back; "forks for the goat" means stabbing him with fingers spread wide; "spur the goat" means jabbing him in the rear. Or lower down, which hurts even more. And with your other foot you can jab him in the head, though that is risky: the "goat" will protest, the fun will be spoiled, and soon it will be your turn to be the "goat". The important thing is to execute your jumps cleanly. There is also "spoons for the goat" and the semi-seemly "knock the goat up" which, presumably, is why the Phys. Ed. teacher Valentina Kirillovna, a very young woman, does not play "goat", although "goat", as opposed to the entirely seemly leap-frog, is a popular and democratic diversion, one that lends itself to schoolyards and sidewalks alike. The occasional little cruelties in "goat" are as insignificant as, say, Sonya's hitting Natasha Rostova with a rubber ball by mistake, though of course in their day there weren't any rubber balls, and I meant that only as an example.

Actually Valentina Kirillovna would like very much to play goat. The slight pain from the "*barankas*", or the "forks", or even the kick below the rump, when she reared her trouser-clad croup, would suit her, if not excite her, though no one guesses as much, least of all her pupils whose foul mouths belie their easygoing innocence. Still, if they — she and the jumpers — had their druthers they would much prefer to play "knock the goat up". But a Phys. Ed. class is a Phys. Ed. class, and therefore Valentina Kirillovna consents instead, though to her own detriment (why detriment, you will see: compensation comes in a couple of pages), to play (after the warm-up exercises, deep knee bends, and free movements) a game of "starting line".

Now here is a truly athletic game! You couldn't ask for more: play it well and by the rules and you will improve not only your jumping ability but your will to win. Here the strongest man wins – meaning he is almost never "it", meaning he doesn't allow himself to be jumped over.

This time the one who is "it" stands with his back to the jumpers who jump over him from behind a line. When everyone has jumped, the one who's "it" moves forward to where the last jumper put his foot down. Then everyone jumps all over again, but on one or another condition, depending on how far the one who's "it" is from the line. The possible conditions are: a running leap from the line (jump "minus one"), or one step over the line and then jump (jump "plus one"), or two steps over the line ("plus two"), or three steps ("plus three"), though it rarely gets to that.

Say a jumper insists that the one who's "it" is too far from the line to reach with a running leap (jump "minus one") and challenges him. This is a chance for the one who's "it" to stop being "it". He then trades places with the doubter and "proves" to him that a jump "minus one" is still possible, in which case everyone must jump "minus one". Including the doubter, who either makes it, or stops short at the last minute, afraid he will wipe the goat out and hurt himself to boot. Or else he races headlong for the starting line, pushes off, and rams with his whole eighth-grade weight right into the goat's fearless rear, thus dooming himself to be "it". Then the game starts all over again.

When the jump is just on the edge of possible, the game looks entirely athletic. With a splendid push, the youth sails into the air, his nearly man-size hands outstretched, for a split second it seems they won't reach their stooped object, but they do, coming down hard on the braced-for-the-worst back, the springy blow gives his heavy, sinking body new impetus, he rises up, hands between the dividers of his outstretched legs in the manner of a hare, and the next moment he lands on his feet, now tucked in under him and, incidentally, already Size 10.

Perky, friendly Valentina Kirillovna is almost always "it". Despite being an impeccable jumper and sailing over the one who is "it" as if over a vaulting horse in the gym, she is mostly powerless to "prove" big distances with a jump "minus one" or "plus one", and so generously and generally volunteers to be "it".

Meanwhile the jumpers are chivalry itself. They jostle genteelly behind the line, waiting their turn to push off, soar up, and come down – gently – on that slim rounded back, while the last jumper, whose landing place Valentina Kirillovna must take, tries to check his flight so as to keep her closer to the line and rule out the challenges that lead to those punishing long jumps. In other words, he tries to preserve a manageable "minus one" situation for as long as possible, and then to create an indisputable "plus one" by flying far over the diminutive woman with the upturned croup.

Little does he know that those challenges are what she craves. The touch of tactful palms is nice, but nicer still is when (every inch of her wants this) some hulking man-child comes hurtling right at her and, to keep from slamming into her, claws her back, just briefly, just where her bra is (once her bra even burst at the seams, but no one noticed), before coming down with all his weight, all his weight, his prodigious weight, on her perfectly arched and waiting back, only to tear himself away and pull up straight on powerful legs, abandoning her to her now pointless pose.

Say what you like, that's just like a man. He comes hurtling at you from out of nowhere, huge and heavy, hands outstretched in his terrible flight the better to come crashing down – for an instant, for life, for a second, for tonight, for this two-week vacation – you don't know for how long, all you can do is wait, tensely but always perfectly attuned, while he flattens you, crushes you, then washes his hands of you so as to amble back to the start in his Size 10 shoes and line up with the other men...

This is why the gentle jabs of her restrained eighth graders always elicit little moans from Valentina Kirillovna, and now... and now, finally, a challenge is in the offing: the man-child at the head of line can't possibly make the required jump "plus one" and so has the right to challenge Valentina Kirillovna to "prove" it. But that would be awkward, especially since the perky, friendly Valentina Kirillovna keeps shouting:

"No, plus one! Come on, you can do it! Plus one! Come on! Pretend you're your Papa going on the attack! Come on, now!" Her voice sounds strange as she sets her feet firmly apart, tucks in her knees like the athlete she is, bends over, and glances sideways at the man-child taking his running start. He thunders toward the line like a paratrooper, takes an enormous step in the air, then... pushes off! She looks away, lowers her head, and arches her quivering back. Oh, God! Oh! She can feel him hurtling at her, huge and heavy, the better to crush her, and she, moaning softly, cheats (and he could have made it!) by raising her back just a hair, imperc-c-ceptibly, so that the enormous palms miss their mark, sweetly and p-painfully, so that the enormous weight of the hurtling male organism does not touch down so as to fly over, but instead slams pants-front-first into his teacher's small, tensed, upturned rump.

"Knocked her up!" comes the cackle of a gaggle of third graders hanging out of a fourth-floor window, and since they won't be able to knock Valentina Kirillovna up for another five years and since they can't bear to wait, they heave a big heavy desk out the window in expression of their longing.

Meanwhile the man-child, depressed by having failed and discomfited by having knocked his nice teacher off her feet, quickly assumes the stooped position of the one who's "it" only to have the fresh air class cut short by the wounded veteran and his bell.

With more gentle jostling, the boys will, of course, walk Valentina Kirillovna home, and she will go knowing that her aching desire is not only undiminished but in no way diminishing, and she will be in a rush to get home and put a record on the record player, and no sooner will she take up a book then she will put it aside distractedly and... if o-o-only the be-e-ell hadn't ru-u-ung...

The book, by the way, is called *Spring Torrents*...

From all the dark corners they come out... and she comes out... a slender girl... all this is born of the silence... of my mood... of the bright morning air... of half tears...

This boy, a second-grader, is still as lazy as the lazy

child who is too lazy even to do nothing and, if he's at home, doesn't even want to do what he wants to do, and doesn't put his ink-pot in his schoolbag though he knows perfectly well there isn't any ink at school and that if some turns up it will be contaminated with carbide on the spot.

He's only a little boy but he already knows something that will stay with him for the rest of his life: the luck of making friends, or enemies, there's nothing in between.

Why does he forget to bring his ink? What makes him doom himself to despair and humiliation? It's hard to say, now. No doubt it is some childish quirk: he has an indelible pencil, after all, and could easily use the lead to make some decent ink with real rust stains on the glossy black pool. Or perhaps it's because the room is always cold at night, and the oil-lamp is burning, and he doesn't want to do anything, and he has three columns of sums to do, and there isn't enough food, and he's feeling so listless. The sum of these childish listlessnesses must be what triggers that terrifying energy in school, always cruel and destructive, but short-lived since the boys' weakness and listlessness makes them want to see results fast.

But still, why does he have to forget his ink? He has a dictation today and Alexandra Dimitrievna always picks on him. Now that I think of it, I can say that for a fact.

A dictation. Some idiotic dictation. Outside the sky is sullen and his crosshatched copybook looks fresh in the grey light. Where they got those copybooks, I don't know. "'Sa-vra-ska has sunk middle-deep in a snowdrift... Sa-vra-ska has sunk' – why aren't you writing?" "I forgot my ink at home," the boy mumbles. "'...middle-deep in a snow-drift...' so you're not going to write anything, is that it?" "I forgot my ink at home..." "Well what am I to do with you?" the scrawny battle-axe's steel-grey curls inquire. "What am I to do with you, always forgetting, always holding up the class, hm?" "May I share?..." "'...For bast shoes that freeze...' freeze, that's when something becomes very cold, as cold as ice..." "We know, we know!" "Alexandra Dimitrievna, may I share with someone?" "Do you mean to tell me you haven't started writing yet?

'to the ledge...' Well, go ahead and share if someone will let you."

"If someone will let you": the whole class knows what that means. A number of the other boys didn't bring any ink either but they have already refilled their pots and vials with borrowed ink, or found seats next to or near boys who have ink.

"Well, go ahead and share if someone will let you!"

"Makar, lemme share?"

"Bring your own!"

"'The top of a cof-fin... en-vel-oped in sack-ing...'"

"Deryug, lemme share?"

"What?" says star-of-the-class Deryugin, diligently spelling the word "koffin"...

"Deryug, you goofed. 'Coffin' is spelled with a 'c'!"

"Alexandra Dmitrievna, why can't he mind his own business? He's even telling me what to write!"

"I'm warning you for the last time! Now start writing! '...Peep out of the mis-er-a-ble sledge...'" the teacher enunciates, wheeling around toward the board and pretending not to notice the desperate begging going on behind her back, for the boy keeps dashing further and further away from his desk looking for someone to share, then rushing back again after each new rejection.

"Prokhor, lemme share? I'll give you some of my baran-kas..."

Note that you could get absolutely anything for a baranka. Just as you could get a genuine gold ducat for a *Dukat* cigarette-butt or, say, a Latvian *Laima* candy wrapper for an almost useable rusty soldier's revolver.

"Prokhor, I'll give you some of my barankas..."

"How many?"

"One..."

"Like fun!"

"O.K., two..."

"Hell with you!"

That was that. He had exhausted his sharing aisle. None of the teachers let you go all around the class sharing. If the ink was close by, you could dip your pen in and go back to your seat, but otherwise...

"Are you writing or not? I told you to share... But you're too lazy to do even that... everything has to be handed to you on a silver platter... Boys, what are we going to do with him, hm? Since he's holding up our dictation. Send him out? Hm?" says the hoary-headed teacher, my first, towering over our copybooks.

"Ye-e-es!" they all cheer, taking advantage of the din to correct the word *coffin* to match Derugin's *koffin*.

The boy sits there, head bowed over his crosshatched copybook, peering through glistening eyes at his pen with the Rondo tip which, as luck would have it, or rather wouldn't have it, uses up more ink than other pens, but the only other pen he owns has a "goose foot" tip, and you're not allowed to write with "goose feet" until the fifth grade, and he's still in the second, so here he sits – on account of his own foolishness, his own childish unconcern – among the ink-sharing class, everyone is sharing with everyone else, but not with him thanks to the tall grey teacher who is blackmailing him – though he doesn't realize it – because she hates him.

"H-Here!" the teacher bellows in disgust and shoves her spill-proof ink-pot at him with such violence that from out of her spill-proof – spill-proof! – pot several astounded drops splash, gleefully spattering the fresh page to which the boy's copybook is open.

"Only I'm not going to go back and repeat the whole thing just for you!" she says triumphantly. "So you'll still get your usual D!"

No. He won't. He knows this poem by heart, and the unstressed vowels – that secret nightmare known to one-sixth of the earth's land mass – are not a problem for him. He manages to blot the merry ink drops but not his dripping tears as he hurries to catch up with his classmates, most of whom will remain his classmates all through school.

"'A fee-ble old wo-man is strug-gling with the bri-dle... Large gaunt-lets...' gauntlets are like mittens..." We know, we know!"... "'of goat-skin she wears... Some drops on the ends of her lash-es are freez-ing,' comma and dash... you haven't studied that yet. 'From mist they must be... or from tears.'"

I don't remember any more when it was that I first saw that strange bird, either it was then, when I was still a child, or it was recently, or else I saw it in a painting, or perhaps it has been flying through this story the whole time? But I don't think so... This bird is called a hoopoe. Its fan-like crest sticks straight up when it's sitting, and flattens back when it flies. It's a beautiful bird. And a rare one. And since it's rare and beautiful I must have seen it as a child. When else could it have been? It appeared from out of the blue, calling in that sinister way hoopoes do: "Sorry lot! Sorry lot!" It appeared from out of the blue, perched, and called: "Sorry lot! Sorry lot!" On second thought, I can't say if it was then or now. But in any case the hoopoe is calling. It must have been then... Sorry lot! Sorry lot!

What's sorry? Childhood. School. Adolescence.

Damn that childhood, damn that school... Damn all of you who became teachers, damn all of you who became pupils, and damn me, too, damn me! Only not her... not that little girl... who would appear every now and then from out of a dark passage... from out of a half tear... from out of a bright summer...

She was doomed as it was.

YOU'RE MY SECOND

"Ya gonna tell me or not?"

"Yes..."

"Hey, get offa me! You're pushin' me off the bed!"

"Darring, darring, junior rieutenant..."

"I'm gonna getcha, Olga!"

"Yes..."

"Whuddaya mean 'yes', ya deaf dumbbell! How many guys ya been with, huh? Say, eight guys?"

"Where?"

"Up the ass of a bear! Gimme your good ear, for cryin' out loud! What I wanna know is, how many guys ya been with?"

"You're my second, Vasiry... I swear to you on my chirdren!"

"What a liar! So who was the first: that Chink ayours?"

"My husband wasn't Chinese, he was Buryat-Mongorian... I tord you."

"Yeah, yeah, ya tord me. So ya mean that people's commissar ayours was the first? An' I'm the second?"

"Prease berieve me. Why are you being so..?"

"Hey, whuddarya cryin' for! Just funny we were the first and second to count off, is all! Hey, c'mon, don't cry! Your eyes'll get all fishy! It's your birthday. Hey, look how smooth your hands are! Y'do all that washin' and they're still smooth and soft! How come they're so soft, huh?"

"Vasiry, darring Vasiry, why do you have to..?

She took in washing though she could easily have found less taxing and more respected occupations on the grassy streets. Say, gluing pins on little celluloid hippopotamuses with acetone glue, or braiding snazzy belts out of film strips, or bending hairpins on a home bending machine on loan. The neighbors would have thought that was fine, and she could even have passed for a cultured woman.

But she chose to do people's laundry. A very strange occupation, you have to admit, if even Rebecca Markovna remarked: "If she takes in washing..." Rebecca Markovna didn't know what it would lead to, but obviously nothing good.

Besides, why would anyone pay her to do their laundry? Everyone did their own. Who would want a stranger to see their holey underwear? However, people with money who wanted to live in style turned up and started giving their washing to Olga.

Olga Semyonovna didn't charge much, and she would pick the laundry up, bring it back, blue it, iron it, soak it in bleach and lye, get out the blood stains ("Heaven help you, Olga, not someone else's blood!"), the spots from summer berries, and even sunflower oil. Washing out the sunflower oil of those days was a major undertaking, and the boy who slipped a sunflower oil bottle in with the other bottles he was exchanging for noisemakers and sawdust balls didn't get away with it: the junk man wheeling his barrow along the grassy street wouldn't take *those* bottles, since the sunflower oil was impossible to wash out. Today it's possible: the water must have become caustic.

But back then no one had the strength or the means to remove the thick sticky film inside that fluted bottle. You poured in some sand, added some water, and shook the bottle for hours, making the sand bang against the flutes like a bad heart. Big mistake! When the swill settled, the bottle's cloudy sides were covered with transparent scratches.

Another time the boy inserted the frayed end of a rope into the bottle's narrow neck, pushed in the rest of rope, and then twirled the bottle round and round the ropy intestines twisted up inside. All this did was to ruin the rope, now grease-stained and worthless for washing the bottles that could be washed – bottles of bluing, say, or ink, though not violet ink, those bottles, too, were unwashable.

Looking back one suspects that the boy simply didn't have the patience, and that his efforts, however endless they seemed to him, were in fact as brief as the brief interval between a child's intention and decision. Still, he kept on trying because once he had seen a sunflower oil bottle washed clean by Leonid, an older boy who lived next door and could do anything.

Having divined the secret of things, Leonid began either manufacturing those things or subjugating them. True, the junk man, for whom the unwashability of sunflower oil was an article of faith, rejected Leonid's bottle, too, but Leonid didn't care: he could make one of those sawdust balls on an elastic string any day, what's more his would look nicer and last longer.

It may also be that Leonid triumphed over the oil because the invincibility of the word "sunflower" didn't frighten him: for one thing he called it "Lenten" oil, and for another there was nothing formidable in the word "Lenten" since his own fare, owing to life's meagerness, was always Lenten and to triumph over it — to clean his plate, that is — cost him nothing. Then again, it may not have been Leonid, but rather the meagerness itself that elicited the last bits of vegetable fat and cleaned the bottle besides. After all, "Lenten" oil was a luxury in Leonid's family, his kashas and his mother's frying pans were generally seasoned with hempseed oil — a peasant balm since sacrificed to the fight against drug addiction.

But the boy's greatest achievement, besides making those scratches, was getting off the label, yellowed and semi-transparent as if it had been soaked in kerosene. The label resisted at first, but then peeled off piecemeal in twisted filaments like the dirt that still stuck to your skin when you came out of the bathhouse.

Olga Semyonovna, as we've said, could get out any stain, and her one large, light room — which doubled as the laundry — was always bright and clean. The fancy hotel furniture ranged about her tidy abode was unaffected by the washing. True, the zinc clothes-boiler, in which the long johns and other underthings were left to soak, stood in a back corner of the communal kitchen.

Her room was flooded with sun, while the iridescent soapsuds and the laundry itself, heavily white against the grey corrugated washboard, added their own joyful light. She never splashed water on the floor which must be why everything looked so neat – anyone else would have sloshed water all over the place, the floor would be soaked, while the soap would be plastered with dry dust after squirting out of their hand and leaving an opaque half bubble on the floor already beginning to buckle from the spilled murk.

Not at all! The floor was painted and perfectly level, sun streamed in the window, the wash whitened, the fizzing foam burst and simpered, the moisture made Olga Semyonovna's immaculate hands soft and improbably white, while the ultramarine in the huge bottle of bluing compelled all this whiteness to shine.

So the room seemed to the boy and girl who so often came by. Sometimes nearly every day. Their parents didn't object: they knew Olga Semyonovna very well. She was young and gay and pretty, but – what could you do! – stupid. She takes in washing when she could – with a war on – be unstitching parachutes or sewing buttons on little pieces of paper. And now that hick Vasily Ivanovich has latched on to her! She, the fool, let him in and now she's living with him. No! I don't mean that! She's not a floozy, but he still has Nyura and their child, and that deaf Olga, she's honest, but she should never have let a soldier in the door: now he thinks he owns the place... As for the children, rather than letting them go off God knows where, why shouldn't we let them go to her?

"So what did Olga feed you?"

"Fried potatoes."

"Fried in what, suet?"

"No, lard."

"Didn't he bring her any sunflower oil?"

"But they taste so good in lard!"

"So she does her washing while you just sit there?"

Actually they do just sit there, but she isn't doing laundry the whole time. Sometimes she stares at them abstractedly, but she is never depressed, there isn't an ounce of melancholy in her, or suspicion, or denial, or salutary distrust.

She also has a sweet way of saying "r" instead of "l" and she doesn't hear very well. Or rather, she doesn't hear at all in one ear, and not very well in the other. She's amused by her own deafness and her unarticulated "l".

"My rittre girrs used to rike it when I tord them this story. You can risten whire you eat. Once there was a barin who had three daughters: Riry, Rora, and Rara (Lily, Lola, and Lara). They arr said 'r' instead of 'r', so no one wanted to marry them. But one day a strange man appeared in their virrage and he saw Riry (Lily) in the window and made up his mind to marry her. Their mother tord them not to say a word so he wouldn't hear them say 'r' instead of 'r'.

"He came to see them and just sat there, and they sat there too. He smoked and didn't say anything because he fert embarrassed, and they didn't say anything either, you know why. But when his ash ferr on the rug, Riry, the one he was courting, suddenry said:

"'Gentre sir, gentre sir, prease, the carpet is burning!'

"Then the middre sister poked her:

"'Riry, Riry, you know Mama tord you to sit quietry and not say anything.'

"Then the youngest sister, grad that she wasn't to brame, said:

"'Thank Rord I herd my tongue and didn't say anything!'

"So they gave the whore secret away! Isn't that a good story? My rittre girrs arways raughed a rot when I tord them it."

Her little girls, meanwhile, are asleep in an orphanage for the children of former VIPs in the city of Ulan-Bator Khoto, in the country of Mongolia, whose postage stamps, though neither triangular nor diamond-shaped, like Tuva's, are also beautiful.

Her little girls are in some other room now, not hers, though they should be in hers, they are sleeping in another room, very far away. So far away and inaccessible that she tries not to think about it or she'll be terrified. She has no idea when she'll see them again. Her third petition wasn't even answered.

Her little girls are sleeping in another room now. Most likely there are three beds in that room and they are sleeping in them. One little girl is homely, another is pretty, but with Mongolian features, while the third is delicate and sickly and, most likely, will die soon.

They are there and she is here. Why?

Because when she was young, she left Polesye (the people there aren't like in Moscow or Ukraine, they're cheerful and open, and they'll do anything – plant radishes or distill tar or take in washing), well so she left Polesye for the Amur since she'd been assigned to settle on the river and fish, but on her way there, at a rally, she met a big man – a people's commissar. Before she knew it he'd left his wife, married her, and the girls were born. Then her commissar got sick, and they had to go to Moscow for treatment, and leave the girls with his relatives. He was in the Kremlin hospital so long they gave her this room and the furniture, too: the nickel-plated bed, the three-leaved mirror, the bedside table, the bureau, the blankets, the whatnot, everything but a ball-point pen – all just like in a hotel so she could live here awhile. Then her husband began to die. And while he was dying, they started something against him in Mongolia, and soon he was under investigation in Moscow, but he'd been unconscious for a month already, and his relatives in Mongolia had gone off grazing and left the girls in an orphanage in Ulan-Bator Khot. When her husband died, they stopped the investigation. But her little girls were still foreign citizens and then the war started. She doesn't think her in-laws want to give her back her girls. But even if they do, who'll bring them to Moscow? It takes two months by train. Or if they let her come get them, then two months there and two back. With little children. And a war on. Besides, none of the furniture's hers, it's the State's, and plus now she's met Vasily Ivanovich.

"Aunt Olga, your oldest daughter's named Narina, right?"

"Yes."

"See, I was right, you said her name was 'Sun'."

"I said her name was Narina and that means 'sun'."

"Aunt Olga, Vasily Ivanovich is a junior lieutenant, right?"

"Yes, but he's going to be promoted soon."

"See, and you said he was already a lieutenant."

"Be quiet, or she'll hear you! You know we're not supposed to ask about him."

This boy and girl are brother and sister. The sister is in her teens, the boy is a boy. Olga Semyonovna likes to fatten them up, but they don't come just for that, just for the chocolate, say, or the American sausage. They come for the love and the attention, not that their own mother denies them, but it's always nicer coming from someone else.

The girl is also drawn by the grown-up secrets here; in a year and a half she will be grown-up herself, she's already writing to the front, and she's even received a letter from section leader Garik Duk, true, Garik would soon stop writing. He must have been killed, though that's hard to imagine.

Sometimes Olga Semyonovna takes the girl aside and explains something to her. The girl blushes, but listens intently, and then, staring down at the floor, mutters something in response. She is mean and snappish, this girl is, and she would never tell her mother the things she is whispering to Olga Semyonovna so her brother won't hear.

She likes to look over the women's underthings that are brought in to be washed, and laugh with Olga Semyonovna over old woman Balina's old-fashioned pantaloons with the enormous slit between the legs. That was the style back then!

And so the children come and go. Perhaps it is their self-preservation instinct, or perhaps it is their survival instinct that compels them to clean their plates of the potatoes and canned stew; that compels the girl to study the fastenings and furbelows of grown women; that compels the little girls to go to sleep in their orphanage so as to wake up and gnaw for an hour on the tuggy, undercooked meat Mongolians like; that compels Olga Semyonovna to try and forget — after a small glass of tarragon vodka with Vasily Ivanovich — her children far away; and that compels junior lieutenant Vasily Suvorov, son of Ivan, from the White Sea city of Kem, to try and fit in on the grassy street.

"Olga!"

"Yes..."

"Hey Olga! 'Jeepers! Creepers! Where'd you get those peepers?'"

Vasily croons the words to the song in Olga Semyonovna's half-good ear, which you can only do if you're lying against the wall.

"Darring!"

"Jeepers! Creepers! Where'd you get those eyes? I'd like to kiss'em right now!"

"Go right ahead, my darring rieutenant."

"Ain't a lieutenant yet, Olgunya. But I am a catch. And I'm gonna be a lieutenant real soon! Hey Olga, didja really marry a people's commissar?"

"But you know..."

"Swear ta me."

"But I showed you the stamp in my passport."

"Who the hell can read what's in that passporta yours? It's not Russian! Oka-a-ay, oka-a-ay, I believe ya. But you musta thrown allota guys over before ya gotta that people's commissar! How many guys ya been with, huh? Say, eight guys?"

"Vasiry! How many times have I..."

"How many ya kissed? Oh, no! You're not cryin' a-gain! First she lies then she cries."

But if they've drunk two glasses of the green tarragon vodka, then Vasily, so as to be able to pour them each more, doesn't lie against the wall. Which means he has Olga Semyonovna's deaf ear on the pillow and he can have some fun.

"Hey, Olga!" he whispers warmly. "Hey, Olga! That's some paira knockers ya got there!"

Olga, sensing something tender in his eyes and half-guessing every other word, replies:

"Oh, but that's not true: my eyes aren't especiarry big and they're brue!"

And she laughs gaily.

Actually, she often laughs gaily. She rarely cries.

True, it does make her sad when Vasily goes off on his quartermasterly duties, sternly declaiming at the door: "'I believe in you, my dear friend!'" or "'Wait till the amber rains rain sadness!" Her sadness is just sadness, though, it's not melancholy, but we've already said that, and she really was a very good woman.

When he hooked up with this good woman and found out her old man had been a people's commissar and used to chow down in the Kremlin with Kalinin and sometimes she went with, Vasily lost his head and didn't know how to act at first. He never did figure it out (and never would have!), but that didn't keep him from bossing her around and fussing an awful lot.

It's easy to see why. A naive and jumpy dunce from outside Kem, he got to give orders in the Army, wound up in Moscow, started rushing around from base to base, shouting at whomever, getting hold of whatever, for which he was never praised, or not getting hold of whatever, for which he was always berated by his beefy superiors; so that the only thing left to do was to take it out on his driver, Lukoyanov, or on that nameless Siberian soldier Vasily called "bum", or on Olga Semyonovna, who had grown attached to his idiotic eyes, though he was a foul-mouthed yokel, as crude and vile as any other clod from Kem.

The one person the junior lieutenant liked to hang around was the boy. Part of Vasily had never grown up: he hadn't played enough as a child, what's more he never could have in his Kemian backwater, no matter how well his childhood might have turned out. And his didn't turn out at all: it was just time wasted having his scrofulous ears boxed and nothing else.

Nobody in Kem knew how to make a ball out of newspaper, nobody knew any card tricks, so that the standard repertoire of the average city kid came as a revelation to the junior lieutenant, now completing his second childhood by correspondence – and clearly getting something out of it this time – especially since the boy, whose repertoire was far from standard, wanted the officer to like him. He had all sorts of tricks up his sleeve, besides which his science classes at school contained a phantasmagoria of marvels: the boy would, say, rub Vasily's buffing cloth against Vasily's comb, and the comb would attract little bits of paper like a magnet, while Vasily watched, open-mouthed. His mouth opens still wider at the sight of a needle slithering across the table or rising up on its own thread towards the magnet, like a dog on a leash, and he even screams when he hears the boy's banter in the telephone – made out of two tin cans and more thread attached to the cans' pierced bottoms with matches – to which Vasily, say from the kitchen, smartly replies.

"Comrade junior lieutenant!"

"Yo!"

"The crow's a joe!"

"Darky!" Vasily sometimes calls the boy 'Darky'.

"Say what?"

"The hag sat on a nut!"

And so on.

It is a sunny morning in May, and the boy and girl have just walked in not expecting to find Vasily Ivanovich, but he is standing by the three-leaved mirror cleaning his freshly scrubbed ears. He is barefoot, in jodhpurs and just an undershirt. The girl usually tries to avoid Vasily, especially when he's in just an undershirt, especially since he never talks much to her, and once – she either heard him or she thought she did – the junior lieutenant said to another officer: "I'd wait if I was you, comrade Captain, she's got big tits, but she's still a kid!" – so the girl slips into the kitchen to see Aunt Olga, leaving the boy with the junior lieutenant still cleaning his ears.

Vasily does this by twisting the corners of his waffle-cloth towel into tight little cylinders and rotating them inside his ears. When he pulls the little cylinders out, they come partly untwisted and the ear's impurities, against the white towel, look like brown car grease. Vasily's hygienic stunts don't startle the boy – everyone on the grassy streets cleans their ears that way.

"I'm gettin' a German revolver soon. With poison cartridges!" says Vasily, wincing because he's jammed the twisted towel end in too far. "And they're gonna issue me a Mauser, in a wooden holster! I've shot with a Mauser three times awreddy!"

"We shoot with interesting things, too!" says the boy. "Like cartridges, and shooters..."

"Yeah, but they don't make any noise! There's no bang!"

"Ever seen one of these?" From out of his pocket the boy pulls a key and a nail joined by a piece of string. One end is tied to the key's ring-shaped top, the other is fastened just under the head of the nail.

"How does it work?" Vasily's idiotic eyes fill with wonder while the boy extracts some matches from a cube of blue paper. (Matches weren't scarce then, but just try and find a match-box: there wasn't anything to strike a match on. True, the boy could strike a match on a window pane, but he still couldn't do it on the marble windowsill at school, though nearly everyone else could. He was never alone in the classroom long enough to practice, and their windowsill was the only one anywhere made of cracked marble.) So then, matches in hand, the boy takes a Standard razor blade out of its sky-blue wrapper worn white along the creases, and shaves the sulfur off the matches into the empty paper, trying not to catch up the wood, while the junior lieutenant, still clutching his towel with the half unfurled reddish-brown ends, follows the boy's every move.

The boy knocks the sulfur from four matches into the key's hollow shank and corks it with the nail. The tip of the nail has been rounded off and ground down, but not as well as it should be — the boy has no more patience for grinding hard nails than for washing greasy bottles.

So he inserts the nail into the key's snug shank, picks up the waxed thread, its ends still attached to key and nail, and tells the junior lieutenant to "Stand back!" Vasily stands way back, while the boy, gently swinging his arm, hits the butt-end of the open kitchen door with the head of the nail.

A loud, percussional bang blows key and nail apart and leaves them dangling from the waxed thread, smoke streaming out of the key's aperture.

The junior lieutenant is dumbfounded, yet no one comes running out of the kitchen: Olga is splitting wood for the stove, while the boy's sister has witnessed these explosions dozens of times.

"Gimme it?" the junior lieutenant almost begs him. The boy holds out his stringy contrivance.

"These're mine, so don't worry!" says Vasily, fussily and clumsily scratching the tops off a bunch of matches.

"You'll blow up," says the boy.

"No, I won't! I was raised on peas!" Vasily Ivanovich replies, decapitating his matches and singing along:

> *One day I went swim-ming,*
> *A bandit on my trail,*
> *I began undres-sing,*
> *"How 'bout that juicy tail!"*
> *Yells the bandit on my trail...*

"Ya know that song?" he asks, evidently hoping to some-how compensate for his newfound inferiority.

The boy has known this song for a long time. He knows all the songs Vasily either bawls or croaks: they're either prison ditties, or what Dostoevsky called lackeys' songs.

Vasily starts waving his contraption and suddenly – "hell with it!" – whacks the varnished door of the VIP wardrobe, the boy jumps back.

"Ta-dah! Wow, sonuvabitch!" yells Vasily. When he sees that the nail is gone from the thread and the key is smashed, he is doubly thrilled: "Wow, smashed it!" But when he realizes that he's ruined what wasn't his, he looks away and says: "I'll getcha 'nother key and I'll letcha aim my German revolver allya want. But better not touch the cartridges, or they'll explode. Once our platoon commander's exploded, and his heart shrank. Ain't nothin' worse than when your heart shrinks. Gotta watch out. At the front allota guys wind up inna hospital with shrunk hearts."

"Are you going home?" the girl's voice asks from the kitchen.

"Hey, whuddaya mean? The wife's just aboutta get the grub on the table!" – to the boy and girl he calls Olga his wife. "Hey, and on Sunday I'm bringin' canned stew. You come, too, and we'll play coin-toss!"

"So you can grab them all with those big mitts of yours!" the boy sasses, taking advantage of his position as the one materially wronged.

"That's right, I got re-e-eal big mitts! So come on over. And bring your sis..."

"I'm going to catch May beetles on Sunday!" the boy says evasively.

"W-wow!" shouts Vasily. "I wanna go to! We'll catch'em, and then... we'll stick'em on girls' tits!"

The boy picks up his undamaged nail and walks out, while Vasily, still excited about his match blast and the idea of sticking girls with scrabbling beetles, starts bolting his food and grabbing Olga Semyonovna, though after last night you'd think he could relax, it's not even noon yet.

"You're some cook, Olgunya! Ya feed me cracklin's! Just like them Hunkies! You're like a Hunky – I guess livin' with 'em you gotta be like 'em. Boy, you're some broad, Olga, o-o-oh, am I gonna stick a beetle ta you... Olgunya, hey Olgunya? Olgunya, come on?!"

"Vasya, it's right out..."

"So I'll pull down the blind! I'm goin' ta X section today, o-o-oh, I may never come back!"

..."Wait for me!" he instructs her sternly at the door. "I'll be by Sunday with the captain."

"Vasiry!" she mutters. "Vasiry, it's true, you're my second."

From the grassy street comes the honk of the truck that has come for the junior lieutenant.

He really is her second. No matter what you think. Because the people's commissar was her first, and before the people's commissar she only kissed Syomka behind the tar-works, but Syomka's long hooknose got in the way, and they never did find out what it is to kiss properly. So he truly is her second. But how to count them, how to count them. What about that man who came by when her husband was sick and said he wanted to know how she was settling in? He hinted that her husband was under some kind of suspicion, and said he'd spend the night, and fell on top of her, while she lowed, and squeezed her legs together, and it c-c-could have been worse, but for some reason he got off her, gave up, after slobbering all over her. So Vasily really is her second. True, when she brings the Balins back their laundry and Sonya Balina isn't home, but Borya Balin, Sonya's husband, is, something happens, because Borya calls her "Olechka", and she always thinks to herself what an interesting dark-haired man Boris Arkadievich is. He's dressed in nice boots and a sort of military service jacket with a stripe on it since he was wounded in the arm. She feels comfortable with him. More comfortable than with her Mongolian husband, more comfortable than with Vasily, not to mention that slobberer. She feels as comfortable with him as she did with Syomka at the tar-works, and she feels suddenly embarrassed that here she is bringing him his laundry and that she takes in washing at all, and she says it's too bad Sonya isn't there, and quickly turns to leave.

No, no matter what you think, Vasily is her second.

Sunday arrives and so does Vasily Ivanovich Suvorov. He's a lieutenant! He got another promotion! He's a lieutenant! He's not junior anymore! Always hated that word: "junior"! You have to be careful with words: remember "Lenten"?

He arrives with the captain. The lieutenant and the captain arrive. In the Willis. Senior Sergeant Lukoyanov is with them and so is that Siberian soldier, you might even say bum.

Olga busies herself over the Primus stove and the three kerosene burners. The lower one smokes, but that's alright! Today she's making a pie with buckwheat porridge called a *knish*. And there's canned stew. And lots of chocolate. And *Ram Attack* cigarettes issued in honor of Talalikhin, the first fighter pilot to execute a ram attack, and green tarragon vodka. There's bread, condensed milk, and potatoes. And sausage, both ours and the canned American kind. And powdered eggs for an omelet, and a delicious broth Vasily snuck out of the penicillin factory in a milk-can for waste.

While he's still more or less sober, Vasily suddenly – see, he knows his job! – starts cleaning his gun – his first pistol. But the ace assembler and disassembler of .375 rifles (1891 model) is so confused by the odd metal parts he dumps them all onto a fresh copy of *British Ally* and shoves the whole heavy mess into a bureau drawer.

Hurry up and have fun! Vasily's idiotic eyes are totally off the wall. The captain has to go in two hours, and Vasily, gobbling and guzzling, is telling him that, see, our hostess here, Olgukha, see, her husband was a Mongol, comrade captain, Mongolian people's commissar for inland waterways, got that? An' see those Mongols an' those Chinks, comrade captain, their waya showin' friendship ista shit – excuse my French – on the other guy's cucumbers, or whatever the hell they got growin' out back, so the inland waterways guy, see, was awways shittin' on the commissar for horse-breedin's cucumbers, right Olga?!"

Raucous laughter! Olga turns slightly red and laughs too, then goes to the gramophone and puts on a record, while Vasily informs the captain that there's this girl, see, who comesta visit my Olgukha, here, comrade captain, and a year from now, see, if ya wanna, ya could.

The dancing begins and Vasily, dancing with Olga, says to her:

"Listen, Olgunya, don't get sore if the captain lays a hand on ya. It's okay by me. He's gotta report ta X section – for active duty. An' besides, whuddayou care? Y'awwreddy been with eight."

But by now Olga's head is on Vasily's shoulder, her bad ear by his lips:

> The night is da-ark,
> The window has been blacked
> The apartment is packed
> With brass, from sergeants on up...

Vasily bawls the officers' famous "response" to the popular

song, purposely turning the "majors" into "sergeants" to make the lyrics a homier.

He is carrying on, singing and talking such nonsense that he forgets to help the captain with his suitcase and only sees him as far as the door, wailing another lackeys' version of another well-known song:

> *Lying in my bed,*
> *An arm across my head,*
> *Is someone else's wife...*

The others are quiet and well behaved. The young bum, fascinated by the mirror, keeps walking up to its gleaming leaves and moving them and being surprised all over again that he can see all of himself at once. This being the case he manages to make a perfect crease running down the back of his field shirt to meet the seam running up the middle of his jodhpurs.

Lukoyanov is scraping the water-repellent substance on the box of powdered eggs off with a strong but cracked fingernail – is it wax? Because it looks just like real wax and the furrow left by his nail on the grey cardboard surface looks exactly like the kind on candles.

The party is winding down. The celebrants have eaten all there is to eat, and drunk all there is to drink. There are more cigarette butts than scraps of food on the table though there seem to be plenty of those, too. Actually there aren't many: there aren't any crusts, they have all been eaten; the bottom of the large frying pan, black and untouchable, reveals a few congealed blotches missed by the bread used to soak up the grease. Shreds of white fat spangle the insides of the stew cans between the bluish streaks of tin. Three empty bottles – so green while the tarragon vodka was in them – are now colorless, though the glass still seems somehow tinged with green, especially the low-grade bottoms.

This all becomes glaringly obvious when Vasily gives orders for the electricity to be turned on. Though Olga has used up her quota and may get in trouble with the neighbors, the electric company, or the police, Vasily instructs Lukoyanov to turn on the lights, a feat the senior sergeant performs by sticking a nail and a sharp steel awl — implements equally prized by our people — into the wires just under the meter.

The electric light is bright and harsh. Everyone looks pale, while the room, robbed of its dusky shadows and generally used to oil lamps, seems suddenly smaller.

Off go the lights.

Vasily is fidgeting and fussing. He is about to get into bed with Olga; the senior sergeant and the bum are billeted on the floor where they have piled anything that can be used for bedding. The situation so excites Vasily, he doesn't even realize he's a little embarrassed.

"Hit the ground quick, hang onta your dick!" he yells, and when the kerosene lamp, after being turned down, is finally blown out and a slight stench of kerosene hangs in the air, and the dusk turns to darkness, he is still running around the room, stepping over his underlings, crashing into the table, and knocking over empty bottles.

"Justa sec', guys, gotta pull back the blind, Olga's gotta get her dress undone!"

So he pulls back the blackout blind — a thick sheet of black paper, now creased and ripped from use, with wooden slats along the top and bottom — and the ceiling lightens to reveal hazy grey shadows.

Finally he climbs in with Olga who, because of her deafness, didn't quite catch what he was saying and replies in affectionate but purposely indistinct whispers for fear of being overheard. Meanwhile Vasily hits the sack with another maxim:

"Bums go to the sticks, Russkies get the chicks!"

He keeps thrashing around in bed, listening to see if Lukoyanov and the bum are asleep yet, they sorta snored once, choked on their spit, and rolled over, but he still can't calm down.

"Lukoyanov!" he screams, just when he seems to have finally calmed down and Lukoyanov is whistling through his nose.

"Who?" Lukoyanov jerks awake.

"I'm testing you!"

"Okay, okay: two!" the middle-aged senior sergeant snaps and falls right back to sleep.

But Vasily is Vasily and in the accumulated silence he barks:

"Bum!"

"Yo!"

"Aim low!"

Silence. The bum really wants to sleep.

"Bum!"

The bum wants to sleep in the worst way but he's fighting it so he can listen in on the lieutenant's love.

"Bum!"

Here the bum's nervous system, whose taiga instinct says there's no use waiting, succumbs to sleep – but orders is orders so the bum hangs on ta what the lieutenant told him ta hang on ta. And soon, instead of the second-hand lieutenant's love, the bum is dreaming of his own love, with such a perfect little crease up the middle, you couldn't miss if you tried, only he can't catch up. Vasily, meanwhile, tired of heckling his underlings, presses up against Olga and whispers in her more or less good ear. In his agitation, he forgot to climb over to his side of the bed against the wall. Even so he's able to talk to Olga because tonight she made the cramped bed up the other way round – away from the strangers – and next to his lips he finds a woman's ear that is tender and always responsive to love.

"Hey, Olga!" he whispers. "'Where'd you get those peepers?! Where'd you get those eyes?!'"

"Oh, Vasiry, do you rearry mean that?"

"I really do! I re-e-eally love your eyes!" Vasily insists and starts pawing the woman lying next to him with an indiscriminate palm. He doesn't do this long, since in his rush he is soon squeezing his knees, all tangled up in his regulation long johns, into the narrow space that has slid open for him on top of the sheets.

"Vasya... Vasya... Vasya..." The bum, chasing his shameful dream under a greatcoat in the corner, doesn't hear a word.

The next morning Lukoyanov and the bum disappear on business. Vasily wakes up a little later, hangover, and hears voices in the kitchen:

"Olechka, please do your best! After all, whatever you do always comes out just fine. Sonya didn't have time, so I had to come myself. And why shouldn't I look in on a young lady? I've got three shirts here and, I apologize, my underwear. Please have everything ready today, Olechka, because I'm leaving first thing tomorrow to get raw materials for work. You mean you don't have one of our filmstrip belts? I'll see that you get one, and your little girls, too. So then, will you do your best?"

"I'rr try, Boris Arkadievich. I'rr dry the shirts over the stove because it rooks rike rain. Would you rike them stiffry starched, Boris Arkadievich?"

"Of course! What isn't soft, Olechka, should be hard!"

"Fine, Boris Arkadievich, they're arready soaking."

"Tut!" says Vasily gloomily. Then he gets up, pulls on his jodhpurs, and walks over to the three-leaved mirror where a bunch of half-dressed men are milling around as if this were the draft board. Vasily stares out of the central mirror at himself, while out of the side mirrors, cunningly adjusted by the bum the night before, five more Vasilys are gazing. And all five have terrible headaches, not counting those who have turned their backs to Vasily in the distance.

"Tut!" says Vasily and walks over to the window. Outside the sky is dull, a sunflower oil bottle lies wet in the grass, the rain makes it sparkle and seem completely transparent, and, if it doesn't clear up by evening, the May beetles won't come out for another three days.

"Tut-tut-tut!" clucks Vasily.

"Tut-tut-tut!" sputters the motorcycle drawing up outside.

The motorcycle's rattling seems to have gotten mixed up with the drumming inside Vasily's hangover head.

The motorcycle is escorting a black motorcar. Military men get out of the car, check their little notebooks, and then the number on the house, while one of them, accompanied by another dragging two suitcases, disappears around the corner, to Olga's porch, no doubt, since there's nowhere else to go.

Still barefoot and in just an undershirt, Vasily jams his forage cap on his head: there isn't time for anything else.

They're already knocking at the kitchen door. Olga screams, a male voice booms:

"Well, hello, hello! And how are we today, Olga Semyonovna! Can only stay a minute. Your daughters are fine, fine, the little one's wasting away, but she's putting up a brave front, a brave front! I'll go into detail later. I just wanted to drop off some things of yours and your late husband's. His medals are here, too. This isn't everything, but it's all I have time for right now. Headquarters wants me. I only stopped by because it was on the way. Your daughters are fine, fine. The older ones are good girls, and the little one's putting up a brave front, a brave front. Here's a picture, I almost forgot! I'll go into detail later, but now you must excuse me. I'll stay with you for a couple of days next time, if you don't mind. How are you settling in, may I take a look?"

"Permission to report, comrade lieutenant-general! Lieutenant Suvorov."

"Well, I'll be! It seems the Army's already billeting men with you. So Suvorov himself is quartered here. I didn't know, excuse me! At ease, Suvorov! Bullets miss, bayonets don't!"

"That's arright! That's arright! I'm grad to have you! Prease stay as rong as you rike. Stay for a week, or even two."

"At ease, lieutenant! Goodbye and... well then... see you soon."

"But what about Narina? What about Tinochka? What about my rittre one?" Olga splutters out the door after her guest.

Vasily goes back to the three-leaved mirror.

"Tut, tut, tut!"

Vasya, Vasya, Vasya, Vasya, and Vasya in the three-leaved mirror agree with him completely.

"Vasya, rook! Here they are, my rittre girrs! I'rr get your breakfast in just a second! My darring rieutenant!"

"Shoot the bitch!" says Vasily to all five selves, all of whom nod their approval: "Yeah, shoot the bitch!"

Vasily races to the bureau, but the lieutenant's first pistol, disassembled the previous evening for cleaning and oiling, is still lying in the drawer disassembled. He starts fumbling with the parts, then stops: it'll take too long to get the gun to shoot.

He walks over to the window: the motorcar and motorcycle have sped away to headquarters and the boy and his sister are trudging up to the back door.

"Tut!" says Vasily.

"Tut!" says Vasily. While an exultant Olga Semyonovna shows her snapshot to the girl in the kitchen, the boy walks into the room and quietly announces:

"There won't be any beetles today."

"No beetles, so..." Vasily repeats quietly, and then suddenly screams: "You bought those stogies offa the signalwoman, ya dung beetle!"

The boy shrinks back. True, his boots do have a slight heel, but his mother said they were for men. Besides, they were the only ones she could get.

And yes, they do look like the signalwoman's, but how does Vasily know that? The boy was all alone the day he spied on that signalman and signalwoman who were dragging a reel during a drill and wandered off into the Bogdanovs' cherry orchard, and vanished, and he spied on them. And yes, in the jumble of boots under the bushes, he did notice those low heels of hers go suddenly limp.

"Darkies like you buy'em offa signalwomen! Offa the Red Army!" screams Vasily. "And ya come here to chow down! Your big sis'as got knockers outta here, an' all eithera ya wants is candy."

Olga Semyonovna doesn't hear this because her bad ear is turned to the door. But the girl, who always hears everything, runs in, grabs her brother by the hand, and rushes out. They shuffle past the window – awkwardly and hurriedly

– and don't look back. The girl walks on ahead, muttering something to the boy over her shoulder, but he is distracted by the bottle in the grass and keeps stopping and wanting to go back for it, he can't keep up with her, and – my God! – how shabby and lost they look! Look at them, remember them, because they are leaving. They are leaving this story, and they are never, ever coming back.

"Tut!" the five madmen out of uniform in the mirror cluck at Vasily, increasing his own resentment and everyone else's fivefold, though some in the glassy distances have turned their backs as if on purpose. And suddenly:

"Yeah, you givit ta her! The bitch! The way she puts out! For every goddamn guy that comes along!"

Vasily rushes into the kitchen looking around for something to grab. Olga Semyonovna recoils, clutching her photograph. So-o, Vasyok, what're we gonna smack her with, with those long johns, the bitch, from the clothes-boiler... all wet... whack that snapshot, too! Thwack go the wet heavy pants! Thwack! Hid it behind her back... Just in time, the bitch... So get her in the ribs. Whack her good! Send that glossy snap flying... Ugh! Smack'er in the face... with the pants... Again! And again! Thwack! Darkies, you whore, generals, you whore... but it's true, you're my second... Thwack! ...prease berieve me... from majors, you whore, on up... Thwack! Thwack! Thwack!

Rebecca Markovna was right, after all, when she said: "If she takes in washing..." And though she hardly guessed what it would lead to, she, as always, knew a fatal mistake when she saw one.

SITTING IN THE DARK
ON BENTWOOD CHAIRS

A light snow fell and filled up
all the little paths trodden in the previous snow.

Everything was fresh.

Pile the snow up to the casements and you would have
a fluffy eiderdown with stove chimneys poking out of the white
folds – if only the windows glowed orange.

But the snow is within reason. The bushes show up darkly.
The cat is nowhere to be seen. And there aren't any fences.
So that the little street doesn't look like a street and the little
buildings on it stand pell-mell. Especially the sheds sticking
out along the backs of the yards. But since there aren't any
fences, there aren't any yards, and the sheds face any which
way: you can't tell whose is where.

The place seems *deserted*. Yet the windows aren't
smashed. There are even curtains in them, and wads of cotton
with colored fringe stuffed between the double sashes. Aren't
these signs of life? Yes, but they are the only ones.

Somebody made some tracks tramping off to work in the
darkness an hour and a half or so ago. Then the snow buried
the tracks.

The air is still turbid, but the sun is up: there can't be
any orange windows. There can't be any, period: the windows
are all covered with thick black paper. Besides, there's no
electricity.

Let's check the time. It's wartime. First someone went
off to the labor front in the grey gloom, then it snowed. Then,

though it was already light out, the children did not go to school: the schools are all closed. So it must be around nine.

But why aren't there any new tracks? Why isn't the cat stealing past? Where's the smoke from the chimneys? Actually, they don't light the stoves here first thing: this isn't the country. This is the capital. The heat won't last if you light the stove too early. Though by now you could.

The slops must rot holes in the snow by the abbreviated porches since there are no slop boxes: they have all been swiped, along with the fences, for kindling. Wade through the drifts to the place where the slops are supposed to go and your felt boots will fill with snow. So you sling the slops off the porch. A door bangs, a woman jumps out, and a thin stream sails from bucket to snow.

There, a door just banged!

There, the landscape has come alive!

Now let's imagine that we are a jackdaw and that we were here a while ago and didn't see anything – even other jackdaws, even crows. No one comes here to feed. We, too, realize there's nothing to be gained and fly away to a nearby dump, huge and fetid even in winter, to wrest something from under the snow.

We peck, we pull, we swallow. We peck, we pull, we swallow.

And we fly back again.

How everything has changed!

Tracks! They lead to the water pump, snake from houses to sheds, circle former yards, outline the street, zigzagging back and forth across it and turning into bygone gates.

Smoke is coming out of chimneys. Not all of them. Then it vanishes from some, and emerges from others. The smoke doesn't belch or billow: the wood isn't that good or the day that cold. And the snow around almost all the porches is pocked with the black hollows and yellow boreholes of human effusions.

We, the jackdaw, fly toward the slop-filled craters, but on their ice-encrusted pharynxes we see only wizened potato peels, a boiled onion's vile snivel, wisps of long hair, sweepings, threads, and scraps of camouflage clothing: there is nothing to peck.

We also notice that by one shed with a chimney (a chimney means it's a dwelling, not a shed), there are no signs of life. The snow is as fresh and fluffy as ever.

We spy a cat, just skin and bones and mange. We caw warningly, if pointlessly: there aren't any other birds in sight, and the cat seems to be aiming for the shed with the chimney. She has two former yards to go, so there's still time to look round for a little something.

We swoop down and see smoke trying to slither out of the shed's incongruous chimney. Three top bricks have apparently fallen into the flue. What do we care? We need to land: there seems to be something by the wall. We land. There is. A thin strip. We tug at it. The strip rips. We hop along with it in our beak, leaving the *first* tracks. We examine our catch. We like these wine-colored strips. Another time we might save the strip for decoration, but this time we are hungry and determined to digest it. We swallow it and fly away, now only half-hungry.

The jackdaw had disengaged a thin strip of leather frozen to an edge of the shed's foundationless wall. The bird's tugging had also broken off a chunk of stucco. The brittle stucco had long since crumbled away here and there to reveal the grids of a clay-smeared lath and old boards with rotten wood dust caulking the cracks in between.

The wall over the jackdaw's find contains a window, evidently the source of the strip. The window contains four small panes coated with antediluvian putty, cracked bits of which have fallen away. These fossilized remains must be lying just under the snow and, come spring, will show up white against the black earth, like last year's dog dung.

The window has no second − winter − sash, but inside a squalid quilt dangles. Dirty cotton wool peeks through the frayed sateen − once red, and now the color of dried blood.

The chimney, from which the smoke was trying to escape, sticks out of a lean-to roof over the shed, part of which is actually a shanty of wattle and daub.

We sensed this: the window is at chest-level and you have to bend down to see in (we tried to see in but saw only the tattered quilt).

To the right of the window is a wall – its lath all coming apart – and then a crooked, makeshift gate of dead boards.

Can this be the entrance to the place where the smoke was trying to escape? Some of the smoke inside is clearly succeeding, someone has curtained himself off with the foul quilt. But how can such a gate lead to a dwelling when it's winter and bitter cold outside?

It can't. The gate leads to the shed. But you must go through the shed to get to the dwelling: inside the gate to the left there is a door covered with bast matting. The criss-cross matting is held together by laths and jammed under the metal door handle with enormous bent nails.

A bench runs along the wall from the gate to the door. On the bench is a tin bowl. In the bowl is something resembling wet bread. It isn't frozen, so it must have been put out recently, but not just now because then there would be tracks in the snow. Perhaps someone left it on their way to the labor front, and the snow swept the tracks clean through the cracks in the gate.

The cat is still making its way toward the tin bowl.

Inside the shed, the dusky light let in by the cracks in the gate and the holes in the roof reveals a desolation under-scored by the crooked handles of the rakes, shovels, and broom slumped in the corner. The tools are all badly hafted, probably dangling on their sticks and barely fastened (with more bent nails) to their wooden handles, shiny from use.

Also in the emptiness stands a tall cage on wooden legs. Its frame is of flimsy slab boards, its wire mesh is rusty. Through the mesh, bristling with smelly yellow straw, some-thing shaggy and warm is visible. Rabbits.

So then, along the wall to the left is a bench with a bowl and a bast-mat door. To the right is the shed's emptiness. The gardening tools and the rabbits belong to people in the wooden former dacha towering in the yard with its turrets and corroded tin trim, lacy and church-like.

The many tenants inhabiting the former dacha use the shed, and the one next to it, and the one next to that.

All this time the cat has been picking her way here, she thinks there's something in the bowl. Of course, some days there's nothing: either nothing was put out, or someone else got there first. Then the only thing to do is to glance longingly at the warm life in the rabbit-hutch, flick one's tail, and stalk out. But if the bowl is not empty, then there's no time for rabbits: one must gobble everything up or make away with it and squeeze under the gate.

The cat spies the unattainable jackdaw flying toward the bowl and quickens her neat step over the fresh snow. By human standards she is horribly underfed, and what she does eat isn't fit for feline consumption. We needn't lament, however, she found a home.

A boy found her at the student dorms outside the cafeteria, an ill-fated attempt to feed people, notwithstanding the odd person who did get fed.

Though the cat was filthy and shivering, the boy picked her up and brought her home. A disheveled cat didn't frighten anyone in that part of the world, they didn't believe cats had worms, but that this cat was freezing to death, the boy knew for a fact. Actually she was sick, she had caught cold, and her fur was matted. Stroking her was like stroking a pocketful of acorns: her entire body, except for her head, paws, and tail, was covered with hard knots.

At home the cat ate some soup that had soured, then climbed into the warmth of the tin oven with which local tile stoves were then equipped. The cat began to drowse, then startled the family with what sounded like a grown woman's cough coming from the stove. Horrified, they opened the door only to see the cat – curled up on the warm grate and gazing back at their huge faces – half-open her mouth and cough.

From then on, the oven was her refuge. She stayed there even when the stove was being lighted. Only when the grate became unbearably hot would she jump out and flop down on the rough floor to cool off. Later, she would scramble back inside.

The cat also had frostbitten ears which she scratched and pummelled and rubbed relentlessly. When an ear went numb, a leg would flash, and she, ripping the gossamer ear, would howl, tormenting it with a furious hind paw or crushing it with a front one. The boy would pin her down while she growled and writhed, determined to finish scratching the hateful ear, or tear it off entirely, but then the urge would pass and she, thumping her tail on the floor, would collapse; the boy wouldn't let her go right away for by then the bloody ear was in tatters.

The boy cut out the fur balls with a dull pair of scissors – the only kind he had. The cat tried to bite him, but he, resorting now and then to a *Standard* razor, got rid of all the knots and even split one open so as to marvel at the contents. The cross section was like felt: the separate threads were so fine as to be indistinguishable, and so tangled as to form a solid mass. What wasn't there in those days?

The cat went around with her corrugated haircut, but the fur soon grew back, meanwhile she lapped up the soup and sour whey. She even licked the spit off the floor.

While we were rambling, the cat reached her goal: the gate, that is. In addition to the jackdaw tracks in the snow, now there are cat tracks. The cat stole up to the bowl and began devouring the contents, but when something banged inside the bast-covered door, she dashed off with the last piece, squeezed under the gate, and ran round the corner past the cesspit.

After a while the ruined flue again began exuding smoke. The color of the smoke kept changing, a sure sign that all kinds of kindling were being used.

No one had thrown any slops out into the snow.

The flue was exuding smoke because inside the shed shanty on floorboards laid right over the earth, near a small pillar-shaped stove against which there was nowhere to lean, a tall man in a bulky coat was down on his knees blowing into the fire-chamber. The fire was not catching, though the man had already thrown in many scraps of colored leather taken from a plywood trunk whose battered scuttle gaped.

He could hardly have gotten the fire going even with birch-bark, a blazing pirate's pipe of which will set any but the dampest logs alight. The frozen bark lying in the fire-chamber could not have been damper. Once a blue tongue seemed to leap up, but then the weary kneeling man began coughing violently and put the flame out with his spittle. In the end he stood up, pulled back the ragged quilt to let in some grey light, and ripped up a pair of paperbacks. The paperbacks — Rybkin's primer and an ancient, tea-colored text — flared up immediately, at first the sodden bark dripped on the jittery fire, but then the bark began to smoke, too. The man kept blowing into the fire-chamber; when he wasn't blowing, he was coughing and spitting, only now on the floor.

When the bark finally caught fire, he leaned out the door and glanced at the tin bowl. Then he dragged a bentwood chair up to the stove, sat down, unfolded some sort of paper, took something out of it, and began chewing, he threw the paper into the fire. The paper burst into flames, and then a hunched creature in a heavy coat, a large torn scarf wound round its head, and large unfathomable boots on its feet, climbed down from the bed in one corner. The creature moved into another corner, gathered up its enormous coat, straddled the bucket standing there with its spindly bottom-heavy legs and made water, messily. But over the bucket, at least. Then it pulled something up around its legs, let something else down, shuffled over to the stove, dragged up another bentwood chair, and sat down next to the man who seemed to have dozed off. From the way in which the creature used the bucket, it was clear that it was a woman. She unfolded some sort of rag, saw something in it, took this something in her fingers and ate it.

"It's empty!" the man said thickly and indistinctly.

What exactly was empty wasn't clear: besides the empty tin bowl, the fire-chamber was almost empty and he wasn't putting anything more in though an icy pile of bark lay by the stove.

The woman didn't answer. She didn't even seem to hear. Then she stopped chewing. Then she started chewing again, though she hadn't put anything in her mouth. They sat there like that, chewing from time to time for no apparent reason. Only once the man got up to give the damper, which had gotten stuck, a shove.

Out in the passage – the adjoining shed inside the gate – something crashed. Neither the man nor the woman stirred, however. A youth had booted the gate. First he had gone by the window, bent down, and made out two figures sitting by the stove. Since going past the window was always a trial and he didn't want to touch the icy gate, he did what he always did: he kicked the gate as hard as he could (he had come out in galoshes over bare feet), thus proving that he had nothing to do with the existence whose shed he was forced to share. He went over to the cage, opened the little door and shoved something in from inside his jacket. Then he stroked the warm rabbits huddled in the straw. With his other hand, he unfastened his pants and, still stroking the rabbits, relieved himself under the cage. Then he fastened his pants and, peeling his wet fingers off the frigid metal, padlocked the little door and ran out, slamming the gate behind him.

Incidentally, the boy and the youth are two different characters. Let's be clear about that.

Inside the shed, on the snow blown in through the gate, the galoshes tracks remained.

Since a frost was coming on and the wind had begun to blow, the youth ran straight home to the former dacha.

"Alive?" they asked him at home.

"Why wouldn't they be?" he replied.

Who they were talking about wasn't clear. The ones sitting on the bentwood chairs or the rabbits.

By late afternoon the wind had died down, but the cold had come to stay. At dusk the youth appeared again and again peered in the window. At first he couldn't make anything out. Then he saw that the figures were still sitting on the chairs, not by the stove, but in the middle of the room – with their backs to the window. Standing there staring, the youth began to shiver, his hands, too, were freezing: one held soggy porridge wrapped in newspaper, the other, four rotten carrots.

He again kicked the gate open, dumped the porridge into the tin bowl, and thrust the carrots into the indiscernible cage where even the white rabbits were opaque. He poked some rabbit feed through a crack in the top of the hutch and ran back, not home this time, but to the black hole to the left of the inhabited shed, and squatted over it. Then he wiped himself with the wet newspaper from the porridge, and fled the cesspit, vilely black even now in the pitch-darkness. The outhouse, which had stood over the pit two months ago, like the outhouses in all the yards, like the fences and the slops boxes, had been swiped for fuel, and everyone managed as best they could.

Running down the incline, the youth lost one of his galoshes, felt the snow — icy as the padlock on the cage — with his foot, swore bloody murder, and ran into the warm house.

"Alive?"

"Why not? Just sitting there."

Again, who they were talking about wasn't clear. The ones on the bentwood chairs or the rabbits in the cage.

Towards evening, the ones on the bentwood chairs had moved to the middle of the room where there was less of a draft than by the walls. They hadn't relighted the stove, they were numb. They sat motionless to keep from touching their icy clothing. Outside it was bitter cold, in some houses they were lighting the stove for the second time that day, though in others they were lighting it for the first. It depended on the dwelling. The billowing smoke shown white in the gloom, especially over the cat's abode.

The woman of that house had managed to maintain a modest warmth all day by cooking on the kerosene stoves and had lighted the fire only after dark, so as to keep from freezing to death in the night. In the room the oil-lamp quivered, in the stove a bright fire hummed, the father stood pressing his stomach to the warm bricks, while his son drew a horse by the cave-like light. The woman, too, sat close to the oil-lamp sewing a white camouflage smock on an unruly, if well-oiled, manual Singer machine, the loudspeaker was mumbling something, the jolting of the machine was making the lamp's flame flicker, and everyone was in high spirits because of the cat's latest escapade.

Too squeamish to warm herself by the fetid kerosene stoves, the cat had fallen asleep in yesterday's ashes at the back of the fire-chamber where wood was eventually and unwittingly piled. When the birch-bark began to crackle, a mournful wail erupted from deep inside the stove. The fire was doused, the wood removed, and the horrified cat hauled out by her armpit with the poker. The mother berated the laughing boy for bringing the cat home in the first place, then kicked the cat who, grumbling and grey from the ashes, slunk away to the soap dish that was her bowl and, in the floor-level murk, lapped up the little water that was left.

In a way the middle-aged father was also numb since he wasn't working then and, barring an emergency, spent his days puttering in the shed, or sitting at home in his cap with the ear flaps, nodding over the paper, and warming himself by the fire. Now, too, as we've said, he was pressing his stomach to the stove bleached to match the plywood walls, which you wouldn't necessarily notice since the oil-lamp's flame was no larger than a capital letter in this story.

Standing, he warms his stomach, then turns his back to the heat, then sits down by the fire-chamber which, with its door ajar, adds its own parallaxes and shadows to the wick's trifling light. Meanwhile, the cat, too, has settled by the half-open fire-chamber and on just the chair where the father will sit after shoving her aside. Once he does, you can see the side of the stove: it is greasy and even shiny in one place from people's palms, otherwise it is rough, with large grains of sand and the outlines of the bricks protruding slightly along with the senseless sinew of reinforcing wire that that fool of a stove-maker attached supposedly to secure the brickwork. The boy, too, as soon as he has finished drawing his horse, goes up to the stove, and blocks out the glossy spot by leaning his back against the unbearably hot surface. And so it goes all evening: first the father, then the son, first they gaze at the fire till the vein stands out on their forehead, then they put on another log, first it crackles, then it hisses: the dampness boils up in the heavy brand and seeps out of its butt-end in turbid, foamy drops which fall on the coals and vanish in the red embers. First the embers darken, then they turn crimson again, and only the mother doesn't look up from her sewing.

When the brick stove is heated through, but a charred log remains which would make no sense to burn – because then the heat would *waste away*, or perhaps because of women's ancient and innate wariness thanks to which Meleager's mother snatched the brand from the fire lest her son die according to the prophecy – then the mother will rise from her machine, take the dustpan, and prod the awkward, smoldering log until it finally rolls out of the fire-chamber, and maybe onto the floor, in which case they will scramble to scoop it back up onto the dustpan while the mother shouts at the boy: "Get the cat out of here!" They will carry the brand outside and dump it in the snow next to the last gaping swill hole while in the house, as if it had been on fire, the strong smell of smoke will hang in the air, and they will close the stove-door, and seal the flue with the damper, and if something is found to cook, it will be put in a cast-iron pan and left in the hot coals overnight, and next day there will be a warm stew that tastes like nothing else in the world.

This is the way they keep warm in all the houses. Some are just lighting their stoves, others are leaving off; some make their fires deftly, with never a charred log left over, others make them from the heart, without measuring; some burn firewood, others burn stolen fences, still others odds and ends; but they all take care to warm themselves before the long night, then crawl in under the covers, and come morning are loath to expose even their nose to the frigid room, stubbornly clinging to that strange number 98.6.

They all warm themselves standing, they all huddle close to the stove, more or less, and only the old man and woman in the shed-shanty are sitting still, preserving their ninety-eight point six – where do they get it? They are sitting on bentwood chairs in the midst of an appalling hovel, at some point in their diurnal oblivion they will move to the beds. What beds, where? In the dark you can't make them out. Actually you can't make anything out, the furniture or the utensils, but one can assume that they won't take off their coats before climbing into the same bed not because they are man and wife, but because it's warmer that way. Also hiding in the darkness – most likely minus their burnable straw mattresses – must be two empty cots because their daughter, who slept on one, was forty minutes late to the labor front three months ago and they gave her a year and a half. This happened because the "little box" tram into which some three hundred people had squeezed broke down making them all late to their battle stations. I don't know if they got what she got, but the stout, shy girl who always avoided your eyes (she felt ashamed before the street of her parents' squalor) went to prison. Her brother, who slept on the other cot six months ago, is growing stiff, pressed against his freezing comrades in a trench where that jackdaw apparently saw him. And saw him, apparently, for the last time.

You might, of course, think that son and daughter were glad to exchange their parents' slum for a trench and barbed wire, but that would be very hypothetical.

The two sitting in the dark on bentwood chairs didn't always sit in them in the dark. What's more, there was a time when – they were still young! – they bought those chairs so as to sit on them in the light in their own house. What's more, they had the gumption to abandon their backwater for the capital, which, one assumes, took everything they had – God didn't give them much ambition, and that was soon sapped.

So long as life went along of its own accord, he made purses and reticules because he was a purse-maker and a reticule-maker – and a master of his craft. He sewed elegant little things, soft and crimson on the inside, brown and supple on the outside, fitted with "little kiss" locks, "rapid" fasteners, "eensy-weensy" snaps and "overbite" latches; there were no zippers back then.

But the New Economic Policy ended, and with it life's

even pace, and they had only just arrived and, in their foolish haste, rented (temporarily, they thought, for the summer) a shed-shanty like the mud-covered hut they left behind, and now they were stuck in it with their scraps of colored leather, but − they were still young! − they soon had a little boy in addition to the little girl they brought with them from the south.

Everyone around them was struggling, many had been laid low by the same events, but they were the only ones who lost their taste for life, and their existence on the bentwood chairs led to the dark time about which we are writing and cannot seem to stop.

She was stupid, arrogant, and a bad housekeeper. When they first arrived, she boasted that her husband was a purse-maker and reticule-maker, and she put on airs with the neighbors. She still does, which her neighbors can't forgive her though now she goes around all bent over in that outsize cloak of hers belted with a Lisle-thread stocking. Everyone pities them and wonders how they can live that way, many would sympathize, but she is as nasty as ever even on her manure pile.

He, with the destructive connivance of his quarrelsome consort, began to go to seed and by the time the war broke out he looked like an old man with his brown, flea-bag face and rotten teeth and wearing that too-large coat − someone's old fur-lined paletot, except that the fur had been ripped out and replaced with sackcloth backed with musty wadding. Of the original coat only the faded seams were still intact, the whole thing was grimy and gave off a foul, telltale smell.

Interestingly, the collar was of sea otter, a bald skin, the surviving bits of which would mean little to the uninitiated. But then the initiated would be suspicious since a sea otter skin, even threadbare, costs far more today, they say, than the sleekest fur.

His wife was also a liar and, even in those terrible days, when she ran into a neighbor on the street, she would say, if she said anything, something like: "I want to make my husband a good pot of borscht today." Her tone was independent, even aggressive. Then she would shuffle off, all hunched over, in her cloak which smelled, despite the bitter cold, like a chicken coop – a small, crowded one on a long, hot day.

Now she was completely unconscious on her chair. They had had barely anything to eat that day. She had a ration card, but she gave him nothing without abuse. He didn't have a ration card since he didn't work and he didn't work because he didn't have the strength: this winter had been so hard it was all he could do to breathe and see.

Having found nothing in the tin bowl that morning (remember the cat?) – the food scraps were put there by neighbors anonymously, anonymously because they felt ashamed of their leftover hand-outs, and because they didn't want to get involved, didn't want to see that awful numbness, and because they didn't want to anger these people who had never asked for charity; so the anonymous gifts were accepted anonymously while both sides pretended not to know of any such arrangement – so then, having found nothing that morning, he, it seems, got up from his chair towards evening, and found, it seems, a lump of freezing porridge in the bowl which, it seems, he gave to her, and she, it turned out, wasn't completely numb because she took it.

All this was going on in the blackness which explains the repetition of *it seems*. And she, it turned out, was not completely numb, in any case not the way she had been the day before yesterday, if it was the day before yesterday – the days had all frozen together, you couldn't separate them! So then, the day before yesterday, in the evening, as she was straddling the bucket, she knocked it over and soaked her ragged left boot. Then she went back to her chair and sank into numbness (that night they didn't get into bed, but dozed till morning on the chairs), and in her somnolence she didn't notice the icy hour or the black night snows, she didn't notice that her boot had frozen to the floor, and in the morning she couldn't pry it loose. True, when they finally managed to light the stove, her foot separated from the felt and the felt from the floor – and only *then* did her frost-bitten toes separate from one another.

She whimpered and whined because of all this and began shouting at her husband insistently and conceitedly, she shouted for an hour or two, though he was long gone, and his tracks in yesterday's snow would soon be covered with new snow, as we've said.

He went all the way to the woodpile, where he scraped together a whole sackful of bark from out of the snowy sweepings, occasionally mistaking a lump of manure and throwing that in, too, then he trudged home with his sack which, except for its sharp edges, looked just like a sack of potatoes.

He had lighted the stove with this bark, of course, that morning, and would have relighted the stove now, in the evening, but he was already ill, and so he stayed in his chair. He wasn't very ill yet, he was mumbling something to his wife, it was fairly late, around ten o'clock. His wife got up howling, and he, wincing, got up, too, and they lay down on the bed, slowly climbing onto some sort of pile in their unwieldy coats, and slowly covering themselves up with something, he kept tucking something in with his long arms, tucking it around him, she kept crawling under something, crawling and crawling.

The cat was in the ridiculous habit of going out in the night when it was coldest in search of food or, more likely, an attic with a warm flue. You see, cold air blew through the rag-stuffed cracks in her adoptive family's floor — whose boards had been carted away from the market stalls torn down off Red Square — how was an infirm little beast to endure such cold on a thin mat? In the middle of the night, the cat would begin yowling. Eventually, after much debating and hoping the cat would stop, somebody would get up, they had to anyway: the saccharine was making itself felt. The cat, in its indecision, would back away from the half-open door and the blasts of icy air only to be ejected with a kick.

Banished this time, too, the cat looked round and set off along the usual path. It was dark, and again the wind was blowing and conspiring with the fine snow to create in nature what should never be. Especially now, especially here, where as it was everything was bleaker than it ever had been. The snowy naphthalene, scentless in the frost, had blanketed all the tracks we saw and once again it was up to the cat to insinuate signs of life.

This time she approached the shed from the back and pushed her way in through a kind of hatch. Somehow the shed was so redolent of rabbit that she forgot all about the tin bowl and decided to do what she had tried to do several times and to which end she must jump up onto the box responsible for the warm stench of wet straw mixed with the rotten stink of carrots and cabbage. Those who have kept rabbits know this smell, those who haven't can't imagine it, though there isn't much to imagine.

Once on top of the box, the cat jammed a paw through the crack and, flaying an armpit, stretched as far as she could. As always, the rabbits were just out of reach and she soon tired of the senseless effort, and then a frost-bitten ear started to itch. Confusing her paws and not wanting to pull the one that was in the cage out, she tried to manage as she was. And it worked. She scratched the source of her torment, achieved the required lassitude, then attacked the same place with her hind claws. Although the paw stranded in the hutch prevented her from luxuriating fully in the nascent pain, the tearing of the ear caused her to howl with pleasure, then something cracked, and the slab-board on which she had been wriggling collapsed under her. The board had been nailed bark-side down, allowing the cramped rabbits to stand on their hind legs and nibble the dry phloem – one place in particular – they needed to survive.

The howling cat was deaf to the other howling coming from inside the bast-covered door. But a man, who had gotten up for work before dawn and come to the pit, heard it. The pitch-darkness meant you could use the pit without feeling shy, so long as you didn't freeze to death. The man had been up most of the night: he'd eaten some bad food and the bitter cold hadn't helped matters. Now he couldn't help but listen to the sounds of a night which, it would seem, was soundless and which might never turn into day.

But then he heard a sort of howl. A howl squeezed out

of somewhere. Since the pit was by the wall of the shed-shanty, the howling must be coming from there. Sometimes a second voice would howl, and then a third, cat-like voice would chime in. The man began to feel queasy, meanwhile the first voice – although masculine, it was thin and therefore pitiful – went on and on howling in the night. Oh, how he did howl.

The howl somehow reminded the squatting man of the strange song the purse-maker and reticule maker used to hum over his strips of colored leather:

> *Pretty, ripe, red raspberries*
> *Grew on a lady's nose.*
> *I picked them myself*
> *On the lady's name-day.*
> *It's true, it's true, it's true,*
> *Oh, I'm not fooling you.*
> *Tula-Tula, Tula-Tula,*
> *Tula, my home sweet home!*

Having finished with the pit, the frozen man walked quickly away and was soon making tracks in the snowy powder towards the tram: he'd get there by five a.m. Hunched and hoaryassed, but he'd get there, otherwise he'd wind up doing time like that girl Fima. In the shanty, they went on howling and howling. He howled, and she howled. He howled continually, she howled when she lapsed into consciousness, smothered in the rags she kept crawling under, even in her sleep. He howled because he had a hernia (remember the sackful of bark?), she howled because her frost-bitten toes burned. It hurt so badly (hurt him all the time, hurt her when she half woke up) they couldn't think about anything else: not about food, not about wood, not about the children they once had, not about the luck they never had. When she lost consciousness for the umpteenth time, he was in such pain that he stopped groaning so as not to provoke it, he probably wrinkled just his nose, and under his nose (wrinkled like a child's about to cry), his upper lip, most likely, began to tremble over the black stumps of his few remaining teeth, and there was only one thing left to do: to get up and stand for a while, then maybe the bandage would help.

Better yet he should lift his legs up and prop them against the wall. But he couldn't because he was lying on the edge of the bed and besides he didn't have the strength, and his legs would have frozen, propped up like that – the wall was covered with frost. Then again, he couldn't just lie there since the bed was too narrow for two people in overcoats, and he kept sliding off and inflaming the already fierce pain.

How he tried to get up! My God, how he tried! He was lying there, after all, in the middle of a merciless winter, only the wind and the snow were kept out. How he tried to get up! But how did he try to get up?! He tried to get up quietly and slowly, while the pain, if it didn't clamp shut like a pair of pliers and rock, would try in its murderous way to pry apart those frozen claws jammed by a rusty bolt, he was in pain greater than anyone should ever be, he was in pain, too, because he couldn't call anyone, and because there was no one to come, and because he couldn't bear such torture, and because his idiot wife, when this happened before, always grumbled: "What if you were having a baby and the head had just come out?"

All the same he gets up. He feels around under what must be a pillow and gropes for his bandage. You can't make it out now, but in the daylight it looks like a harness made of grey inner skins. Dirty from use and shiny from his body. When he tries to unbutton his coat, his hands refuse to obey, and when he tries to unhitch his pants, his hands – shaking from the pain and from everything – let them slip. His hands started shaking after the sackful of bark that brought on the hernia, and they're shaking now because that's all they can do when the horrible pliers clamp shut. He couldn't keep his drawers up either: one pair after the other fell down around his feet. Now how would he cope with that useless bandage? The pain started up with a jerk as soon as the cold surface touched his skin, stopped, then gripped him again: he couldn't wrap the stiff belt around his hips, and when he could he couldn't get the copper pin to go into the hole. He knew how to do this, his fingers remembered far smaller and more intricate clasps, but his tangled legs, those outlandish hands, and the icy bandage flaying his bare skin made him clumsy and he lost his head.

He kept tugging at something, kept turning numb, kept muttering and cheeping, and when he suddenly stopped – in the dark, and in time – the pin went in. Now all he had to do was pull up his pants and drawers but, worn out by the pin, he lost his balance and collapsed, or rather fell flat on the floor. Instead of coming undone, the bandage began to strangle the painful place and it was as though all the frozen bark were sticking out of the burst sack of his body, gouging haphazard holes in him with its jagged edges, and life would have left the desecrated body if the body had not reached down to the frigid floor for some reason and begun pulling up the jumble of drawers and pants. Then he got down on all fours (all this in a huge, ponderous coat) and, leaning on one hand, hiked the drawers and pants up further, to his haunches, fastened them just, and got up, grabbing on to the back of the chair, he must have been ashen, but it was dark – you couldn't make anything out – it was very dark, and most likely he wrinkled his nose and his upper lip began to tremble.

The pain, muddled by the inane fiddling, slightly humbled by the bandage, seemed to dull, as if it had given up trying to outdo itself, and he, strangely, conceived the idea of eating something, especially since it made no sense to lie down in the bandage, especially after that struggle to get up.

He dug around in his pocket and, finding nothing, went out into the passage. He felt around in the bowl, discovered a lumpy glob of dried-on pearl barley, scraped it off and began chewing. Now he wanted to relieve himself. By the rabbit-hutch for some reason. We can guess the reason. So as to hang onto the roof, shaggy from the rabbit's frosty breath. But then his shaking hand slipped through the roof and landed in a warm pile of animals whose skins, under the lightest of fur, were as thin as the skins used to line the little pockets of the smallest and most expensive purses.

Suddenly the pliers clamped shut again. He lurched, squashed one of the rabbits, and felt a sharp stab of pain.

His hand jerked back, slid along the wet straw and fell on something. When he pulled the hand out, it was clutching a carrot end: the nasty-tasting part with the coarse yellow middle that sticks up out of the earth. The smelly end was dampish and smeared with his blood (his blood was still flowing!), even so he bellowed in pain as he raked and kneaded the stump with his gums. Then, ignoring the frantic rabbits, he groped around for another carrot end, and another. He brought them all into the house, he was tired of standing and wanted to sit: his hernia ached, his bleeding finger smarted, his back was stiff and his trembling muscles weak.

He sat down on his chair and went limp. He began groaning, cheeping and wrinkling his nose, then he chewed the carrot, then he groaned some more.

The cat came by later than usual, and a lump of something was lying in the bowl. So they hadn't come out for it. When the youth came by, he saw tracks in the swag of snow that had swept into the shed, tracks going from the bast-mat door to the rabbit-hutch and back. He didn't care, he was in a rush and shivering, but then he noticed the hutch's gaping roof: one of the boards had split in two and fallen in. Who could have done that? And one of the full-grown rabbits was missing. He looked round, searching for the rabbit with savage eyes, and almost thought it had run away. Then he remembered that the rabbit couldn't have gotten out through the roof by itself, and he was struck by those tracks in the snow.

He was frozen in his bare feet and galoshes, but he knocked the bits of board back together and, as he was leaving, dumped out the bowl's contents and ground it up in the snow.

A quilt hung in the window.

"Alive?" they asked him at home.

But he, tense with intentions and decisions, said nothing.

The jackdaw had reappeared in the grey skies now that there were intimations of life – tracks in the snow, slops by the doors, smoke from the chimneys. Only the mud-covered hovel made no attempt at smoke. The tired jackdaw was on its way there. The jackdaw was tired because it had flown with the crows far beyond the city to a place which, though undisturbed beneath the snow, was alarming for the noise, the din and the sudden disappearances of air. The crows were unperturbed. They knew that the noise and din meant there would be plenty to peck. But at the first terrible bang, the jackdaw jumped away from the supine man over whom the crows were strutting. The jackdaw couldn't bring itself to peck the man, and when the next monstrous crash again displaced the air, the bird rushed up sidelong into the sky and flapped as hard as it could for the city.

Hunger and cold forced the jackdaw to slow its flight, but by then the reports were muted. Thanks to the wind, the bird was soon over familiar territory and remembering that the scrap of leather it had tugged at yesterday under the window had come away, so that now it had only to hollow out the snow and earth and extract the rest. The jackdaw veered towards the window, checking at the same time to see if the cat was anywhere. It wasn't, nor were its tracks, so the jackdaw swooped down. It got so carried away gouging the frozen snow (the scrap was right where the bird had left it) that it stupidly took fright at the sound of footsteps – they were too determined for the local winter rhythms – and flew up onto the roof of the two-story former dacha. Scraping along the cold roof, the jackdaw peered down and realized for some reason that it couldn't see the leather scrap.

The youth was walking away from home, this time not in galoshes over bare feet, but in thick felt boots and his mother's quilted jacket. He strode up to the gate and kicked it for all he was worth. The gate flew right off its hinges and the jackdaw jumped up onto the ridgepole.

The youth booted the bast-covered door, then ran out of the shed and stood in front of the shack. No one came out. He listened, again ran inside the gate, pounded the door, then tugged spitefully at the bast which came off in clumps – together with all the laths, oakum and tiny nails – and fell on the fine snow. The youth again ran out and again planted himself in front of the hovel.

Something was going on inside. The jackdaw was certain: inside they were moving about. Someone seemed to have pulled the quilt back from the window, if only briefly. The youth stood there and waited. Edging open the door over the clumps of bast, a man in an ungainly coat came slowly out and stood in the gate. He held onto the gatepost and peered uncertainly into the grey light, he didn't seem to realize that it was the youth loitering there who had banged on the door. He didn't even seem to see him.

"Why'd you take that rabbit, you parasite?" the youth shouted.

The man looked at him but didn't answer.

"Don't just stand there, you parasite, say something!"

The man turned clumsily around and retreated into the shed.

"Fix the cage! You hear me, stinker! Give the meat back! You sponger, you parasite!" the youth screamed his demands.

He had no way of knowing, after all, nor did the man know that in the tea-colored text that had gone into the fire the day before along with Rybkin's primer, in that text whose letters were as spidery as the spiders in the shed, it said:

"These *are* the beasts which ye shall eat:

"Every beast that pateth the hoof, and cleaveth the cleft in two claws, *and* cheweth the cud among the beasts, that ye shall eat.

"Nevertheless ye shall not eat of them... *the hare*: for it chews the cud, but divides not the hoof; *therefore* it is unclean unto you."

Truly the man did not know this, yet the book's unequivocal style, the stern will of its myriad little letters ruled his age-old wonts, and the youth's accusations were senseless.

"Give me back the skin at least, you bum! Rotten bastard!"

But here she emerged, and an idiotic scene ensued: she shuffled toward the gate, while the man retreated toward the door. Since there wasn't anyone inside the shanty (it wasn't fit to live in anyway), the furious youth did what any teenager on our street would have done and hurled a shard of ice at the window and smashed two panes, while through the sash, serene and unsurprised, the minus-thirty-degree winter slipped in and curled up, naturally, on the bed rags – it was tired of knocking around outside those idiotic lath walls.

At the sound of the glass shattering, the jackdaw jumped again.

The man turned. Behind him his small raggedy woman shown darkly. Then the man began, of all things, to bark. His bark was loud and guttural. This stunned the jackdaw because people, like cats, don't bark.

But that man was barking.

The youth, too, was stunned and backed away even before he had the chance to gloat over breaking two panes at once.

In the yard no one heard this tenant's loud, even animated, voice. They heard the muttering, they heard the gruff phrases, the groans – last night, for instance – but not the loud voice. But that loud voice was his, and he was testing it for the first time, which is why even he didn't recognize it.

The man stood there and shouted in a loud, yet very soft, guttural voice, and *what* came out seemed to be a sound *from a long way off*, a sound at the end of phonation, for the phonation itself had faded somewhere in the larynx, or in the rotten bronchial tubes, or just in back of the bad heart, even before taking on the turbid air.

What the jackdaw saw was a sad and unusual sight. It saw a boy, and opposite him two old people, one of whom was shouting. The jackdaw had figured out that he wasn't barking but shouting, and all because it reminded the bird of some futile squabble on the scrap heap. If the jackdaw knew the old man wasn't barking, to the youth it seemed that the man – staring into space and with tears in his soft voice – couldn't stop barking.

But then the jackdaw noticed that the leather strips it had all but extricated were buried under the shattered glass, glass it couldn't possibly lift. It wasn't a crow. Now the hungry black bird with the grey neck began to regret that it hadn't stayed with the crows and hadn't jumped up onto the face of the man lying in the snow. Who the man was, the jackdaw didn't know – we can guess, though, if we want – but that he was young the jackdaw and the crows both knew, for they could easily distinguish young from old, and were always on the look-out for some aged creature tottering on the edge of that immobility they also knew and prized. But unlike the jackdaw, the crows had understood what a rare piece of luck it was to jump up on the face of *young* flesh (in that alarming place there was all you could eat) and had sharpened their claws with particular care.

1979-80

Translator's Notes

RED CAVIAR SANDWICHES

p.7   *Ostankino Park*: The park surrounding the summer palace by the same name built by Count Nikolai Sheremetev in the 1790s.

p.8   *Without the Bird Cherries*: A sentimental love story by Panteleimon Romanov (1884-1938).

p.13   *Blok*, Alexander (1880-1921), the symbolist Russian poet whose principal symbol was a beautiful and mystical female figure.

p.13   *mounds of earth*: These mounds of carried earth round simple wooden houses served as added insulation from the weather; roughly as high as the foundation (2 feet), they were also very comfortable for sitting out on.

p.19   *Sumarokov*, Alexander (1717-77), poet, dramatist, advocate of Classicism.

SEMYON'S LONELY SOUL

p.20   *the three train stations*: Yaroslavl, Leningrad, and Razan are adjacent terminals in central Moscow.

p.24   *sixty rubles in today's money*: *The Grassy Street* was written in 1979 and 1980 when the average monthly wage was 175 rubles.

p.31   *Ferapont Golovaty* (1890-1951): A collective farm worker and beekeeper, Golovaty was an initiator of the national movement to collect money for the defense fund during the Second World War.

p.34   *rasshibalka*: An outdoor game that involves hitting a stack of coins with a small lead disc; players pocket those coins they manage to make flip over.

p.35   *Budyonny's March*: A martial anthem named for Marshal Semyon Budyonny (1883-1973). During the Civil War, Budyonny led the First Cavalry later immortalized in Babel's stories.

ONE WARM DARK NIGHT

p.41   *pointed helmets*: Known as budyonovki, these helmets were worn by Red-Army men from 1919 to 1941.

p.43   *skittles* is an approximate translation of *gorodki*, a game that originated in Russia in the 1820s. Using bats, players attempt to knock various configurations of five cylindrical blocks out of a square (6.5 x 6.5 ft.) from a distance of 21 or 42 feet in the least number of turns.

p.43   *Mikhailov*, Maksim (1893-1971), famous Bolshoi Theater bass.

p.47   *Young Pioneers*: A communist organization to which all Soviet children were required to belong.

p.47   *Rozov*, Viktor (b. 1913), a famous Soviet playwright.

p.49   *Taras Bulba* (1835): A novel by Nikolai Gogol set in the 17th century in which an old Cossack, Taras Bulba, kills his traitorous son.

TWO TOBITS

p.60   *alatyr stone*: In medieval legend and folklore, the alatyr was the "father of all stones" invested with miraculous powers.

p.60   *with a hard sign*: The orthographic reform of 1917-18 did away with the hard sign following hard consonants as well as four other letters in the pre-revolutionary Russian alphabet.

p.61   *Khimki*: A suburb northwest of Moscow, Khimki is less than 14 miles from the Kremlin.

p.61   *Petrovsko-Razumovskoye*: Another northern suburb, midway between Moscow and Khimki.

p.61   *Old Believers*: These strictly Orthodox Russians broke with the Russian Church because of the liturgical reforms – e.g. one must cross oneself with three fingers, instead of two – imposed by Patriarch Nikon in the 17th century.

p.61   *bread and salt* are traditional Russian symbols of hospitality.

p.62   *the holy archpriest*: Archpriest Avvakum (1621-1682) was a leader of the Old Believers.

p.64   *Salade Olivier*: Named after the French chef who introduced it in Russia before the Revolution, Salade Olivier became a household name only in the 1950s when ordinary Russians began using mayonnaise. In addition to mayonnaise, the traditional recipe calls for boiled potatoes, meat, canned peas, pickles, onion, and hard-boiled egg.

p.64   *between the cosmopolitans and the cosmonauts*: The "cosmopolitans" were mostly non-Russians (i.e. Jews) perceived as purveyors of Western influence and ideas. Stalin's campaign against cosmopolitans began in 1948 with the murder of Mikhoels, artistic director of the Moscow Jewish Theatre, and ended with his own death in 1953. Soviet cosmonaut Yuri Gagarin became the first man in space in 1961.

p.64   *the zampolitans*: Deputy commanders in charge of political work, zampolitans existed in every section of the military and were responsible for the ideological "health" of their subordinates.

p.64   *the panic* began on October 16, 1941. With the Germans less than 14 miles from the Kremlin, government institutions began evacuating and people began looting.

p.67   *the Germans have already named the day*: The Germans had planned to arrive at the Kremlin on November 7, the anniversary of the Revolution, and celebrate their victory with a parade on Red Square.

p.68   *the black loudpseaker*: All radios had been confiscated at the start of the war to keep Soviet citizens from listening to enemy propaganda. Instead, people had to rely on loudspeakers with only one station that broadcast programs over special wires.

p.69   *he hasn't planted potatoes in the middle of the street*: As a special dispensation during the war, people were allowed to plant potatoes on the dirt roads outside cities and in the country.

p.69   *Molotov's speech*: Foreign Minister Molotov announced Russia's entry in the war on June 22, 1941.

p.70   *kulaks' henchmen*: The kulaks, or comparatively prosperous peasants who could afford to hire labor and buy machinery, were destroyed as a class in the '20s and '30s. Here their 'henchman' refers to the slightly better off Nikitins who could afford a cow.

p.70   *Burdenko*, Nikolai (1876-1946), the Soviet Union's pioneer neurosurgeon.

p.72   *a dirigible went up every evening*: During the war, dirigibles trailing long cables served as a primitive form of urban air defense.

p.76   *who's registered on First Meshchanskaya?*: Food ration coupons could be used only in the particular store where one was registered. Some stores (like the one on First Meshchanskaya Street) were better than others.

p.80   *those three fingers you just crossed yourself with*: As an Old Believer, Nikitin crosses himself with two fingers and is outraged at Hymie's allusion to three fingers.

JULY

p.82   *Vladykino*: A suburb north of Moscow.

p.83   *trophy horses*: German horses captured during the war.

INASMUCH AND INSOFAR AS

p.93 *"Well, he's dead, but... soon they'll be kicking him in the moustache and out of his tomb!"*: A reference to Stalin who died March 5, 1953, and was originally buried in Lenin's tomb on Red Square.

p.95 *in our land of the Soviets we overfulfilled the plan*: An ironic remark given that plans were "overfulfilled" by substantially reducing the original plan.

p.96 *the two most famous of all*: Lenin and Stalin.

p.100 *The Tale of Igor's Campaign*: Based on the unsuccessful campaign of Prince Igor against the Polovtsian army in 1185, the original manuscript disappeared.

p.100 *the tsarist letter "yat"*: The "yat" was abolished by the orthographic reform of 1917-18 and replaced by the similar-sounding letter "e".

p.108 *everyone thought the mayonnaise was tainted butter*: Unfamiliar foods (e.g. canned crab or cod liver) were rejected in favor of familiar ones during the war when any purchase meant giving up scarce food coupons.

p.109 *cavalry sword*: During the war, Stalin reinstated various tsarist traditions (from cavalry swords and shoulder straps to separate education for boys and girls) so as to bring the people (those who supported the Soviet government and those who didn't) together against the Germans.

SORRY LOT

p.114 *the great Czech educator Komensky*, Yan Amos (1592-1670).

p.114 *the great Russian educator Ushinsky*, Konstantin (1824-1871).

p.114 *the great Soviet educator Makarenko*, Anton (1888-1939). Makarenko worked with groups of juvenile delinquents in prison colonies and wrote a number of books, including *A Pedagogical Poem*.

p.118 *there is in early autumn* – the first line of a poem by Fyodor Tyutchev (1803-73).

p.119 *baranka*: A hard, ring-shaped roll the size of a silver dollar.

p.119 *pre-Petrine*: Before the rule of Peter the Great (1672-1725).

p.119 *Zadonshchina*: An account by a contemporary of the Battle of Kulikovo Field (1380) in which Grand Prince Dmitry of the Don defeated the Tatars.

p.120 *Vasily Lvovich Pushkin* (1770-1830), eccentric poet, ardent bibliophile, and uncle of Alexander Pushkin.

p.120 *Musin-Pushkin*, Count Aleksei (1744-1817), specialist in early texts. The single 16th-century copy of *The Tale of Igor's Campaign* is thought to have perished in Musin-Pushkin's house during the Moscow fire of 1812.

p.120 *svaika*: A pre-revolutionary game resembling darts in which a thick nail or spike serves as the dart, and a ring on the ground serves as the bull's-eye.

p.122 *Peter's assemblies*: Social-business gatherings for men and women held in the houses of the Russian nobility, instituted by Peter the Great in 1718.

p.122 *Lefort*, Franz (1656-99), Swiss-born Russian admiral and member of Peter the Great's "Great Embassy" to the West in 1697-98.

p.123 *Ilya Muromets*: A Russian folk hero, Ilya Muromets was a peasant's son and born unable to walk. He sat on the stove-bench for 33 years and then was miraculously cured.

p.123 *Pomyalovsky*, Nikolai (1835-63), author of *Seminary Sketches*.

p.127 *The Republic of SHKID* (1927): A book about the re-education of home-less children by L. Panteleev and G. Belykh.

p.138 *Spring Torrents*: A novel by Ivan Turgenev (18i8-1883) in which the hero, Sanin, is seduced by the temptress Mme. Polozova.

p.141 *this poem*: *Red-Nose Frost* by Nikolai Nekrasov (1821-78), translated by J.M. Soskice.

YOU'RE MY SECOND

p.147 *Tuva*: Now part of Russia, Tuva was a semi-independent country from 1912 to 1944. As such, it issued its own postage stamps, some of them triangular.

p.148 *Polesye*: A marshy region partly in southern Belorus, partly in northern Ukraine.

p.148 *she'd been assigned to settle on the river and fish*: Like many Komsomol (Young Communist League) members, Olga had been recruited to work in Siberia. On her way there, she attended the Communist rallies (red flags with slogans, music, congratulatory speeches) staged for recruits at stations or in towns through which their train passed.

p.150 *Kem*: A small port on the White Sea.

p.155 *coin-toss* is a crude equivalent of *pristenok*, an outdoor game requiring a few coins and a wall, post, or fence. The first player flicks a coin at the wall and it falls to the ground. The second player follows suit, trying to make his coin fall near the first. Then, if he can span the two coins (with his thumb on one and middle finger on the other), he takes both. The bigger your hand, the better your chances of winning more money.

SITTING IN THE DARK ON BENTWOOD CHAIRS

p.165 *the labor front*: During the Second World War, many of those who were not drafted (women, boys, students) were assigned to dig trenches, build fortifications near the front, rebuild railroads, etc.

p.171 *Rybkin's primer*: A book of physics problems for secondary-school students in wide use during and after the war.